Stuart White was born in Lan Hong Kong and Los Angeles. widely in Europe, Africa, Asia, America.

He covered the drug wars in on Israel, and the civil war in Yugoslavia.

He lives in Teddington, Middlesex. This is his fifth book.

Also by Stuart White

FICTION
Death Game
Operation Raven
The Shamrock Boy

NON-FICTION
Zeebrugge: A Hero's Story (with Stephen Homewood)

STUART WHITE

'Til The Fat Lady Sings

BLAKE

Published by Blake Paperbacks Ltd.
98-100 Great North Road, London N2 0NL, England

First published in Great Britain in 1992

ISBN 1–85782–0045

British Library Cataloguing-in-Publication Data: a catalogue record for
this book is available from the British Library.

Typeset by Falcon Typographic Art Ltd, Fife, Scotland

Printed by Cox and Wyman, Reading, Berkshire

Cover design by Graeme Andrew

1 3 5 7 9 10 8 6 4 2

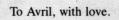

To Avril, with love.

'The opera ain't over 'til the fat lady sings.'

Dan Cook, baseball commentator, US TV April, 1978.

Often wrongly attributed to Dick Motta, coach of the Washington Bullets, who adopted the phrase.

PROLOGUE

The soldiers were all around the car, hemming it in like encroaching jungle creepers, blotting out sunlight, a human foliage in camouflage and olive green.

Jungle faces peered through the windows, denizens of a strange kingdom, their noses disfigured blobs squashed against the glass of the car windows. Dark brown unshaven faces, some young, others creased in the fat rolls of middle-age.

The fourteen year old girl followed their eyes, and they followed hers, and she held their gaze, neutrally observant.

She could feel fear in the car, could smell it like a poisonous odour, and she could see the sickly luminosity of fright on the faces of her brothers Ramon and Raoul.

The heat in the car was stifling, and the white cotton dress began to darken with sweat where it touched her armpits and her small breasts beneath the cups of the stiff brassiere.

It seemed a relief when they were ordered out of the big Peugeot, but then the harsh noon sun cut across the skin of her bare arms like a lance blade.

Her mother and father were arguing, but the soldiers pushed them all across the dirt road to the edge of a dry ditch, and ordered them to face away, across the fields.

She could sense the fear, feel it crackle like static electricity around her, but still she felt insulated from it, earthed and immune. It was a quality that always seemed to have been with her; a detachment, a feeling of non-involvement.

She looked over her shoulder, saw the men whispering

1

to themselves, a fearful, dangerous look on their faces. She saw weapons being fumbled with, and the fear at last touched her.

She remembered a black and white clip of TV film, taken long ago in some foreign land – had Papa said Russia? – of people before a ditch, men with rifles, puffs of soundless smoke, and the figures tumbling one after the other into the ditch, like shapeless puppets.

The terror began to beat its wings in her heart, like a trapped bird frantic to be free. They were to be killed, all of them.

She saw her father turn, saw the naked terror in his eyes, heard him scream: 'No . . . No! This is madness, take the car, take the money. Kill us, but not the children.'

Something moved in her, something pivotal, something to change her for ever. She turned and faced the soldiers. She saw men. Men. Men as never before. Heavy faces, young faces, cruel, innocent, frightened, full of bravado, and all deadly dangerous.

It was as if she had been given wisdom beyond her years, some ability to really *SEE*. She realised she was smiling, and felt a curious, incomprehensible and previously unknown heat in her belly, spreading like a liquid stain to her loins.

She observed the bodies, saw the men shuffle and move, experienced a weird, floating sensation, and it was as though some psychological alchemy had transformed her fear into power.

Strained faces, all eyes on her, and suddenly the knowledge exploded within her. They want me. They *WANT* me, like men want women. They want *ME*.

She took a step forward. One. Another. Three steps. Her father screamed out: 'Angelita – no!' But another step and another; first steps on an unknown journey away from the past and the normal.

2

A soldier's hand reached out, grabbed her and imprisoned her against his chest. She smelled sweat, tobacco and cheap cologne. It meant danger and challenge, but also safety now, and it had something to do with the spreading warmth in her groin, in the strange hardening of the small nipples.

She heard Mama give a long, high-pitched wail, and then there was a terrible deafening burst of gunfire that made the girl flinch and close deeper into the body of her captor.

And she thought: I know what has happened. Why don't I cry?

Her clothes lay before her in a neat pile where she had carefully folded them after being ordered to undress. A neat pile among the flattened shards of cornstalks, the bundle crowned by the optimistic white cups of her brassiere, like twin spires of religious innocence pointing to Heaven.

She lay down, as she was told, and felt the corn stubble sharp on her bare bottom, and the warmth of the soil, strangely luxurious on her skin. A bee buzzed furiously somewhere near her face, but outside her vision.

Her legs were parted, and she felt the crushing weight of the first man. Would there be pain, like Mama had said there would be on her wedding night? Would it have been like this after the ceremony, the Mass, the incense, the wine and the rejoicing?

The pain jolted her, and she gave a little cry. She bit her lip and tasted blood, then felt the rasp of unshaven stubble against her face, and smelled the garlic and the days-old sweat.

She was crushed and rocked in a strange motion, and when the man cried out she feared she had somehow hurt him.

But then he was gone, and another shape lowered itself upon her, blotting out the cobalt sky. So that was the act

3

of which we whispered and giggled and dreamed, the girl thought.

That was the mysterious act of love and pain? And now she knew she must lie in the dirt until all the men were done. Eleven men. Did that mean eleven babies? She felt the pain of the invaded sexual wound, then closed her eyes, leaving, flying off somewhere into space.

And there was something else too, beyond the pain and the humiliation, the degradation of what was being done to her. Something else as she watched her indignity from a distant planet.

She was learning a lesson.

They left the youngest soldier to kill her. They had told him she was an agent of the Sandinistas, so she must die too.

The rest of the soldiers, lust and bravado spilt like their semen into the girl and the soil, left him to do the killing work they could no longer stomach.

This one had felt the terrible heat of lust and adolescence, but now the poison was out, the boil of passion lanced by his violation of her. Now he hung his head, ashamed at what he had done, and must do.

The girl knew she had seconds to save her life. She spoke to him, and his head came up, jerkily, alarm on his face, for they were the first words she had spoken since they had taken her. There had been no pleas for mercy, no oaths, no prayers or appeals to God. Just mute acceptance.

She said: 'You have been left to kill me.' She said it as a statement, and he looked away, unable to bear her gaze.

'You cannot kill a woman you have known carnally. It is in the Bible – a mortal sin. You will go to perdition.'

His head turned, face set in a parody of defiance, but the gun spoke the truth while his face lied, the barrel lowered as if in shame.

4

She said: 'My name is Angelita, and I have taken Communion. What is your name?'

'José.' The name slid, like dribble, from his mouth.

Time hung suspended under the blazing sun, then she saw the barrel lift. She held her breath as it traced upwards from the dirt, across a line with her legs, her thighs, her stomach, breasts, as though caressing her, violating her once more.

It stopped, pointing at her head.

She said: 'Angelita – little angel.'

He hesitated. Long seconds, then the barrel tracked upwards, up, up until it was vertical to the sky, and he fired. She winced and covered her ears.

The boy soldier said: 'They must hear the shots. Then they will think I have killed you.'

She moved a step towards him: 'Thank you José.'

He stepped back before she could reach him, the unformed, immature face struggling to slip back on its mask of cruelty. He fumbled in a pouch pocket of his fatigues, and threw some crumpled notes at her feet.

'Puta!' He spat into the dirt.

She was a whore and he had paid her like his comrades told him they paid the girls in the big house in Managua. And being a whore was worse than being dead.

The girl picked up the worthless banknotes, smoothed them, and folded them into the palm of her hand as the soldier trudged out of the field, onto the road.

Then she took her clothes, dressed slowly, and walked away in the opposite direction. Back towards the capital, away from the ditch, away from childhood, away from innocence.

Chapter One

Bianca excused herself, left the studio and climbed into the back of the waiting Mercedes. As she left, the men with whom she had been talking watched her go with scarcely disguised longing.

Two were internationally renowned photographers, the other was the editor of a famous fashion magazine. Each was rich, each frequently had affairs with beautiful women.

And each, in their turn, had tried and failed to sleep with Bianca who was now probably the most famous model in the Western world.

She graced the pages of every fashion magazine in Europe and America. Her personal income was estimated at around a conservative two and half million US dollars a year.

Bianca – the world knew her simply as Bianca – held a United States passport, but chose to live in London rather than New York, whence she had moved 18 months previously.

On the passport her family name was given as Vasquez. That seemed to be the most anyone knew about her family, or her background.

She had appeared in Manhattan, as if from nowhere, five years previously. She paid for a series of photographs of herself and then sent them to the top American fashion photographer, Sven Carlsson. He sent them back, unopened, as he did with the hundreds of other unsolicited pictures he received each month.

So Bianca took a sleeping bag, and a Thermos, and camped outside his Tribeca studio. Each time Carlsson stepped out, or in, she handed him the pictures, and each time he waved them away.

It was 12 degrees below freezing, and on day four, infuriated but reluctantly admiring her guts, he asked her in, thinking he could tell her in five minutes why she was wasting her time.

The pictures were awful, amateurish, badly lit and badly posed. Although she was relatively slim, she had weight in the wrong places, and she appeared gawky. But there was something in her face, her eyes, something in the way she posed – amateurish as it was – that hinted of better things.

He told her to go away, lose 21 pounds, get in shape and return in a month. She did, on the day and the minute, and she'd lost 22 pounds and working out had improved her muscle tone.

Carlsson cancelled two days work, and spent it in the studio with Bianca, working her until she was exhausted to the point of weeping.

A year later she was on the cover of Vogue. She appeared on the Tonight show with Johnny Carson, was witty and warm, modest but forthright – Johnny liked her, vital – and suddenly she was the face!

It was around that time she acquired United States citizenship in a quiet deal struck between a US Senator with extensive publishing interests, and the State department.

The suggestion was she had come from Cuba, and therefore was a refugee from Communism. The tabloids delved a little deeper, narrowing it to Central America. Certainly she had been in Costa Rica for a while.

No-one cared. The dregs of the world had poured into America in the 80s, it seemed like half the country couldn't speak English, and Bianca could, perfectly.

No-one knew how. But she was an asset to whichever country she belonged, and there were ungrateful murmurings when she eventually took up residence in London.

She told the Press she felt safer there, but there were other reasons, reasons no-one could ever be told, something that had shocked her. A man's face at a diplomatic reception on Park Avenue, a ghost.

From her house in Belgravia she could be at London's Heathrow Airport in 45 minutes and in the centre of Manhattan less than five hours later, thanks to Concorde.

She had a two-level apartment on the Upper East Side, a house near St. Paul de Vence in France. Bianca could appear and disappear at will.

That had become, very, VERY, important to her. The media set its pack loose on her. A downmarket American tabloid claimed she was a beautiful Brazilian trans-sexual, another that she was simply a transvestite.

Two Costa Rican women came forward and claimed they were her lesbian lovers, a Cuban defector told how she had been his lover, and how he had risked the firing squad to smuggle her out of Castro's island.

Bianca added an estimated million dollars in libel payouts and settlements, to her bank account.

She refused to speak of her background, and that only added to her allure and her appeal. That and her by now legendary beauty, for Bianca had become the most desirable woman in the world.

Bianca had escorts, but never boyfriends. She was squired to Hollywood premieres and London society bashes by famous names; a top British actor, a Japanese millionaire, the helpful US senator.

The latter talked of running for President, and the media ruminated on Bianca as First Lady. But the cognoscenti of London, New York and LA, said that the escorts had not seen the inside of Bianca's bedroom, nor had they been given the privilege of her body.

And when the cynical asked how those things could be known, the cognoscenti answered that these things were whispered in salons, sensed, or smelled on the wind.

In London she lived quietly, dining infrequently, at San Lorenzo – her table was two away from The Princess of Wales – NEVER at Langan's. She never went to nightspots, not even Tramp.

Bianca-spotting was a difficult game, and the gossip columnists paid well when she was.

One minute she was public, high-profile, smiling for the cameras, for the chat-show hosts, and then she was . . . gone. The phantom mystery girl.

She paid a full-time travel consultant to book her tickets, and the woman concerned had signed a detailed legal document admitting to severe penalties if details of Bianca's movements were disclosed.

She was Dr. Jekyll and Miss Hyde. Where she walked at night, where she went, and what she did, no-one knew. She ignored the rumours. Was she celibate, was she lesbian, was she nymphomaniac, did she trawl bars incognito for rough trade?

The public dismissed it all as malicious gossip. Bianca kept her life private, it was as simple as that.

Only Bianca knew – along with a selected few in whose interest it was, never to speak.

Wearing dark glasses and carrying a small Louis Vuitton piece of hand luggage, Bianca alighted from the Mercedes at Heathrow's Terminal Two.

The automatic glass doors of the building parted for her like courtiers, she turned right and walked towards the Air France Première Classe check-in desk.

A silver sable fur coat was wrapped tightly around her, an Hermes silk scarf around her head, and she left it until the last possible moment before going through to the Departure Lounge.

She saw no airport photographers, so went straight to the gate. Fifteen minutes later she was airborne, and after she cleared passport control at Charles de Gaulle she climbed into the Citroën with darkened windows that awaited her.

As it sped down the autoroute, into the Northern suburbs, she glimpsed the dome of the Sacré Coeur off to her left, and into the centre of Paris.

At the Place Vendôme the Citroen sighed slowly into the kerb outside the Ritz, and she quickly went inside and registered. Within minutes she knocked on the door of a suite next to hers.

The door was opened a crack, then wider by a swarthy man in a light beige cotton suit. He wore sunglasses, and did not speak, which Bianca thought was unnecessarily dramatic. Soundlessly he showed her to the bedroom, then closed the door behind her.

The bathroom door was ajar a few inches, the light was on, and a disembodied voice said: 'I shall be with you in one moment.'

She waited, observing the Louis Quinze furniture which she found hideous, until the man appeared.

He proffered a hand and she took it. Soft and warm.

'Bianca, a long time.'

'Six months, Ahmed, no more.'

She hated this, the preliminaries. He said: 'I'd like to do business now.'

'Business is what I am here for.'

He gestured with one hand to a thin, lizard-skin briefcase propped against the legs of one of the repulsive chairs: 'Thirty thousand francs.'

'Thank you.'

'Let us start the business.'

Bianca took off the sable fur she had worn since leaving the studio in West London, and beneath it she was naked except for a tiny pair of black panties

11

that narrowed to a string beneath the cleft of her buttocks.

The man was stark naked, and had a huge erection. Detached now, observing, her soul a camera hovering above her, she knelt before the man, and took his penis in her mouth.

When it was over, and they had cleansed and covered themselves, the man said: 'Can we talk?'

Bianca laughed: 'Joan Rivers.'

'I don't understand.'

'A comedienne called Joan Rivers uses that phrase. An American would understand.'

He looked at her without humour: 'I am not an American. They are my mortal enemies.'

'I am American, Ahmed.'

'You . . .' the man, struggled, 'you are Bianca.'

'What do you wish to know? And what do you want?'

He told her, clear headed now that he was freed of the imprisoned lust.

Early the next day Bianca paid her bill in cash, took a taxi to a discreet Lebanese bank off the Champs Elysées, and deposited thirty thousand French francs, using a small private room reserved for such occasions.

She left the briefcase in the car, and the Romanian refugee taxi driver later sold it, to his delight, for six hundred francs.

Back in London, she checked her messages, but responded to only one. It was a Whitehall number, and the first digits of the seven figure number were 230. The last four digits were known to less than five people.

The man answered, instantly, and when she spoke, he replied, rather stuffily, in that distinctive Old Etonian voice the public knew so well: 'May I call you back in five minutes?'

She agreed and replaced the receiver. Clearly he had someone in the room with him. Within three minutes her telephone rang.

'I couldn't talk, I'm dreadfully sorry.'

'I understood. You wish to come to the house tonight?'

She heard the intake of breath: 'Yes, may I?'

'You know the terms?'

There was something approaching a sexual choke in his voice: 'I know. Look, you have to understand something. I'm not a rich man.'

'Oh, but you are, Jeremy, I *KNOW*. Does the public realise how rich you are?'

There was silence, just his anxious breathing.

'What was that game you told me about, the one you like, with the houses and the companies you buy, and the little stacks of money?'

'Monopoly.'

'Then think of it as Monopoly money. If there's time we can play, and you may win your money back.'

'I could RUIN you Bianca.'

'You could ruin YOU, Jeremy. Samson, temples, worlds crashing. You don't want that. Remember what I know.'

'I've never known a woman like you.' She heard the stress on WOMAN, and noted it. It helped confirm what she had come to suspect.

'Your detective?'

'Is discreet. He borrows money at very favourable terms, and anyway . . .' his voice trailed off.

And anyway, Bianca completed the sentence in her mind, he would not think of you and a woman, would he, Jeremy, and certainly not a woman like me? For you could NEVER possess a woman like me, even if you wished, could you, not under normal circumstances?

13

And these were not normal circumstances.

She knew what the man in Paris wanted her to do, and she knew it could be done. Jeremy would do it for her, and he had the power to see it done.

Bianca did not know what Ahmed and his people wanted with an entrance pass to the House of Commons, but she could imagine. And she did not care.

If she was to be the angel of chaos, then she would rejoice in it. Let the men destroy each other, she cared naught for their politics, their petty nationalism and their blood feuds.

She thought of the users and the used, the ones who ripped and savaged, and those who were devoured. She had been used, and was used still, but now with her deliberate consent.

There was no end to it if you were a woman. Men had changed her, twisted and deformed her at that moment of brutal possession as surely as a broken limb badly set.

She remembered the moment she had watched those lust-sweated faces as they lowered themselves onto her unbroken girl body.

They had taken something then, something that had been already there, like a devil seed that may never have flowered, and they had fertilised it with their act of rape.

And over the years it had grown in her like some evil weed that choked any goodness out of her.

It was like a sickness. She had to have sex, any sex, perverted sex, and it had to be a stranger. But most important of all there had to be money, MUCH money, and the money had to be THERE, in the room, so that the act had meaning.

Then the act could never be confused with love, or passion. Only with money could there be satisfaction.

Tonight the Minister would come to the house, and she would do the things for him she knew he liked. And this time after the vital aphrodisiac, the money, she would ask him to get her an entrance pass to the House of Commons.

In truth was she the user now, or still the used? Had she been reborn, a phoenix from the flames, or was she some psychological, warped grotesque?

Perhaps she would never know.

Bianca lay on the bed in a Janet Reger slip over soft-silk cami-knickers, and watched the man's confused middle-aged lust with detached amusement.

She knew with cruel satisfaction the power she possessed.

'Undress for me Jeremy.'

He did so, believing absurdly that this gave her some pleasure. Off came the regimental tie, and the ministerial white shirt with its detachable collar. Off came the military brogues and the heavy wool pin-striped trousers, creased and ill-fitting.

Off came the grey socks, and lastly, with a hint of embarrassment, the baggy white Y-fronts. She thought: How absurd men are.

He knelt on the bed, naked and pathetic. Thin white body, a half-moon of sagging belly, and a half-hearted erection.

He was a Minister of State in Her Majesty's government, a respected politician, devoted husband and father. And, Bianca suspected, a man who also slept with other men.

When he took her it was always from behind, He had tried and failed to persuade her to indulge his public school vice, and recently she had noted bruises and weals on his body he was unable to explain away.

His touch, the way he spoke, certain things he said, or

15

had started to say, made her suspect he was a homosexual, perhaps even a promiscuous one.

All these Englishmen were the same – the public school educated ones at least – sent away as toddlers, preyed upon sexually by the older pupils, then starved of female company.

No wonder some of them could only be turned on by their own sex.

But something in Bianca excited the Minister. He had once told her he had a Seychelloise nanny, and Bianca wondered if in his mind she was a re-incarnation of that long, lost female, the one who had shown him the touch and affection his own mother had denied him.

She said: 'Come to nanny.' And he did, like a small, grateful boy. Grateful for her embrace and her pastiche of caring, for the kiss and touch of surrogate love fifty years too late.

Bianca brought him to a climax, sensing once again that he reserved his real sexual passion for males. And as she soothed and coaxed him into half sleep, she gently put questions to him, things the man in Paris wanted to know.

Later, as he snored, she went through the contents of his red despatch case, making brief notes, then copying several of the more important documents on a copying machine she kept in her dressing room.

Two hours later the Minister was on the green leather front bench of the Commons making a speech deploring recent corruption in local government.

Bianca counted out the five thousand pounds, and put them away for later banking in Paris or Switzerland. Ahmed wanted her to go to Tripoli to meet the leader, and she had agreed.

She liked the danger, the risk of discovery, perhaps death. Anything to lift her from this wasteland of detachment.

16

But she intended to call a halt to her relationship with the Minister as soon as was practicable, because sleeping with homosexuals in the Nineteen Nineties could mean the new Black Death. Even Bianca feared that.

Chapter Two

Long miles upriver and seemingly a world away from that of Bianca and the Minister, the Thames was narrower, lazier, the wharfs giving way to tree-lined banks and footpaths.

It meandered past sleepy islands, moored boats, under arched bridges, past houses where lawns swept down to the river's edge.

The Thames of Magna Carta, of Jerome K. Jerome's Three Men in a Boat, of rowing skiffs and Sunday walks along the towpath. A dreamier, sleepier river, adolescent to the drab grown-up it would become later as it raced, grey, wide and unfeeling, past the House of Commons where the Minister spoke.

But like an unwitting umbilical cord it linked the politician, the famous model, and the man and woman who now lay hostile and unsleeping in their marriage bed in their house a scant half mile from that ancient river.

They could not know it, but their lives were about to collide like meteorites, with consequences for all of them that would alter their existence.

But, mercifully, for Nick Carter that was the unknown future. Now he faced the terrible present as he lay, illuminated by the glare of the bedside lamp and the merciless beam of his wife's accusing gaze.

'Are you, Nick?' she demanded. 'Are you sleeping with someone else?'

'For *God's* sake, Jenny . . .'

She had woken to his restlessness, as he tossed and turned in the big bed, trawling back over the years, sifting through the memories like a treasure seeker, searching for

19

lost explanations, for misplaced reasons, for something that would tell him how, and why, and where?

Where had they gone, the years, twenty-two of them, counted out like playing cards, useless fours, Jokers, Jacks, and Kings?

Twenty-two years since that damp day outside the hideous modern, Sixties-montrosity church. Nick in a Burton's twelve quid Saturday Night Suit and shoes that let water in.

Jennifer's hair in a lacquered tower over the rented dress and enough mascara to camouflage a Commando's face. Warm, sparkling wine they fibbed was champagne. Silly speeches, his mates getting legless on pints at the bar, a small fight, someone puking, then six hours wait in Manchester Airport departure lounge for the charter flight to Paris.

Looking at the wedding album now was like looking at strangers. Nick's pasty white face, shouting of beer and fried food, hair down over his eyes, a hint of cockiness in the stance.

Jennifer a stone heavier than she was now, bigger-busted, but both so naive looking, so accepting and trusting. Ten days in Paris, a leaky bathroom, and a corner café that kept them awake all night.

Back, exhausted, to the rented terrace house on the hilly streets of that Northern mill town they called home. Back to the whistling kettle, the black and white TV, the cheap imitation G-plan sofa bought on hire purchase.

Other pictures in the big box they kept now in the front room. Jennifer in her starched white nurse's uniform standing outside the grim stone facade of the town's general hospital.

Growing out of her head, in classic photographic error, the extended glass bulb announcing: 'Casualty.' were he, and this woman in the bed next to him, those people?

They lived in Richmond, now, the soft South some of

Nick's surviving relatives called it, in a detached house a few minutes' walk from the river, from the shops and the wine bars.

They had a small cellar, in which they kept their wine, nothing special, perhaps a hundred bottles, mainly spared for dinner parties. Stripped pine doors, fabric on the walls, ageing but quality sofas, knick-knacks, modern and old, a few antiques, Bang and Olufsen TV and video, Sony sound system.

Everything in the house blended, it didn't hold itself up to be liked or disliked, it was comfortable with itself. A large eat-in kitchen, an Aga, a pine dresser and a large, scuffed table which Nick's father had made.

Polished floorboards in all but one of the rooms, littered with rugs, one valuable, most picked up at jumble sales and small shops. Always a statement. It didn't matter, none of it mattered really, did it? Possessions are not important to us. And meaning, of course, precisely the opposite.

A Volvo in the drive, a conservatory with cane furniture, and hundreds of books. Most read and treasured, for he and Jennifer had educated themselves the hard, lonely way, but some bought optimistically and then abandoned to be seen, their spined titles part – unconsciously perhaps, they wouldn't have dreamed of doing it deliberately – of the statement of who they were, what they had become.

Nick turned in the bed, hugging the pillow. From that, to this. How? Why?

He had been twenty-two, a reporter on their local evening paper, a Jack-the-Lad with a byline. Once there was a multiple pile-up on the motorway that curved past their town.

He was in the Casualty department, trying and failing to persuade a young, simpleton Irish nurse to give him the condition of the injured. Someone took hold of his arm – hard. It was Jennifer. She was brunette, slightly shorter than him, with what was then a full figure, very popular in the Sixties.

'When we know something we'll tell you, AFTER we've informed the relatives. Now leave her alone.' Her voice was correct, a bit nurse speak, get-back-into-bed-you-naughty-boy-Mr. Smith, and also, by the standards of the town, a little posh. But it also had warmth and strength.

Her name tag said she was Jennifer Fairhurst. Nick thought about her, told his mates about her, and they all knew what nurses were like, cor, and he made a bet that she'd go out with him.

Next time around he introduced himself, asked if she'd remembered him, she said she had, and he asked if she'd go to the pictures with him and she said she certainly would not.

Jennifer was engaged to a clerk at the Town Hall called Derek. She was twenty, and she wanted to be married by the time she was twenty-two. She and Derek were 'saving up' for a house, probably a bungalow on one of the new estates springing up at the edge of town.

Nick learned this over several visits, and by chats with other nurses, also that she was the daughter of a builder, and had an elder sister and a younger brother.

And he made a vow to himself that she was not going to marry some prat from the Town Hall. Jennifer, almost despite herself, because no-one approved of reporters, liked Nick. He was a bit cocky, a bit of a cowboy with his too tight trousers and his too pointed shoes, but he had a directness and a kind of confidence she respected.

But she had a vision of orderliness and respectability. A marriage, a house, children, perhaps even the continuation of her career part time.

She'd been going out with Derek since school, and he was steady, reliable. She wasn't going to ruin that for a flirtation with a boozy local reporter – all reporters drank too much, didn't they – someone who no doubt thought nurses were 'easy'.

She was not easy. She had seen what easy led to. Her 18 year old brother had got a girl into trouble and had 'had' to get married. Some girl from the local estate, a girl with a reputation as 'easy'.

Her brother's new wife smoked, had ladders in her stockings, and broken veins from sitting too close to the electric fire in her council flat.

Jennifer went there every couple of weeks, out of duty, into that bedlam of quarrels, a screaming baby, cigarette smoke, damp nappies and a blaring TV. Her elder sister had married a solicitor in Grantham, so if Jennifer needed a comparison, a way to go, a way not to go, she had it.

Ironic, she would think in later years, given Nick's job, that a newspaper would change her life, would bring her to him. It was an article on Voluntary Services Overseas, and a project in Botswana in which a local girl was involved.

It was like an itch. She kept the cutting, taking it out furtively, transfixed by the hungry, sick eyes that peered out of the photograph at her.

The bottom drawer figuratively, and the rest of the drawers in reality, were filling for the wedding; sheets, pillowcases, tea-towels, bath towels, kitchen utensils.

She made a decision, wrote a letter, went to London for an interview, and was accepted. A year training girls to be para-medics in Uganda.

She broke the news to Derek in a small, genteel tea and cakes cafe in the centre of town. She had it all ordered. She could leave in two months, add twelve to that. They could be married on schedule.

Derek said: 'I forbid it.' He used those words. A 23-year-old clerk in the Planning Department forbade Jennifer Fairhurst from going to Uganda.

He looked stern, forbidding, and precociously middle-aged, and suddenly she saw the clerk's dim vision, took in the frayed cuffs, the row of pens in the top pocket, the tunnel mind.

She saw their life stretching before them, cosy tea-times, TV and Rotary dinners, of holidays in the Lake District, sensible shoes, pipes and slippers and Sundays with her in-laws.

And Jennifer laughed. Perhaps if Derek had laughed with her, there might have been a chance, but he was hurt and angry, and thumped the table, drawing attention to them, saying: 'No bloody wife of mine is going off to the jungle for a year.'

She mailed the diamond engagement ring back the next day. When Nick came into Casualty next she told him she was leaving for Africa and his eyes lit up: 'Great! Africa, marvellous. Always wanted to go to Africa.'

Mainly, he said to himself, because he suspected it meant the end of her thing with Derek. But it ignited something in her, and she invited him to her farewell drinks at a local pub. He came alone, and as she was leaving, handed her a small clumsily wrapped package.

With a kind of choked embarrassment he said: 'Little something to help while away the dark African nights.'

She opened it in front of him. It was Hemingway, The Green Hills of Africa. He said: 'Read it?'

'No, I haven't.' In reality she had read very little, 'thank you.' She hesitated then gave him a brief peck on the cheek.

'I'll bloody miss you, matron.'

'You too. Any stories out in Africa?'

'Not unless a local's involved.' He sheepishly took out a scrap of paper with his address on it. 'Drop me a line if you get a minute. Postcard or something, if you want, you know, if you're not too busy saving lives.'

And then he was gone, the glassed door of the pub clicking shut behind him.

She wrote; long letters written by the light of the storm

24

lantern on those pitch-black African nights, rain tattooing onto the corrugated roof of her hut. She wrote not quite knowing why, telling not only of Africa, or Uganda, of the bush, of sickness, of the kindness of the Africans, but, despite herself, of herself too.

His letters were shorter, less weighty, pithy with day-to-day tales of newspapers, booze-ups, stories, the town, local politics and scandal, but vivid, and an important link with home.

As Nick had wrestled sleeplessly with his memories downriver at Richmond, a black Citroen saloon with diplomatic plates made the journey from a small, rather run-down embassy just off the Bayswater Road, down Park Lane, skirting Buckingham Palace, and into Belgravia.

The chauffeur kept the engine running, while a swarthy man got out, and was let into Bianca's house. She recognised him as the bodyguard from Paris.

She noted, clinically, that he would realise she had performed a sex act for the Leader. In the vestibule of her home she handed him the copies she had made of the documents taken from the Minister's despatch case.

She said 'He will find them interesting.'

The man quickly and professionally scanned the three sheets in silence, then said: 'Yes, it's the inconsequential things that are often the most important.' He folded the sheets.

She noted: Not bodyguard, aide. It might make him more difficult. For she sensed his tension, could hear the quickening and thickening of his laboured breathing.

'Goodbye.'

He remained immobile, then his hand came out, tentative at first, then bolder, and he laid his fingers on her lower arm.

'You are desirable. You and I could –'

Her voice cut him off like a dagger.

'You will leave now or I will kill you.'

She felt him stiffen, but the fingers raised only a fraction from her skin.

'Or better, I may let them take you back home. Then the Leader can kill you personally. He has been known to take more than a week.'

The man jumped as if hit by an electric shock, and he disappeared like a shadow, the big front door slamming shut behind them.

She went to her first floor bedroom and carefully ejected the magazine from the tiny .25 Raven automatic pistol she had concealed in the palm of her hand, and put gun and bullets back into a drawer.

Bianca was ice-cold. They thought because you could be purchased, that you could also be taken freely, without choice. No-one, she vowed, did that. Not to her. Not now.

The man could not know it, but by threatening him with a painful death at the hands of the Leader, she had saved his life.

For had he persisted in trying to have sex with her she had planned to shoot him and think about the consequences afterwards.

Nick met Jenny at the airport, and they shook hands, formally. He said: 'You've lost weight. Suits you.'

She said: 'Worms.'

He winced: 'Honest?'

'Honest.'

'Oogh, gruesome.'

She laughed: 'Common there, and anyway gone now, they won't attack you.'

They talked in the car, fumbling perhaps, towards something that may have been hinted at, or understood in their letters, but could not be known until they were face to face again.

26

He excused himself from the family reunion, and met her two days later in the main park. He'd had lovers, quite a few for his age, in fact there was a girl in tow now, but somehow he was nervous, off his stride.

Finally, for she was a different person after Africa – some things that had mattered didn't any longer – she said: 'Well, if you won't Nick, I'd better.' And she kissed him.

They were married 14 months later, and during the engagement Nick got first a trial, then a staff job at the Manchester office of a national daily.

They honeymooned in Paris, bought the terraced house next to the one they'd rented, upgraded their car, and suddenly they had more money than they'd ever known.

Nick earned twice the national average wage, Jenny worked. They discovered food, started to drink wine, and swapped Majorca for Greece as a summer holiday destination.

Two years later he was offered the London office, and hesitated. He was on familiar territory here, he was a Northern lad, London scared him, perhaps he'd screw up there, blow it, perhaps he couldn't handle all that.

They had everything they needed, money, house, Jenny was on her way to becoming a Sister. Why risk it all? He could always come back if it failed, but then he would be the guy who'd gone to head office and crapped it.

Jenny was furious: 'Are you CRAZY? You MUST go.' They flogged the house, bought a flat in Mitcham right at the moment before the first London property boom. Prices soared, and over the years they soared and moved with it.

They discovered they had a knack for timing, a knack for location; what was coming up, what down, taking advantage of their double salary status.

They moved West, Twickenham, a town house, then a semi three streets away, then they saw the estate agent's ad for the big detached house in Richmond, seedy, run-down and unloved.

Nick said: 'It's a fortune, it'll bankrupt us.'

'It's a snip, we'll have to live in squalor for a year, some work we can do ourselves. Next boom – weeeee. up it'll go.'

The house around him, Nick reflected, was worth almost £400,000. Say they liquidated everything, car, furniture, savings, pension, Christ they'd probably be worth half a million pounds!

Nick was the only son of a railwayman, and he was worth half a million. He could remember vividly borrowing ten bob – what was that, fifty pence? – from his Mum so he could go to the pub the night before pay day.

Rebecca was born at the end of the Seventies, planned. Jennifer was thirty, and they felt it was the optimum time. They had the house, jobs, money and security. And they quickly admitted to each other that one was enough.

She still did some supply nursing, but they hardly needed it now. Nick had joined the Enquirer in 1985. It was a Canadian venture and they were paying almost a third more than most British newspapers, with expenses to match.

It was aimed at the best selling News of the World market, trying to match it for showbiz, sex, sport and scandal. Soon it had 3.5 million readers.

Nick had discovered style, like a singer might discover his voice. Much earlier Jennifer's middle-class instincts had tamed his wilder sartorial fantasies, and London had smoothed him, given him a shape and a substance, and a feel of his own.

He favoured Churchill brogues, or Gucci loafers off duty, shirts from Turnbull and Asser, silk ties, understated, bought where the fancy took him, and suits he had made by a former Savile Row tailor who had become a personal friend.

28

At first he'd baulked at the prices, that deep working-class fear of spending, the preference for short-term cheap over long-term value, but his growing awareness and confidence, and Jennifer's encouragement, had over-ridden that.

They loved holidays, and travel for its own sake. They had long weekends in European cities, Berlin, Rome, Venice, Madrid and Bruges, touring galleries, monuments, eating in good restaurants.

In Summer the South of France – they had access to friends' homes there, and had considered buying one of their own – or the Greek Islands; Ios before it became overcrowded and spoilt.

Winter too, the West Indies, Bali once, Hawaii, even Africa, though not Uganda for the situation made it impossible. They lived the archetypal good life; dinner parties, the theatre, private film screenings sometimes, thanks to Nick's job.

He travelled a lot, doing mainly showbusiness inter-views, Los Angeles, New York, the Cannes Film Festival. And he and Jennifer still loved each other, more impor-tantly perhaps, still LIKED each other.

The sex had declined, that was to be expected, but they still made love when they could. If Rebecca was away staying at the home of one of her friends, or on a riding weekend, they would stock up with Veuve Cliquot, lower the lights, put on a movie sometimes, and the old magic was still there.

Neither had succumbed to the metropolitan sport of musical beds. They'd both been tempted, who wasn't, Nick once VERY seriously, Jennifer once in a kind of craziness, but neither had given in to it.

It was an unspoken thing between them, a rock, an anchor to what they were and had become. It said, we've come this far, together, joined, united.

Once they'd been listening to Barbra Streisand, her duet

with Barry Gibb, and Barbra had sung: 'And then you found her, you let the stranger in, who's sorry now?'

And Jennifer had said to him, with a kind of intensity he had never seen before: 'Don't let the stranger in, Nick, don't ever let her in.'

Jennifer, had a full life, some private nursing, voluntary work at the local hospital, long hours with Rebecca with her passion for horses; hostessing their dinner parties, watching their finances, remembering the birthdays and the anniversaries of parents, brothers, sisters, friends.

They were both slimmer, they had given up jogging, but there was an exercise bike in one of the rooms. Jenny's breasts were smaller, utterly different, but better, more erotic to him. She had less around the hips and bottom, thanks to exercise and good diet, and her skin was good.

She was ageing slightly, they both were, but when he looked at their early pictures, and then one, say, of them on the beach in Antigua, brown and confident, in good shape, it was like they'd been remade.

They had, EVERYTHING, and they had EACH OTHER.

Yet over the last year Nick had felt the first minor touches of unease about his work, like symptoms of some creeping illness. The business was harder, more ruthless than he could ever remember it. The pressures were greater, the rewards too – he acknowledged that – but the penalties more severe.

The Enquirer had fired two people they did not think were keeping up. More extremes were gone to to get stories, and more and more people were being alienated.

Some showbiz agents put the telephone down on him as soon as he mentioned the Enquirer's name, before he could even ask to interview their clients.

He felt like a man on an iceberg; that every story he

did cut off a chunk, and the space on which he could stand became smaller and smaller.

Now he was required to do more general features, buy-ups and exposés. Miles the editor had addressed them, saying: 'There is no room at the Enquirer for prima donnas.' Nick felt Miles Rimmer was looking directly at him. And Nick realised he was late forties, geriatric in career terms.

He had the money and the lifestyle, but could he keep it? He couldn't go back to that other world now, it was not just 200 miles away, it was a solar system away. He was a different man.

And that was another issue. Somewhere during the metamorphosis from Formica to stripped pine, he had lost focus of what he was, of what he stood for, if anything.

Some nights he lay awake and thought. Who am I now?

There had been just one aim and it had consumed him for so long, that the question had been cast aside. Money and lifestyle, security, success. He had discovered a streak of ruthlessness in himself he had not previously believed he possessed.

He learned he could compete, win, that he had talent, that he could work, hard, do whatever it took, go the extra mile, and that that way lay victory, material success, things he had believed as a youth were beyond him and his kind.

Three months ago the careful world had started to unravel in a manner that stunned him. That night he lay next to Jennifer, her bottom curved into his, the cleft of her buttocks defined between the silk pyjamas.

It was a familiar ritual. It would have risen, hungry for the kill, pushing at her, Jenny shifting as though in discomfort, but in reality in a delightful ease of expectancy, as she felt the presence and the hard probing head emerge beneath her pubis.

31

He would reach up, pushing his hands under her pyjama top, cupping her breasts, stroking her nipples, as his face slid up her pyjama jacket, kissing the exposed clammy softness of her back.

She would thrust her bottom backwards on him, entrapping it in the folds of silk, bringing her hand down to grip its head.

And at length, with no words spoken, he would pull down the pyjamas over her bottom, and slide in wet and hungry, through the foliage of her, deep into the core.

Impaled like this, she on him, him on her, sexual Siamese twins of their desire, they would rock back and forth. And after the moment of fission and fusion, they would lie, half-awake, each floating on a personal ocean, but linked, conjoined, glued together.

And still with virtually no words except for sleepy grunts of enquiry to welfare, and slurred reassurances of reply.

It was older than caves, natural, normal, spontaneous. And they had assumed, he and Jennifer, that they were the players in this love story, Abelard and Heloise, Romeo and Juliet, but that no such tragedies would befall them.

And then, on that darkest of nights of the soul, the beast had refused to rise, to move from his cage. And the oldest fear of all welled up in Nick.

The fear that the natural and normal is not. That that which has always happened, may not. It was also the fear of the master for his slaves. That one day they will rebel, will say No, and that no threat, no punishment, no inducement or reward will make them obey again.

Jennifer had been marvellous, and understanding. But all her coaxing, her gentle and kindly disguised skills had failed.

That night he had slept fitfully, and unknown to him so had she.

His doctor said there was nothing organically wrong,

advised him to eat and drink less, exercise more, avoid stress.

He had tried to imagine other women, women he had secretly desired, film stars, strangers on the train; he imagined unspeakable perversions, read erotic books.

Nick had everything, but without this he had NOTHING, WAS nothing. Had they come all this way, through almost three decades to reach this point?

Now his wife looked at him in the glare of the lamp, looked through him as if he were glass. He felt she could see every organ, every nerve and vein of him.

'Are you sure you're not sleeping with someone else?'

At that moment he hated her with the kind of ferocious, if temporary, hate that is possible between spouses.

For he knew what would be asked, eventually, and he felt that if he had been faced with such a situation, the enormity of someone's shame and humiliation, that he would have pulled back, sensing their pain, embarrassed into compassion.

But it was three months now; too long.

He prayed for reprieve, for a stay of execution.

'Good God, Jenny, how can you even ask that? I've always been faithful to you, you know that. I have told you, I am NOT having an affair.'

There was no mercy in her face now, no reprieve, no stay.

'Then tell me, Nick,' she said, 'I have to know. Why can't you make love to me anymore?'

He looked back at her blankly, mind gasping like a stranded fish.

'WHY, Nick?' she put a hand on his arm with appalling tenderness.

It could be avoided no longer, and there was something approaching terror in his voice:

'I'm impotent Jen. I'm impotent and I don't know why.'

33

Chapter Three

Jessica Alexander was, in most people's opinion, including Nick's, one of the best reporters in London and she had the track record to prove it. Now she wanted to have lunch with Nick, and she wanted to pay. That bothered him, and made his pulse run a little.

Sex had nothing to do with it. Jessica didn't fancy Nick, and if he had ever fancied her he'd forgotten.

You spent enough years around their periods, their PMT, the overheard or directly related accounts of their sex lives, and you almost literally ceased to think of them as women you might fall in love with, die for, marry, or run away with.

And they in their turn saw you at close hand for years, heard the petty deceits, the silly boastfulness, listened to your problems, your oft-recounted tales, witnessed your occasional maudlin drunkenness and flatulence. So if ever there had been the slightest glimmer between them it had long gone.

Today people seemed to mostly keep their sex lives out of the office, and anyway Nick had enough problems in the sexual arena.

The pulse increase was professional.

Jessica was the genuine article, and she wanted to buy him lunch, which meant, from his knowledge of her, that she wanted to involve him in some story on which she was working.

That would not be charity or foolishness, no-one gave away their own stories, and only shared them if they couldn't do them alone. She must need something he had, a skill, a contact, perhaps even his very maleness.

Perhaps it was just someone to go double-handed on a job.

Sometimes a man and a woman worked well together on a strange doorstep. Hard man, soft woman, or vice versa, sweet and sour, sometimes just a voice to fill the gap when one faltered.

The restaurant was deep in the city, away from the normal journalistic haunts, among the bankers and brokers. She poured the Rioja:

'How's Jenny?'

'Fine.' He didn't return the question. Jessica's marriage was on the rocks, a new man in tow, but he had a feeling that one was also being jettisoned like excess cargo.

'I've got a good one, and I need you to make it work.'

Ah, so that was it. He felt the familiar skin crawl, something akin to goose pimples, and a faint coldness in the pit of his stomach.

It was anticipation and instinct. Nick loved the feeling and hated it a little too. He loved it like policemen love car chases, firemen fires. Because it was why you did what you did.

He hated it for what it really said about himself. In some area of his imagination he sat in a book-lined study, a fire crackling in the grate, writing the great English novel, or lovingly crafting pieces on rock n'roll and politics for *Rolling Stone*.

But in his veins, his guts, his balls, where most men really lived, he liked the instant fix of what he did, the heroin buzz of popular journalism.

You got a tip, some little snippet of information, and off you went after the quarry. And quarry was not an imprecise analogy, for whoever you sought was being hunted.

Human quarry, guilty, if that judicial word could be applied in such circumstances, of an infraction – usually

36

only of the unwritten and applied morals and mores set down by newspapers that year.

That was the fundamental purpose of popular Sunday newspapers, their raison d'être. Big prey sometimes, small fry mostly, but every once in a while they must find a BIG name. Find the sin, discover the lie, the peccadillo, then fire the salvoes.

A TV star perhaps, a sportsman, a politician, the more respectable, the less previously blemished, the better. Then the downfall was undertaken with elaborate care lest the victim escape.

Dispatch had to be swift and total, for the victim must not turn on his attackers with libel writs. It had to be right, pinned down, legally water-tight, planned with careful timing too in case injunctions were sought preventing publication.

Even after twenty years on what used to be called Fleet Street, it still made his pulse race, and his bowels tingle. And he could see it on Jessica like a halo, he could smell it like the perfume of blood. She had something, and it was good.

'Tell all.'

'Who is Bianca, Nick?'

'THE Bianca?'

She nodded.

'Silly question. World's top model, mystery girl, could be gay, could be a sex change. Probably none of those. Swimming in money. Why? This about her?'

'Yes. Bianca has a secret.'

'Drugs?'

'Not drugs.' Jessica waved her free hand dismissively. 'Forget drugs as far as she's concerned.'

'So . . . ?'

'She's a hooker, Nick, she turns tricks, five grand a time and more. Top drawer client list. She is at the centre of everything, politics, terrorism . . .'

Nick laughed, couldn't help it.

'Jess, come on . . .'

'Shut the fuck up, Nick, and LISTEN.'

'Hey,' he spread his hands, 'why so touchy?'

And he felt a stab of disappointment. Bianca? She didn't need the money, half the rich men in London would willingly make her their wife or mistress.

'I'm touchy because this is true. Turning tricks here, New York, Paris.'

'Why?'

It was too much like the amateur's view of a good story. The US President is an alien, Margaret Thatcher is a heroin addict, Bianca is a hooker. It was too extreme, too unreal. Bianca and drugs maybe, but this? Crazy.

'I'll get to that. Her client list is what interests me . . .' she saw Nick's eyes wandering, grabbed his hand and dug her nails in.

'Nick, for Christ's sake listen to me. This is not fantasy. We could be at the centre of the biggest political scandal in this country for thirty years.'

He lifted off her hand, saw the tiny white marks where her nails had driven furrows in the fading tan: 'I've heard that, oh, fifty or sixty times since I came to Fleet Street.'

She drank a long draught of wine and stared out through the full glass window at the City throngs, then back to him:

'I sometimes think cynicism is our worse enemy. I'm going to name some names and I want you to listen and not interrupt.' She started. A Cabinet minister, a US government official, a famous Saudi royal, an international arms dealer and playboy; the head of a Palestinian terror group with Libyan links.

'Impressed?'

'Sure.'

'That's for starters.' They fell silent as the waitress

38

brought the food and fussed around trying to fit too many plates and glasses and bottles on the absurdly small table.

And Nick wondered: Has she lost it? He hated himself for even thinking it, for he respected Jessica. But reporters did. One minute right as rain, the next embroiled in half-fantasies involving conspiracies and the CIA, murder plots and famous names, bizarre fiction born of some original information then cooked in a stew of falsehood, something that would never, EVER be printed.

She read his mind: 'Don't look at me like that. I'm not one of those front door jobs, the loonies who bring their files with them, writing in the margins of newspapers, believing the police have put radio transmitters in their head.'

Nick laughed. It was a shared experience. He said: 'And when you try and help them, to explain to them that the police are too busy to implant radio transmitters, they always say . . .'

'You're-in-it-with-them.' They said it in unison and laughed together.

'But . . .' he swirled the Rioja around, then looked straight into her eyes, 'Bianca a hooker? It has a kind of loony feel about it Jess.'

'It's true.'

'Who is your source, can you tell me?'

'Yes. Annabelle Delane.'

Another stab of disappointment. Annabelle was an ex-Page Three girl who had disappeared from the scene a couple of years earlier. There'd been a little story saying she was working towards an Open University degree, some bright snapper had put a mortar board on her head, nothing since.

If that was Jessica's only source, only proof, then it was a non-starter, because to run a story like this your evidence would have to be massive, overwhelming, and as tight as a lawyer's conscience.

Jessica said: 'You look disappointed.'

'She's hardly big time.'

'She KNOWS, Nick, she's given me everything.'

'Why?'

'She's been on the game too.'

'That's not an answer.'

'Let me tell you a story. A man comes to town from Birmingham, or Hamburg, or Tokyo. And he's lonely.'

Nick laughed: 'So he calls a number given to him by a friend.'

'Who got it from a friend, and so on. La Ronde. A very discreet middle-aged lady in Marble Arch or Kensington is on the line. She just happens to know a lovely, young intelligent, discreet girl, who would be happy to have dinner with him.'

'For a price.'

'We pay for our pleasures. She has dinner with him and if she doesn't find him too repulsive, she may go back to his suite or flat with him for the night.'

'Annabelle was doing this?'

'Yes, she was broke, she had a habit. And the mornings after she was three hundred or five hundred better off.'

'And she's made a new friend.'

'Absolutely. And if he should come back to town, what could be more natural than to call her and arrange a meeting. Then perhaps an antique here, a Cartier watch there. If it gets serious the rent is paid, perhaps even the mortgage.'

'That's a story in itself, Annabelle was Page Three.'

'Small fry.' Jessica called for another bottle.

'Get to the point Jess.'

'She's doing OK, flat of her own in Epping, Peugeot 205 convertible, a studio flat in Marbella. And three years ago she was broke.'

'So why did she come to you – she did come to you, didn't she? For money?'

She hadn't received any, Nick thought. Not yet anyway, unless Jessica had paid her out of her own bank account, and no reporters did that, for that way lay financial ruin.

And the Enquirer hadn't paid her, Nick regularly checked the payment sheets. He liked to know who was getting how much, and for what.

'I went to her.'

'What was your lever? How did you persuade her to talk?'

'I blackmailed her.'

Nick gave an uneasy laugh: 'What you mean is you offered to let one story go, if she'd tell you a better one. And she gave you this . . .' he nearly said, "crap", couldn't help it . . . 'this story about Bianca.'

Jessica looked him straight in the eye: 'I know what I mean Nick. I blackmailed her.'

Across London the Minister climbed out of the large bed and walked unsteadily to the bathroom. He looked at himself in the mirror, hardly believing that he could do this.

The risk was immense. His political career would be ruined if he was ever exposed. And the cost was becoming phenomenal. He had already given Bianca over £200,000.

It was becoming harder to hide, both from his wife and his financial advisers. Now he had arranged with an MP, someone who owed him a debt of gratitude, to get Bianca a pass to the House of Commons. And God alone knew why she would want one.

She told him she was doing some project or other, something with ABC television in New York, but she was a model for God's sake. He'd had his MP friend list her as a temporary researcher.

That alone was enough for a scandal, the egalitarian-minded British public was always on the lookout for examples of unearned privilege.

The Minister had his excuses ready; close friend of Bianca's, she a good friend of the country, giving to charity – he could arrange that – deep interest in British system of government, possibility of her seeking British citizenship, etc. etc.

And why shouldn't she have access to the Commons, half the researchers in Parliament were young Americans from various universities?

And if she did want to do this damn silly project with American television, she'd need access to the House. She'd be quietly vetted by Special Branch, everyone with a House of Commons pass was.

There was no untoward connection with himself. He had visited her home, of course, but those visits were unrecorded, and if they were mentioned, the TV project came to mind, and his reputation preceded him. No-one would think, certainly not the narrow-minded bigots of Special Branch, that the Minister would be getting sexual favours from Bianca.

But the Minister was still sweating, as he sat, naked on Bianca's toilet, unaware of the closed circuit video camera that filmed him.

Propped up in bed Bianca fingered the tiny, plastic-embossed card with its House of Commons portcullis insignia, and her name upon it.

She had the pass, and soon she would go to Tripoli.

The Minister returned and lay next to her. She would give it a month at most and then end it. She had no further use for him, and today he had haggled over money.

And then, instead of his nanny, which had always sufficed, she had had to pretend she was a boy.

*　　*　　*

Nick said, incredulously: 'You REALLY blackmailed her?'

'Sure.'

'Blackmail is illegal.'

'So is ivory-hunting, whaling, drink-driving, paedophilia. Or if they're not, they should be.'

'Come on, Jess. be serious.'

'I am being. A lot of things are illegal, poverty should be too.'

'You're not poor.'

'And don't intend to be. I've been lagging behind, Nick, getting older, slower.'

'Christ, you're not forty yet.'

'Soon, and forty is old in this job.'

He noticed the unintended snub, rode it quickly. Sometimes Jessica's intensity alarmed him: 'OK, OK. So how did you blackmail her?'

'I learned she was on the game, and that she's heavily into coke. She's dropped all that Open University crap too.'

'Who told you about Annabelle in the first place?'

Jessica tapped the side of her nose: 'I have my spies. Actually it was an anonymous client, a man, well-spoken, presumably a disgruntled client. Anyway, I know from whom she buys it, where she keeps it, and more importantly to whom she sells it.'

'She deals?'

'A natural progression.'

Nick pushed around some tired quiche, sliced off a piece and chewed it without enthusiasm:, 'So you fronted her,' he said with his mouth full.

'Discreetly. By arrangement. All I wanted was a list of her clients, sexual and narcotic. I would have let it go at that.'

'But she offered you more.'

'Yeh,' Jessica lifted some of her quiche, and examined

43

it like a biological specimen, 'I was surprised she caved in so quickly. She said for twenty grand and no mention in any story she'd give me something better.'

'Bianca?'

'Right.'

'What does she know?'

'Six months ago she was offered a big job. A rich Arab prince on a private yacht moored off St. Tropez. A week, five grand in cash. A private jet to Nice, Roller to the yacht, as much as she could eat, drink and stuff up her nose.'

Nick nodded. Somewhere along the line would be the flaw that would make this apparently priceless diamond worthless.

'Second night out, somewhere off Sardinia, she is called in to screw the Prince's second cousin. Third night, a storm, one of those Med specials, thunder, lightning, sea like the Big Dipper, everyone heaving their guts. She goes on deck and sees Bianca throwing dinner, stomach, lungs, everything over the rail.'

Nick toyed with his fork, mainly to avoid Jessica's eyes: 'A glimpse of a woman in a storm?'

'Night four . . .' Jessica pressed on, 'Annabelle is summoned to Princey-baby's master suite, and there, naked on the bed next to him is Bianca.'

'Doesn't sound very secret,' Nick said, as evenly as he could.

'According to Annabelle, Bianca hadn't realised it was going to be a threesome. She was furious, threw a wobbly and walked out, back to her private cabin. Back in St. Tropez, Annabelle gets an extra five grand and strict instructions from the Ay-rabs to keep her trap shut.'

'So Bianca has a weird sex life on the ocean wave. None of this means she was screwing for money.'

'The Sheikh says she was.'

'He told Annabelle this?'

'Sure, he was pissed, rat-arsed, these oil-sheikhs are famous for getting legless, then they chop the hands off those who do it back home.'

Nick poured out the new Rioja, with a sense of deflation. None of it was enough, he was surprised Jessica couldn't see that. Great for gossip, great for a piece in Private Eye, not enough for a national newspaper.

'Not enough.'

'Of course, it's not enough. Back in England Annabelle gets a call from our friend Bianca. Dinner, drinks, friendly chats, advice, help. Suddenly she is Annabelle's best friend.'

'Doesn't make sense.'

'Does. Annabelle knows her secret, so better her in the tent pissing out than pissing in. Better involved, embroiled, making money, than tempted to sell what she knows.'

'Still needs more.'

'Of course, we'll prove it. And until we do, unless we do, Annabelle doesn't get her twenty. And unless we do, it'll be Annabelle in the frame instead of Bianca. And she knows it.'

Nick looked at his colleague long and hard: 'I never believed Jess, in my wildest dreams that you could be such an out and out cunt.'

She gave him a bitter smile in return: 'Interesting the way you men use the Anglo Saxon vernacular for the female sexual orifice as an insult. Would that imply latent homosexuality would you say, Nick, a kind of reverse penis envy?'

'We've been friends a long time, but I think this –'

'Colleagues, Nick, is what we've been, and will you love me when I'm old and grey?'

'You're a good operator, you don't have to worry.'

'But I do, Nick love, I do. What about Leadbetter and Dixon, they were good operators and now they're out. I see Susie and Heather, the bright young waves of

45

the future; younger than I am, keener than I am, more importantly prettier than I am.'

'They're nothing.'

'They're a threat. I need this job, and I need this story Nick. It'll put me back at the top. I like the money here, I like my flat – my mortgage will be paid in seven years for Chrissake, then fuck 'em – I like the holidays, my car, my bloody independence, I'm not giving it up without a fight.'

'Early paranoia?'

'Maybe, but being paranoid doesn't mean people aren't out to get you. They're more ruthless, more ambitious, I've got to keep up, and if I have to blackmail the likes of Annabelle to do it, I will.'

These women in newspapers today took no prisoners, any of them. They seemed like a risen, de-colonialised people out to prove they could be as tough as their masters, and inflict as many cruelties – especially on their own kind.

Did we make them like this, Nick thought, Was this the legacy of men?

'So, how will you prove it?'

'Don't you know?' She had an amused little smile on her lips.

'No.' And then he realised he did know, and felt foolish for not knowing all along. Why the lunch, why the confidences, everything.

He said: 'No, absolutely not. Not in a million years.'

'Don't be silly.'

'No, I refuse. End of story. Let's get the bill, it's on me, my treat, no problem.'

'Nick, you look the part.'

'Which is what, exactly, a punter?' he waved a hand, trying to draw the attention of the waitress.

'A rich man – in the right place, right setting, right circumstances.'

'Bollocks.'

'Confident, insouciant when you're in the mood, good shoes and suits, shirts too. A certain couldn't-give-a-stuff attitude when you want to.'

'I'm not doing it . . .' he raised his voice, 'could I have the bill here, please . . . I'm not doing it. A decoy, a tethered goat, it's not journalism, and anyway . . .' he found that he was spluttering, 'it's sexist.'

'Get you.'

'When we used to say we needed a "girlie" on a story,' he stressed the quote marks, 'all the women used to call us chauvinist.'

'Times change, Nicky, love. Look, forget the bill and put your bloody arm down, you look like you're at Nuremberg. I don't just need a man, I need the right man. You. The others are wankers and tosspots.'

'This flattery is pathetic.'

'One word, one wrong gesture, and it's blown. The story of the decade blown. She has got to go into that room and believe that you are a genuine punter. She's going to offer you sex for five grand or whatever it takes, and we are going to tape her. If she smells anything wrong, we're done.'

'Jess, just remember. You don't give me orders, I don't give you orders. We're equals, just little old reporters.'

'Yeh, but who runs the story, calls the tune. I've danced to yours before now.'

'It can't work. Christ, you know my background, trouble at t'mill. All this, the suits, the shoes, camouflage.'

Her eyes burned with an almost religious zeal: 'Yes. Yes! Self-made man, clawed your way up, bring the accent back. No-nonsense, spade a spade, where there's muck there's brass. You can do it. And then we share it, all of it, me and you, Jess and Nick, the reporters who nailed Bianca. We'll be STARS.'

'Thanks, but no thanks.'

Her face hardened: 'Then you'll be the laughing stock of every newspaper in Britain. The man who turned down the chance to see Bianca with her pants off. The man who didn't want to have Bianca offer him sex. The reporter who –'

'How would they know, Jess?' He saw her face: 'Oh, you'd tell them, right, you'd make it known I'd turned it down?'

She shrugged. 'These things get out.'

'Blackmail seems your stock in trade these days.'

'Persuasion, not blackmail. DO IT, Nick, for God's sake.'

He upended his wine and took a long swallow.

'To start with Jenny wouldn't stand for it, and we'd never be able to set it up, and if we did, she'd suss me straight off. Forget the whole thing.'

But Jessica knew that it was just excuses now, rationalisations, reasons to be put up and knocked down, one by one.

And deep within him he knew it too, and he knew also that he wanted her to knock it down. He was frightened of the effect it might have on Jennifer, but he WANTED the story.

It was an outside chance; odds against it ever happening, but if it ever did, it would be a sensation.

And he, Nick Carter, would have been the man who pulled it off. His career would rocket.

And maybe it would be better not to tell Jennifer, not in view of the way things were.

He had tried so hard, and so had Jenny. He bought two bottles of Veuve Cliquot, Rebecca was at Jennifer's sister's in Grantham, telephone off the hook, a horny video poised in the mouth of the machine.

Jennifer had bathed, put on a silk slip and tiny briefs, and they sat sipping the second bottle watching the action.

As a kid he and his mates had pushed their noses against the window of the town's only dirty bookshop trying to see the naked girls.

In those days they put stars covering the nipples. The first time Nick touched a girl's breast – astounded that they were soft and not hard – he half expected to find a five-pointed star where the nipple was.

And now you could watch pornography in your own living room if you wished, hard or soft The world had spun revolutions.

Jennifer said: 'Which one do you fancy, or would you rather have them . . . both?' A Brazilian girl, luscious and dark-skinned was doing bizarre things to a blonde, gamine German girl she had just picked up on the Copacabana.

Two women. Together. He knew what his wife was thinking. It never fails to excite a man. Nick was nervous, like someone before an important speech, and he assured himself. It'll be fine, the smells, the stimuli, everything is there, and none of it can fail.

Jennifer said:

'I never feel entirely comfortable with this stuff, I'm never sure if it's disgusting, or horny. It makes me feel strange, you know, seeing women . . . together like that.'

Nick kept his eyes on the screen, on the bodies, black and white, intertwined, and he felt like a doctor in a surgery. A scene like this must have excited him once, surely?

She turned her head: 'Remember this?' She took a long, drink of champagne, kept it in her mouth, leaned over and kissed him, gradually opening her mouth so that the wine flowed into his, and they transferred it back and forward.

'Mmmmm . . .'

'Save money, share champagne . . . hey I can't say "share champagne," I must be getting pissed.'

49

'I remember when I met you, two Babycham and it was the Fleet's lucky day.'

'Liar . . . Your lucky day maybe . . .' She slid off the sofa and stretched out at his feet: 'I'm not an old bag, am I?'

'Not in a million.' She stretched up a hand and pulled him down. He said: 'This rug has just been cleaned.'

'Then . . .' she kissed him playfully, her tongue caressing his teeth, 'we might have to have it cleaned again.'

She pulled her slip up and over her head, and flung it into a corner of the room. Then she pulled off her pants.

'We should watch more lesbian sex, I think I've come over somewhat randy. Do you think I'm a secret dyke?'

'Secret lush. More champagne madam?' She leaned back: 'Mmmm.'

He took the bottle, knelt down next to her and poured gently into the passage from her breasts to her navel.

'Oh yes, yes, yes.'

He bent over, drawing his tongue along her skin, feeling the wine spill across her body.

'Some friends of mine are thirsty too.'

'Then we must supply them.' He took a swig straight from the bottle, put his mouth over first one, then the other nipple, and released the champagne. He sucked and licked, feeling the nipples stand up under his tongue, and the wet, slightly sticky feel around the aureole.

'Yes?'

'Not bad, not bad at all.'

And the fear hovered around him like stage fright. This was good, though, this was familiar and sensual. It was what he liked, what she liked, it would be OK.

'Take the robe off, I like you in your knickers. I like your bulge. Did I ever tell you that I like your bulge? Your bulge is horny.'

He laughed and kissed her: 'You are a little pissed.'

50

'In vino veritas in vino randiness.' She giggled, but there was a rasp in it.

He slipped out of the robe and let it fall. Tactfully, despite what she had said, she kept her eyes closed.

'Any other special friends thirsty?'

'A very special friend is dying for a drink.'

'At your service.' He knelt and poured again, this time from her navel down, saw her arch her back deliberately to help the stream of champagne flow over her pubis.

'Better?'

'Lacking a certain body?'

'The champagne?'

'My special friend.'

'Any body in particular?'

'Suck it and see.'

He lay down, gently parted her legs, and saw the tiny rivulets of champagne on her inner thighs. He took a sidelong drink from the bottle, kept the champagne in his mouth, and put his mouth across the lips of her vagina.

He released it, working it into the crevices of her with his tongue, slowly then more vigorously, listening for her familiar cries, sensing the movements of her body.

He heard her moan, felt one thigh, then the other go up in delicious response. He loved this, loved doing it, knowing how much she liked it, and knowing – selfishly – that when it was done she would sit astride him as he liked.

He had minutes, precious minutes. He tasted the delightful cocktail of the wine and her juices, and wondered how he had ever been squeamish about this. Then the slight stickiness of the drying wine against the soft membrane of her pudenda.

Her hands came down and clutched his head, her fingers deep in his hair: 'God, Nick, if you knew how good that was.' He found her clitoris, sucked and swirled with his tongue, feeling it grow in between his lips. He

51

heard her moans, low at first, then higher, then felt her thighs contract, clutching his head like a vice, felt her shuddering, almost painful convulsions, and her guttural sounds.

When she at last lay still, he prayed; let it be enough.

At last she sat up, a half-glazed look in her eyes, gave him a long, slow kiss, and then reached out her hand to his leg, upwards to his pants, touched, then brought her hand away as though she had been burned.

'I'm sorry, Jen, God knows why. I'm enjoying this, I'm loving it, I swear to God. It doesn't matter for me, as long as you –'

'Hey, sshhh. It's not over.'

She put a finger to his lips, pushed him gently backwards and he stared at the ceiling as he felt her pull his white cotton briefs over his legs and feet.

Felt her hand, then her mouth, then her tongue find him, felt her small mouth encircle him and tighten on him. And there was nothing, just a dead, ice-cold feeling.

She coaxed with her tongue, her mouth, her hand, using those little combinations of movement she had learned from experience over the years that he liked.

He gritted his teeth, hating himself. Why didn't it happen? Godamnit, he wanted it to. At length he put a hand down and raised her head: 'Come up here Jen, leave it for a while, please.'

And she did, crushing herself against him, and he recognised the unsatisfied desire, the need for that core of him inside her.

Her tongue found his, and she tongued him vigorously, almost anxiously, and he returned her kisses, but a pace behind, keeping up, not in harmony.

And her hand went down to him again, withdrew, and she threw herself back with an impossible to suppress cry of irritation and frustration.

He swung her away from him, got up, and went to

the bathroom to shower. When he returned she was wearing his robe, sitting on the sofa, knees under her chin, watching a video of Far From the Madding Crowd.

There was no point in saying anything, least of all sorry, so he just sat next to her, glumly, watching the movie. After five minutes of the artificial silence, she turned to him, something like concern in her eyes, searching for an explanation.

And she seemed to find none in his avoided eyes, and eventually she said: 'It's not enough, Nick, the rest of it. Maybe for some women, but not for me. It's not complete.'

'Yes,' he said, bitterness trying to match the shame, 'it's certainly not complete.'

No, better not to tell Jennifer at all. If she thought he was going to go into some room with not only a beautiful woman, but with Bianca, there was no telling what she might do.

'What?' Jessica was speaking to him.

'I said, she's your wife, not your boss. And you make your excuse and leave in the best traditions of British Sunday journalism.'

'Save the sarcasm Jess, I happen to love my wife.'

'Then tell her, not me.'

'It really is the most awful bollocks. It's probably not true, and even if it is Miles won't go for it, and if he does, the chairman won't. Too dangerous, she's too big, too rich.'

'It'll happen,' Jessica said doggedly.'

'Well, let's say it does. And you get me in this bloody room with Bianca – I can't believe I'm even saying this, she'll suss me straight off.'

'No,' Jessica shook her head, 'she won't. I know you. If you do it – when you do it – shush, Nick – you'll do it right.

53

And do you know why, because you're a professional, my son, you'll make it work.'

'Save the flattery Jess. It won't get that far. Let's say, hypothetically you tried to do it, who'd fix it, Annabelle?'

'Sure. They're thick as thieves now.'

'Wouldn't Bianca suspect?'

'Might. Risk we take. Has to be presented to her in the right way.'

'And Annabelle will?'

'No option remember?'

'Big mortgage, needs the money, and doesn't want the Old Bill swarming all over her place.'

'Correct.' Jessica smiled inwardly. He was hooked; details now, a little more flattery, some needle, perhaps a few sober reassurances, but he was in. Men were simple. All ego.

'We tape it – Nagra?' Jessica was nodding. 'Pix man outside the venue?' More nods.

'OK . . .' Nick took another swig of wine, and pondered. 'She's in the room, she incriminates herself, it's all on the Nagra. What then?'

'What when?'

'How do I tell the most beautiful woman in the world I don't want to screw her?'

Jessica lifted her shoulders in an exaggerated shrug:

'Don't.'

'Whaaat.'

'Get a free screw on the company. She'll say you did anyway, they always do. Anyway the public doesn't believe all that make an excuse and leave crap.'

'Except it's mostly true.'

She winked: 'If I was a man I wouldn't turn down Bianca.'

He said slowly: 'Look Jess, I'm faithful to Jennifer, you know that for God's sake.'

'Word is you're a good boy.'

'I don't believe this ridiculous fucking scenario will ever play, but if it ever does, and by some act of stupidity I am part of it, nothing happens in that room.'

'Fine by me sailor.'

'And if that screws your story, TOUGH!'

'Read you loud and clear.'

He finished his wine: 'Up yours.'

'Say, but you're beautiful in yer wrath.'

'Stuff it.' He began to pick leaves off an adjoining rubber plant.

'Oh come on, lighten up. Make something up. Tell her you're jet-lagged, tell her you're impotent.'

He felt the blood rush to his cheeks.

'Tell her anything.'

'She'll sue the sodding arse off us, we'll both get fired, and we'll be lucky to get work on the Kidderminster Bugle.'

Jessica raised her glass in toast: 'We'll be mega-stars and Bianca will be finished.'

Nick looked at the new Jessica, the one he had never really known before: 'And is that why we're in this business, to finish people?'

'We're in it to get stories.'

'At any cost?'

'Save me the moralising and check your cuttings. You've finished a few people. A couple of people have gone to jail in the past thanks to you, and the choirmaster in Berwick . . . ?'

Had tried to gas himself six months after Nick exposed him as a paedophile, back in the Seventies, before the Enquirer. Jessica either had a good memory or she'd done her homework.

'OK, you've made your point. Just lately, I think . . .'

She grabbed his hand and squeezed: 'Well, don't. Don't think, DO. Just lately it's all think with you. Remember who you are, where you came from. This is what you do for a living, Nick. And you do it bloody well.'

'Too bloody well sometimes.'

She called for the bill and fanatically insisted on paying it, pushing back his proffered notes. In the taxi back to the office, a thought struck him, and he turned to Jessica who was looking out of the rain-streaked window.

'Jess. We never got to the why, why she does it. She's got everything, looks, fame, money, rich suitors, why would she screw Arabs for five grand?'

She turned to look at him and her face was triumphal.

'Maybe she doesn't know herself, but I think I do. She screws for money because that's the only way she can screw. For money!'

Chapter Four

She felt no personal fear, but she could recognise the danger to herself. Perhaps it was part of the reason she did it, the thought that one day the secret Bianca would be discovered.

The tiny frisson at the prospect, was all that reached her, all that worked against the detachment and the distance. Only by going to the edge of the precipice and looking over could she feel any *involvement* with the life around her.

Only those who face death, a philosopher had said, could fully appreciate life. And discovery for Bianca would be akin to death.

It was like executing the perfect turn on a ski-slope, or missing another car by inches on a busy highway. You knew that somehow, somewhere you must plummet, tumble, crash in a tear of metal. But until then you had the awesome power of your secret.

Bianca left the Mandarin, crossed the road and took the covered passageway to the Star Ferry. The breeze was soft off the harbour, humidity down, and she could see the lights of Kowloon glittering ahead of her. She kept the wide-brimmed hat low, but no-one appeared to recognise her.

The shoot had finished at five, and the camera team and other models were exhausted. They would bathe, rest, then dine later. But Bianca had an appointment.

She was carried along in the tide of disembarking passengers, over the shifting ramp, up the incline, then down the steps onto the ferry concourse. She skirted the bus station, crossed at a traffic light, and headed in the direction of Nathan Road.

The head of Xinhua was waiting in his suite at the Peninsular, and opened the door himself. He wore a quaint, old-fashioned Chinese suit of hideous and formal blue, a left-over from the strict days of Mao.

Xinhua was the official Chinese news agency with a base in Hong Kong. That was the official story; the reality was that the head of Xinhua and its senior officials were Peking's unofficial representatives in Hong Kong.

The man, in his early sixties – a youngster by Chinese government standards – was an up and coming politician. Bianca studied him closely, but there was nothing to distinguish him from a dozen men of other nationalities.

He had the Man look, a demeanour of both lust and helplessness. He looked at her as an addict gazes at his narcotic. Whatever was for sale he could afford, but *she* had the power for *he* had the need.

It was there in the too eager eyes, in the parting of hungry lips, in the sweat on the brow and the restrained and terrible swelling in the groin.

In the bedroom he produced a brown envelope, and she tore it with her thumb, feeling the bundles of high denomination Hong Kong dollars that tomorrow she would deposit at her account in the North Point branch of the Hongkong and Shanghai Bank, a branch few Europeans used.

She held the currency, feeling its weight and potency, smelling its newness. She pulled out one note, and held it, crumpled it, feeling it crinkle unwillingly, not ready yet for its inevitable, worn-out ignominious end. The delicious crackle registered on her ears like the note of a piano key.

The man watched her, impassive on the surface, boiling within. Now the aphrodisiac of the dollar bills was working its magic on her, and slowly she eased herself out of the short black dress until her pubic hair became visible.

The man gasped, and Bianca smiled. She was naked

from the waist down, the top half of her body still covered by a tiny black under-bodice.

The Xinhua official strained forward like a dog on a leash, but his feet seemed rooted to the ground. She pulled slowly at one strap until first one breast then the other, was exposed. Slowly, deliberately she pushed the first finger of her free hand into her pubic hair, searching for herself.

Satisfied she was moist, she took the note, straightened it, curled it into a crude cylinder, then slowly inserted the note into her vagina. She beckoned to the Chinese. Power. The power of money and sex. Sex/money/money/sex, indivisible, merged, one whole. The man walked over to her. She had whistled and the dog had come.

Bianca worked on him, mechanically, as she moved the note rhythmically in and out with her free hand. Self-aroused she took him.

Would this be the one? Was this the moment of betrayal; the ultimate danger? She watched, detached.

Miles Rimmer and the lawyer sat side by side on the leather sofa across the smoked glass coffee table from Nick and Jessica on the matching sofa.

He and Jess were the supplicants, Miles Rimmer and the lawyer were the judges, and the reporters were awaiting the judgement. Rimmer splayed a hand across his elegant blue shirt-front, with the other, easing off his tortoise-shell glasses and pinching the bridge of his nose.

It was Miles's affected, world weary, I'm-a-busy-tired-man-much responsibility, gesture. He said:

'I'll go for it Jessica, Nick. But it is not without its dangers, eh Conrad?'

'Quite,' the lawyer said.

'I want Bianca nailed to the wall before we use one word. Conrad?'

'Quite.'

'I need an affidavit from the other girl –?'

Nick said: 'Annabelle.'

'A detailed affidavit. Then I want a clearly audible tape, two if possible. One of Bianca on the telephone to the girl Annabelle when she, as I understand, makes the assignation.'

'OK,' Nick said, thinking: Thanks for telling us all this because we couldn't have figured it out for ourselves. What the hell did you think we were going to do, write the story without any evidence?

'And I want those tapes analysed against Bianca's voice on TV or radio. And if those patterns don't match, *exactly*, the story is dead.'

'Quite,' Jessica said, before the lawyer could, and Conrad glared.

Miles put his spectacles back on.

'This has got to be *right*. If it isn't it'll make the Jeffrey Archer settlement look like ". . . A vicarage tea party, Jessica mouthed under her breath . . ." a vicarage tea party.' Why, Jessica, wondered did everyone compare everything to vicarage tea parties. She had heard a politician, say seriously, that a nuclear holocaust would make Hiroshima look like a vicarage tea party.

'No problem,' Jessica said calmly, 'she's doing it, she's been doing it for a while, I'm surprised it hasn't come out before.' Jessica paused. 'I think she is too.'

The lawyer splayed his hands into a church steeple. 'Ah, reporters. They feel all they have to do is come galloping back with the story and that's the end of it. Life and the law is a little more complicated.'

'Conrad,' Jessica asked, 'if we tape Bianca offering sex for money. If Nick here is in the same *room* with her when she makes that offer. If she *takes* our money, do you think she would *dare* to sue us?'

How she hated newspaper lawyers. Their job was to find ways and means of getting stuff *in* the paper, not keeping it out, but Conrad seemed to work on the reverse principle. If it wasn't 100% reliable he wanted to kill it. But no newspaper stories were 100%, the business was risk. Everyone wanted to get it so right the bastards didn't *dare* sue. But you could bring Conrad a thousand affidavits signed in blood, a million tapes, it was never enough.

'Well, young lady . . .' Conrad gave a pulled face look of scepticism.

Jessica quelled her anger: 'Bianca Vasquez is a prostitute and we are going to prove it. But if you are going to start umming and aahing over dots and commas . . .'

'Legal points . . .'

'Then Nick might as well not go into that room with her.'

'You people think it is *so* simple.'

'*You* people!?' Jessica exploded, 'We make the fucking paper Conrad. Without us there is no paper, and all you lawyers and advertising Yuppies are out on the streets. Without stories, *stories*, remember those Conrad, there is no Enquirer. And this is a great story.'

Nick closed his eyes in despair and Miles said: 'I know you're very keen on this Jessica, but kindly don't lose control, Conrad has his job to do, and so do I.'

'Sorry,' Jessica said, grudgingly.

Miles said: 'Are you happy about doing this Nick? I could get one of the young, keen lads on it. You're a married man after all.'

'No!' Jessica got up from the sofa, 'No, Miles, it's got to be Nick. Those East End barrow boys in there wouldn't fool Bianca for a minute. She'd smell a rat and be off in a minute. They've as much class between them as a three week old dog turd.'

The lawyer shook his head.

'Nick?' Miles said, 'OK by you?'

'Yeh,' Nick replied, 'I'm in. No problem.'

The lawyer said: 'I do have a rather deep worry about all this?'

'Mmmmm?' Miles said in query.

'Agent provocateur. Jessica, you might not be aware –'

'I know what agent provocateur means Conrad.'

'Well, my worry is that we are encouraging Bianca to do something she might otherwise not do if we weren't offering. It might be construed that we have actively engineered the situation.'

Nick interjected: 'If Bianca was a starving actress that might be a point. Offering a starving person five grand for their body and then exposing them as a prostitute, would be agent provocateur. But not a woman worth *millions* . . .'

'Anyway,' Jessica added, 'it's the only way. She doesn't patrol the streets. It is word-of-mouth recommendation. And I make you a promise. The day after we use this, the floodgates will open. Other names will start coming into the frame, and we'll have got it first Miles. No matter *what* the others get, it will be the Enquirer who broke it.'

The four of them sat silently for a moment, the silence broken by the lawyer. 'Of course, what would absolutely clinch it . . .'

Jessica moaned, audibly.

'. . . ask her to spend a weekend with you some-where, Rio, San Francisco, offer her twenty thousand, *thirty* . . .' Conrad's eyes lit up at the dramatic potential of it all . . . 'get her to specifically agree to spending a *further* time with you *for* sexual purposes, *for* money.'

He beamed: 'That should seal it. It also gives you the perfect excuse for not . . .' he giggled, 'consummating the matter there and then.'

'Good idea,' Miles said, 'bring that into your scenario Nick, Jessica.'

They nodded.

62

'And hopefully, before or after this strategic with-drawal . . .' Miles smiled slightly as if to seek acknowl-edgement for his pun . . . 'Nick here will have got some names out of our Miss Vasquez, using the charm for which he is legend in Fleet Street.'

'Of course,' said Nick, meaning it. Of course. What did you think I was going to do? Twenty-odd years in the business and they still talked to you like naughty kids, not giving you credit for any street savvy at all. Wonder what was the last story Miles did? The Tunbridge Wells garden party, probably – in 1951.

'We'll use Paddy Barrow for the taping, if that's OK?'

'Absolutely; good man. Does he have access to these new radio mikes? That way we could tape it, *and* simul-taneously listen to everything going on in the room.'

'No way!' Three heads swivelled to Nick. 'Absolutely no way. Look Miles, I'm going to have to put on the performance of my life up there just to convince her I'm kosher, that I'm this Far Eastern businessman she thinks I am, not to mention probably walking on three legs.'

The three smiled. That was *another* problem.

'And you don't want to give a live performance?' Miles asked.

'No, no way. If I think Jess and Paddy are sitting in a suite drinking wine and listening to me make a prat of myself, I'll bottle it, I swear I will.'

Nick saw the other questions behind the amused eyes.

'And if anybody here thinks, for even one *minute*, that anything untoward is going to happen in that room, they don't know me, or my marriage.'

'Don't worry Nick, a tape will do fine . . . eh Conrad?'

'Yes, quite.'

'When and where, Jessica?'

'A month, perhaps less. Bianca is out of the country at the moment. France probably, she feels safer out of the country.'

'Pictures?'

'I think we should have a snapper try a long shot of her when she leaves the hotel if the light is good enough, but not before, and no flash.'

Miles said, 'I spoke to the chairman in New York this morning. He'll be here on Tuesday and he'd like to see you both.'

'No question of him turning it down is there, Miles, us being a multi-faceted media corporation now?' She bit into the ludicrous sounding words.

'No – well, almost certainly not. But he made it very clear to me. Well, he indicated . . .' Miles grin was like a hungry piranha, 'that if I didn't get this right I would be fired.'

The Editor laughed, and after a polite interval the lawyer, Nick and Jessica joined in.

'And I rather don't want to queue at the DHSS with my UB40.' After, Nick thought bitterly, you get through the one hundred and fifty grand compensation, and the seventy five the Express gave you five years ago. After you sell the house in Kensington, the farmhouse in the Dordogne, the Daimler and the horses.

'And us?' Jessica indicated Nick. 'Do our heads roll too if this goes wrong?'

'Absolutely not,' said Miles, the smile agape enough to swallow Captain Ahab. 'After all,' he added with total insincerity, 'you're in a union, aren't you? What could the chairman possibly do to you two?'

Nick, Jessica and Annabelle DeLane sat on high stools in a West London cocktail bar. Their feet dangled in space and Nick felt like a sausage on a stick.

Annabelle wore a black chiffon dress with a ra-ra skirt and a low cut top. Her large breasts were spread out on the platform of her re-inforced bra like ripe fruit on a barrow.

She drank the champagne Jessica had ordered, upending the flute glass as the three of them sipped and smiled and made small talk about names and places and faces. It was the practised cement-between-the-bricks gossip of people in their business.

It would continue into dinner, until the end of the hors d'oeuvres, then either he or Jessica, probably Jessica for it was her story, would raise the matter in hand, almost as an afterthought.

Annabelle spooned the last of her avocado crab into the fleshy mouth, defined by the bold, fashionable again red lipstick, and Jessica said: 'Is your friend back yet?'

'Uh-uhn,' Annabelle shook her head, 'I understand she'll be back at the end of the week.'

'Can we do it at the weekend then?' Jessica asked. 'It' being the supervised, tape-recorded call when Bianca would hopefully take the first unwitting step into the trap planned for her.

'Yes, why not. You'll have to come to my place, in case she calls me back.' Annabelle shrugged: 'In for a penny.'

Nick couldn't resist it: 'In for twenty thousand pounds.' Jessica glared at him, and he saw Annabelle's face go sullen and resentful.

Nick knew he was being unprofessional. It was a golden rule in cases like this that you never reminded an informant by word or gesture, of the fact that you weren't all sitting here at dinner because you were chums. That instead you were sitting there because some expedient demanded that you all co-operate. There was money, and betrayal and deceit and lies.

And in Annabelle's case, even blackmail, with the added twist that the blackmailer eventually paid her.

Annabelle looked up, met his eyes, raised her glass: 'In for twenty grand – and why not.' Nick saw something like a reluctant amusement in her eyes. He suddenly liked her,

65

and thought, why not, we're all on the game in our own way. At least she knows what she is. I hopes she gets her twenty.

Jessica said: 'Don't forget to sign your contract.'

Annabelle kicked her handbag. 'It's ready and waiting.'

'Because Nick and I won't screw you, but don't trust anybody else at the Enquirer. At least with your contract you're safe. But you deal with *us*, no-one else, Nick or me. OK?'

'Sure.'

'When will I get the money?'

'On publication,' Nick replied, 'just like it says in the contract. You nail our friend, and the moment it appears you'll get your cheque. Normally it takes six weeks, but we'll personally hand it to you in three days.'

A waiter appeared and took their plates.

'And suppose you prove it but don't use it?'

Nick looked at Jessica, and said: 'No problem, they'll use it.' But thinking. This one has the Grand National to run; luring Bianca in, proving it, getting it past the lawyers and the proprietor. The Enquirer was part of a multi-national company now. Suppose something someone was doing involved Bianca? A movie deal, a magazine shoot. Would the proprietor stamp on it?

Nick felt that Annabelle's twenty thousand was a long, long way off. Stories had been pulled for lesser reasons of law than confronted this one, even if they *did* get Bianca cold. Apologies and corrections and even damages had resulted from stories everyone, including the victims, *knew* to be true.

On many occasions the craven back-downs and pay-outs had been made to protect or salvage some future or ongoing deal. The whole business stank, and there was no guarantee that when it came to it, Bianca wouldn't

66

be able to wriggle out of the mess she was in without the facts seeing light of day.

And for Annabelle it was no play, no pay. She'd end up with no cash, just a reputation as someone prepared to double-cross a friend.

So unless the horse went the course, Annabelle with her stupendous breasts, inviting mouth and come-to-bed eyes would find herself cast in the role she had planned for Bianca. Victim.

'Bianca, it's Annabelle.' There was a moment's hesitation, then Bianca said: 'Of course, well how *are* you?' Bianca stressed the 'are' in that falsely sincere American way.

'I'm just great, absolutely marvellous. Silly really, but you wouldn't happen to be in Paris on the 27th?'

'Darling, I wouldn't know without looking at my diary, why on earth?'

Nick mouthed to Annabelle. Be careful.

'Well, just the craziest suggestion, but there is a former *dear* friend of a friend's, he lives in Hong Kong, and he's going to be in Paris that weekend, and I know you *love* Paris, and I thought you might like to have dinner with him, or something . . .' The 'or something' hung in the air like a vapour trail.

'Well, of course, why not, if I'm there. I know Hong Kong, what does he do?'

'He's a banker, some small-ish merchant bank, but pots of money, darling, oodles of it, and he gets so bored. And he's so generous.'

A slight pause: 'Annabelle, are you alone at the moment?'

'Of course.' Her eyes flickered up at Nick, at Jessica, at Paddy, earphones clamped on, eyes fixed on the unfolding spools of tape. 'Bored and lonely.'

'I have your number, I'm sure,' Bianca said politely.

67

'Don't bother looking it up . . .' Annabelle gave her number.

'I'll get straight back to you, I'm expecting a call.'

'Bye.'

The four of them sat in the gathering darkness, no-one wanting to break the spell and switch on a light. They stared at the telephone as though it was a God gone silent.

Six hours and she had not rung. Jessica said: 'She suspects. It's all too pat. We screwed it, we should have thought up another scenario.'

She bit at her bottom lip, savagely: 'I'll never forgive myself.'

'There's time yet,' Paddy said.

'Straight back,' Nick said, 'that's what she said.'

'She'll call,' Annabelle said, doggedly, 'she's curious. She knows what I mean, and she knows I know. She might not bite, but she'll want to know more.'

'Then bloody call her for Christ's sake,' Nick said angrily, the tension getting to him.

'No!' Jessica's voice was iron. 'that *would* blow it. It's up to her now.'

The darkness deepened until they could barely see one another's faces, and the flat got cold.

The telephone rang. Once, twice, three times . . . Annabelle's hand poised over the receiver.

'Five full rings,' Jessica said, and on the fifth Annabelle lifted the receiver. 'He-llo.'

Jessica flipped on a table-lamp.

'Darling, it's Bianca, I am so-o sorry I've taken so long.'

'Don't be silly, actually I had some shopping to do so you would have got my machine.'

'You were talking about Paris . . .'

'Paris, yes, look don't worry about it if you're busy, I thought it would be nice, he'd love to meet you, and he's so generous, but some other time.'

68

Jessica glared at Annabelle and Nick mouthed: Don't overdo it.

'Well you're in luck. I'm in Paris the 26th, 27th and 28th. Where would he be staying, the Crillon, Ritz?'

'Crillon' Annabelle said instinctively.

'That's great. I have a suite there.'

'Snap for him.'

'Of course, there are considerations . . . you'd understand . . .'

'Absolutely.'

'Which we'd have to discuss, not on the telephone . . .'

'Naturally. Tea at the usual place?'

'Why not. Thursday, four o'clock?'

'Darling, I shall be talking to him today, a guideline would help. I mean even bankers have to make withdrawals.' There was mutual amplified laughter at the double entendre.

Then Bianca's voice was harder. 'Ten minimum. Would that be a problem?'

Jessica and Nick's eyes widened. Ten? they mouthed. Annabelle said: 'No problem, he'd be only too happy.'

'Thursday.' Annabelle put the telephone down.

Jessica said: 'When did five become ten? Ten thousand bloody pounds for a non-screw. Are you out of your mind?'

'The Enquirer can afford it, eh Nick?'

Nick shrugged. 'It's not my money.'

'We may just take it out of your share, Annabelle,' Jessica said viciously.

'You won't,' Annabelle said, flatly. 'You want this story so badly money is no object, I can smell it. And if I get cheated by either of you you'll both regret it, I promise.'

'Forget it, Jess,' Nick said.

'Don't tell me to forget it. It's *my* bloody story, and don't you forget it.'

Nick gave a mock bow: 'At your service.'

Jessica turned to Annabelle: 'Where are you having tea with her. You said, "the usual"?'

'Where else would two degenerate whores meet for tea – Fortnum and Mason of course.'

'You said "the usual", just how well do you know Bianca? She's taking an awful lot on trust.'

Annabelle smiled: 'Why should professional liars expect to be told the truth.'

They had a long-distance telephoto shot of Bianca in dark glasses going into Fortnum and Mason in Piccadilly. Another shot of her and Annabelle drinking tea, taken by a concealed camera.

Then there was the transcript of the tape which Annabelle had worn during the meeting. It was as specific as it was possible to get. Bianca had said, in as many words, that if the man did not prove repellent to her she would 'go into the bedroom' with him – her phrase, for ten thousand pounds sterling in either French francs or US dollars.

She had asked was he 'weird', as she would entertain no extreme perversions. A joking Annabelle had even said she thought Bianca could get away 'with a blow job.' Bianca had not demurred. The evidence was damning.

They sent the voice tapes to an analyst who swore on affidavit he would not reveal the contents of what he was examining. The voice patterns were matched, peak for peak, trough for trough on a graph, against the previously recorded voice of Bianca Vasquez. They were identical.

Nick dropped Annabelle at her flat and reluctantly but politely accepted her offer of coffee.

They talked about Paris, the scenario, the chances of success, and as Nick's appalling powdered coffee cooled, he said:

'You must hate us.'

She looked up at him: 'Your feminist friend is doing the blackmailing, not you.'

'I'm part of it though.'

'And I get twenty thousand quid.'

'Is that enough compensation for this?'

She took out a cigarette, lit it and drew heavily: 'No, but it'll do. It's all rotten, all of this, my world, yours, and I'm getting out the very second this is over.'

'What will you do?'

'Settle my debts, flog this place and the others, sell everything and start somewhere else, somewhere far away.'

'What about –' Nick faltered.

'Coke? I'll kick that too, and I can do it, believe me. I'm not going to be blackmailed ever again or lie on my back and be screwed by someone for money.'

'Why did you start in the first place?'

She looked at him in sheer amazement: 'Why? *Why*? Why do you bloody think? I was a counter assistant in Boots in Chingford, I got spotted by a photographer and eight months later I'm on Page Three of The Sun.'

'That is not prostitution,' Nick replied.

'Depends on your point of view. Suddenly you're into it all, nightclubs, flashy cars, modelling trips to Bali and the Seychelles, blokes with money. My boyfriend was a car mechanic, we were engaged.'

'What happened?'

'The usual. He got ditched. Kevin, his name was, he had a battered Ford Escort and grease under his fingernails. He didn't stand a chance really.'

'Bigger fish? It's a familiar problem.'

'Sure is.' She stubbed out the barely touched cigarette, 'suddenly you're mid-twenties and the photographers are not as keen, and the work drops off. Some models get better as they get older, look at Linda Lusardi, others don't. Your boobs sag, your chin goes, your skin loses its elasticity.'

71

'Must be tough,' Nick said it sincerely, but Annabelle gave him a vicious look, 'you don't know the half.'

'Was that when . . . ?'

'Yes. In a way I'd been doing it for years, we all had. The flashiest guy with the best car, the biggest house, the best holidays. You were selling yourself, you just hadn't realised it.'

'But there's a difference . . .'

'Yeh, it isn't formalised. Then you find yourself sitting in the one-bedroomed flat which is all you managed to save out of seven or eight years of flogging yourself to death, you've got an overdraft, no skills, no work, no boyfriend, and you're desperate. And the telephone rings and it's someone you once met, and she says there's a guy in town, and . . .'

'I know the story.'

'And you think, just the once because you need the money. But it's not the money, it's the glamour, being in restaurants and clubs and mixing with colourful people, people who matter, or seem too.'

'And you get sucked into it?'

'You know what you're doing, I did, still do, if I'm anyone's victim, I'm my own.'

She lit another cigarette, nervously:

'Then I got into coke – and don't look so bloody moral at me Mr. Boy Scout – the terrible thing about coke is not that's it's horrible, it's that it's wonderful. Don't try it because you'll love it, I did and I still do.'

'What's the attraction?'

'Just like you've heard. You feel *great*, you can party all day and all night, and when you've got to screw some fat, bald, middle-aged businessman it makes him seem like Robert de Niro.'

Nick laughed, then remembered: 'One thing taking it, how about pushing it.'

'Pushing is a *word*, Nick, just a word. Do Harrods *push*

72

food, does your wine merchant *push* alcohol? People want cocaine, I soon learned that, so I learned where to get it and how to make a profit on it. It's a narcotic just like alcohol – or sex.'

'Take your point.'

'No you don't, none of you do, otherwise Jessica couldn't force me to do this.'

'Well, it's illegal.'

'So's polluting the rivers and starving the Third World and locking up people without trial, or it should be.'

'Didn't realise you were a Guardian reader, Annabelle.'

'I'm a lot of things, Nick, that you'd never dream of. Hookers have brains too you know.' Out went the cigarette, barely smoked, like a reflex.

'I never said otherwise.'

She cocked her head to one side and looked at him, strangely, 'You're an odd one in your own way Nick, I thought that the night in the wine bar.'

'Couldn't be less.'

'You don't come across like the ordinary run-of-the-mill punter.'

'Punter as in client? I'm not a client, never have been, never will be.'

'How can you be so sure – never is a long time?'

'Because I love my wife.'

She laughed: 'Oh boy, which B movie did you get that line from?'

'Yes, I suppose it does sound a bit old-fashioned, but it's true nonetheless.'

'You both still fuck?'

Nick went deeply red: 'Annabelle, why not mind your own bloody business.'

'Been married long?'

'Long enough.'

'Then the chances are you don't, so where are you coming from, sexually, I mean?'

Nick felt unsteady, off balance.

'I think that also comes under the mind-your-own business category.'

She got up from her chair and sat next to him on the chintzy sofa: 'Go on, I'm curious. Between you and me. I won't breathe a word to your wife or Jessica. By the way, do you and she . . . ?'

'Colleagues,' Nick said, 'just colleagues.'

'Yes, she's a bit man-eating tarantula for you. So . . . ?'

'Annabelle, we have to work together, it doesn't mean we have to like each other, so if this is your way of winding me up, forget it, because it's been done by experts and you're not that.'

She put a row of red-painted fingernails on his shoulder: 'Actually, I'm genuinely curious.'

Her perfume was powerful, unsubtle and strangely attractive and Nick realised with a professional disappointment that it was having no effect.

'OK . . .' he said reluctantly, 'I'm not queer, don't like little boys or girls, rubber, leather, dressing up or being spanked. I don't go to massage parlours, and I love my wife. That's it. Boring isn't it . . . almost indecent by today's standards.'

'No,' she said, the hand resting on his shoulder, 'it doesn't make you indecent. Just a liar.'

Nick took her hand off his shoulder, the hand was soft, and quite cool. He said: 'Actually Annabelle, I may look like a Boy Scout to you, but I'm not. I've been dealing with people like you for twenty years, and you all have one thing in common.'

'Which is?'

'You always assume everyone thinks the same way you do and shares your grubby view of sex. Well, my sex life is just fine thank you.'

'Oh – kay, Nick, whatever you say. But let's just see how much in love with your wife you are when

74

Bianca takes her clothes off and offers to go down on you.'

'Time will tell.' Nick got up from the sofa. 'I think I should be going.'

'Frightened of something?'

'No.'

She moved closer to him, and he was aware that under other circumstances, if she was another person with another history, she would be attractive, but noting it like a paraplegic notes from memory the running of others.

'Know what your trouble is . . . ?'

'No, but I think you'll tell me . . .' He fastened the inner-button of his double-breasted suit, almost defensively, pulling the flap across, buttoning the outside like a raised drawbridge.

'Well I have a few theories.'

He gave her a practised patronising smile: 'Free country.'

'You're a little out of the ordinary, I'll grant you that. You have a brain, a certain style.'

He gave her a quizzical look. This wasn't the Annabelle of the ra-ra skirt, all-tits, no-brain Page Three girl. She had a kind of confidence they hadn't suspected – or she'd kept secret – when they'd first dealt with her.

'And you'd be a judge of this would you Annabelle?'

'Maybe. You have it all together, or think you have, and you're right, you are tougher than you appear on the surface. Like there's two of you, fabric, and then steel.'

'I've learned to survive.'

'More than that Nick. You've realised you can compete in their world.'

'Their?'

'You know. You've got some of the glittering prizes and you want more – and you don't want to ever lose what you've got.'

'We all want more,' he tried to deflect her, like parrying her sword. It was all too close for comfort.

'Yes, but what about down there, Nick,' a red fingernail pointed to groin level, 'what do you want down there?'

'I think,' said Nick, as evenly as he could, and as though he was seriously considering her question, 'I think I want what I've got. Now if you'll excuse me Dr. Ruth . . .'

'*I* think Nick, that you're climbing uphill to fifty and you still haven't the faintest idea of what you want down there.'

He moved to the door: 'Either Jess or I'll call you.'

'Or maybe,' she moved closer to him, 'you do have an inkling of what you want, and it bloody terrifies you with its possibilities.'

'Whatever,' he said it with more nonchalance than he felt. She had this way of crawling beneath his defences and peeling him like a snake shedding its skin.

'Because maybe if you got into it – down there,' the red fingernail was like an accusation, 'perhaps it would shatter the rest of the careful world you appear to have constructed around yourself.'

He opened the door: 'Very good. Borrow Jess's old Olivetti and bang out a piece for Guardian Woman.'

She had the decency to smile: 'Yes, sir.' Her cleavage was in deep shadow, like a canyon at dusk. A few things about Annabelle were beginning to disturb him.

'But remember, if you feel you have to play by the rules with Bianca, fine. But making an excuse and leaving applies to her . . .'

She paused: 'Not to me Nick.'

He left.

Jessica said: 'Once more into the breach dear friends . . .' as they got out of the lift on the executive penthouse floor and took the small, thickly-carpeted spiralling staircase up to the reception level.

A woman in her mid-fifties wearing pince-nez got up from a Scandinavian glass desk and greeted them warmly. Dolly-bird secretaries were strictly for amateurs, senior executives liked their secretaries efficient and discreet, which today meant over forty-five. Miss Bird had been the chairman's secretary for ten years.

She pressed her intercom: 'Miss Alexander and Mr. Carter.' She swept them into the chairman's office, to see him in shirtsleeves getting up from an armchair set in front of his desk.

He shook their hands and offered them a drink. They knew that meant juice or tea or coffee, for the chairman kept no alcohol in his office and openly disapproved of its consumption during working hours. They declined, as neither wished to spill a cup of tea out of nervousness.

'May I . . . ?'

He took the folder containing the transcripts and the pictures, and studied them quietly for several minutes. When he looked up he said: 'Are you confident of getting this – In Paris, I mean?'

Their yesses overlapped.

He looked back at the folder: 'Fascinating. I've actually met Bianca . . .' Nick thought: Oh no.

'She came to a party my wife gave in New York, and she's been connected with some of my wife's charity work.'

Which means? Jessica thought.

'I suppose you realise the implications of all this?'

Jessica said: 'After we expose her I think a lot of other people's names could come sliding out of the woodwork.'

'Precisely. Who knows how deep this girl could be in, if she is what you imply she is.'

'She is,' said Jessica doggedly.

'In fact, this is all a little embarrassing. Bianca has just ended a very important fashion shoot in the Far East with one of my American magazines. It's all linked with

77

a detailed holiday promotion scheme, and if we prove she's a whore my magazine is going to look pretty sick.'

Nick felt clammy and cold, his stomach tight, he wanted to say. Don't suppress this, you bastard, not if we get it, don't you dare, but he felt like a victim, powerless to act.

Jessica wasn't, she said: 'Sir, do we have your guarantee that the Enquirer will use this story, if we prove it to the lawyers' satisfaction?'

He looked at her sharply: 'I *never* give guarantees. But I don't suppress either. I was a cub reporter in Saskatchewan before you two were born, and I saw enough of all that.'

'I'm sorry, I didn't mean –'

'Forget it. If you get it – *right* – I'll use it. And it will have to be right. After what the courts did over Mr. Archer we would be looking at the wrong end of a million pounds.'

And we'd be looking at the end of our jobs, thought Nick, careers in ruins, the twosome who cost their newspaper a million. When Miles had said *his* job was on the line, he'd said *they'd* be OK because they were in a union.

Nick knew differently. Unions meant bugger all in reality, certainly after the Wapping experiment. No-one associated with a catastrophe that big at first hand would get out alive.

He thought of the salary, of trying to freelance or get another staff job in his mid-forties, of the house, the car and the holidays, of Rebecca and her love of horses, and wondered why he had consented to get involved. He could have just coasted along as he had been doing. The name of the game was not to take risks, now he was taking the biggest.

'That's enough guarantee for me, sir.' Jessica said.

'Call me Jack, both of you, I find sir very English and very obsequious.'

'OK, – Jack.' Jessica replied, smiling.

'And of course, if you get it right, I would imagine the company would express its apreeciation in material terms.'

'Thank you – Jack,' Nick said.

The chairman went behind his desk, as if to signal that the audience was over. He said: 'Miles has my authority to spend whatever is required.'

Jessica said: 'It won't do you any good, or your wife, socially I mean, if we use it, will it?'

The chairman eyed her carefully: 'Occasionally the social world benefits from having its neck scruff shaken.'

They left, and the chairman wondered why it was the women who seemed to have all the balls today.

'Pushed your luck a bit there, didn't you?', Nick said, as they got out of the lift on the editorial floor.

'Not really, just wanted a commitment that was all.'

'He can still chicken out, what he said doesn't mean sod all, he's got promises like pie crust, ask some of the companies he's taken over.'

'Well, he won't break this one, what about all that stuff about being a cub reporter -'

'Was forgotten the moment he said it.'

'Not today, thanks to the miracles of Japanese technology.' Jessica retrieved a tiny Sony tape recorder from her handbag, the red recording light still glowing.

'ta-ra-ra-ra . . .'

'You're fucking crazy. You *recorded* the chairman?'

'Why not?'

'Sometimes I think you're from another planet.'

'Yeh, the Planet of the Women, you wanna visit sometime.' She switched off the tape and fumbled for coins for the drinks vending machine.

'Do you tape all your private conversations?'

'Only when they're useful, and that wasn't private, that

79

was business. If he double-crosses us on this, I'm out and off to the nearest TV station or satirical mag. No-one is suppressing this story.'

She found coins and began to feed them into the machine, then punched out a sequence on the display.

'I don't know what you do to the enemy Jess, but by God you frighten me.'

A plastic beaker appeared, then a grey liquid began to gush from a concealed pipe. 'But that's your trouble, if the truth was known, Nick,' she was giving him a look of barely concealed scorn.

'Oh yeh?'

'Yeh. You frighten too easily. Your wife frightens you, your boss frightens you, the stories you do frighten you, I think, to be honest, your bloody life frightens you.'

She handed him the plastic beaker, and he was too bemused to reject it. He took it and it burned his hand.

'Actually, I'll tell you exactly what frightens me Jess . . . this . . .' he waved his free hand, 'this place, this business, what we do and who we do it too.'

'Really?' she fed more coins into the machine, and cursed when the cup failed to appear and the liquid went into the overflow grille: 'Poxy machine. You may look and try to act like Mr. Smoothiechops Nick, but I know one or two stories about you from the old days.'

'Pray tell, I could do with a good yarn.'

'You know exactly what I mean. You've conned the punters, you've massaged the quotes not to mention *invented* one or two, so don't start getting pious, not now. Just because you think you're on some road to Damascus try not to make me feel guilty.'

He turned on his heel and tipped beaker and hideous liquid into an overflowing rubbish bin. She came after him.

'Don't walk away from me.'

He stopped: 'Jessica, why don't you fuck off and play

80

reporters like the rest of the morons in here. I don't want to be Kirk Douglas in Ace in the Hole, not today, thank you.'

'And you think you're not? You want to see yourself with your tie undone, feet on the desk, smooth talking them down the line, what was it Miles called you once, 'Best telephone chat-up man in the business?!' All you're lacking is the dimple.'

Nick breathed deeply: 'Actually Jessica, for me you could take every tabloid newspaper in the country and dump them in the North Sea.'

'You're kidding yourself.'

'I'm not.'

'You love it.'

'Did. Now it frightens me, but then as you say –'

'Come on!'

'It does Jess. Some of the stunts we pull, the con tricks, the lies we tell . . .'

'Lies! The whole bloody country is built on lies from the royal family down. What's the hereditary peerage if it's not a lie? You take a bunch of ruffians to the Crusades, ten centuries later your great-grandson squared has a title and forty non-executive directorships at five grand apiece . . .'

'Spare me the Socialism Jess, it's like a record.'

'Screw the Socialism, talk about the system. And this, the Enquirer, you talk about lies. All newspapers are liars, all TV programmes, all magazines, it's all perspective, points of view. The Rashomon theory . . .'

'I'm one of the few people who saw the movie, Jess, so don't ram Rashomon down my throat. I know, each witness looks on an event with a different view, a different perspective, a different memory . . .'

'Right, so don't talk about lies.'

'I think you know different here.'

A reporter pushed past them, and Jess greeted him

81

warmly, then, when he was out of earshot, said:, 'Twat. Tried to pinch one of my contacts last week. You talk as if we were the only ones doing dirty tricks, poke your nose into the City of London, Nick, Wall Street. At least we don't steal people's pension funds.'

'I'm glad you can rationalise it.'

'Every week I pick up UK Press Gazette and turn to the Jobs pages and that rationalises it bloody quick. Seen this week's? The Northumbrian Water Authority want a Press officer, willing to work weekends, must have own car, telephone. Nine grand a year, £190 a week!!'

'Point taken.'

'You've got the best job in the world, travel, independence and you're paid a king's ransom by the standards of this God forsaken country.'

'I said point taken.'

'Well, then . . .'

'And prostitute ourselves . . .'

'Jeesus! The bin-man doesn't? The bloke on the assembly line, the bird frying hamburgers in McDonalds? It's work, curse of the drinking classes. Ninety-nine percent of the population would cut your throat to do what you do.'

'OK. OK. It's just that this last couple of months, I dunno, some of the stuff we've been doing, makes me feel ashamed sometimes.'

A kind word would have done it, a cosmetic sense of sympathy with his moral dilemma, real or imagined. Instead she plunged in the dagger.

'Maybe you've lost it. Maybe you've gone soft. Perhaps you should pack it in and become a Press officer somewhere. Frinton's quiet.'

He looked both ways down the corridor, then said softly: 'Actually Jessica you're about ten seconds away from me grabbing your head and shoving it right up your arse.'

'Ah, violence, the reasoned argument of your average male. Just try it and I'll put your balls in a sling.'

'Like I said, Jessica, a different planet.' He left her, went through the swing doors, across the main editorial floor and sat at his desk.

He felt – diminished.

Later she came up to his desk.

'Nick?'

'Yeh?' He didn't look up from his Evening Standard.

'Nick, I'm sorry, most of that was uncalled for, I wouldn't have said it if I didn't like you.'

He snorted derisively: 'Got any hate around?'

'Come on man, I mean it. I hate to see you losing your –'

'Bottle? Is that what you were going to say? Are the white feathers on their way?' He folded the Standard: 'I thought you were a feminist and I thought feminism meant *we* could revise our roles too. You know, no cutesy-mumsey for you lot and we were free to say that hunting lions scared the shit out of us.'

'No, not bottle, you've got bottle, I've never seen you shrink from a confrontation.'

'Thanks, grateful I'm sure.'

'More your edge, that sharp edge you had, I wasn't being rude about your family –'

'You could have fooled me.'

'I was trying to say, don't let all the good things, Jenny included, let you forget how you got there. You're the best when you're on top form, you can charm the birds off the trees, don't let Jenny –'

'Will you for God's sake leave my wife *out* of this, you know nothing about Jenny.' His face was red with anger.

'I know that if you stopped being so godamned pious over your marriage it might be happier.'

'My marriage is in a damned sight better state than yours. When *is* the divorce finalised by the way?'

'That's not what your face says in the morning, it says everything ain't fine and dandy down at DunRoamin.'

Nick got up from his chair, face working.

'Can you lip read Jessica?'

'Nick!'

'Well, fuck you.'

'What I'm saying is if you've got a problem –'.

'I'll discuss it with a friend, I don't need your advice, as a matter of fact I don't think you're qualified to give anyone advice.'

He stared down at her, looking big and angry, feeling small and shrivelled like one of those awful shrunken Borneo heads.

'Do you read me?'

'Loud and clear, but I'm going to give you some advice whether you like it or not. . . .'

'Sincerely and genuinely fuck off Jess –'.

'Be a man. If you want something, take it, stop apologising for yourself. If you get the chance to screw Bianca, *do* it. Come out of the closet, be *you* for God's sake, not someone you think Jenny wants you to be, or your daughter . . .'

'One more fucking word, Jess . . .'

'Just be you . . . and that's it . . .'

He subsided into the chair, stunned by the ferocity of her outburst. He felt like an old, tired man.

'Nick, I'm not your enemy.'

'Well tell me then, Jess, since you seem to know all about me, and my family, and how I function, who would 'me' be?'

'That's for you to know – don't you?'

'No, I don't. I did, but this . . .' he waved his hand to encompass the editorial floor.. 'this changed it, and now I haven't the faintest idea who I am.'

And he realised it was true, he didn't.

*   *   *

Bianca took the framed picture from the drawer in the escritoire and looked once more at the dead strangers who had been her family. At Mama and Papa, Raoul and Ramon, at Angelita – little angel – the girl she herself had once been.

She had retrieved the photograph from their house in Managua after she had trudged painfully back, body aching, feet bleeding, back against the the columns of fleeing refugees like a salmon fighting its way upstream.

The power had failed and as darkness fell she fearfully climbed into her parents' big bed. The sheets had been changed, the pillow cases smoothed down, made tidily before their departure, like an orderly farewell kiss at a railway station.

Her sexual opening burned with a slow buzz of pain, and she put her fingers there, beneath her pants, in an effort at self-comfort.

The girl had never touched herself before, not there, not like this, Mama had said the church forbade it except for cleansing or sanitary purposes.

But the opening hurt so much, and she had been told even saliva had some healing properties, so she put the tips of her fingers to her lips, moistened them with spittle, and put the fingertips back against her vagina.

The faint oyster fragrance of herself lingered on her lips.

At first the wet touch of the spittle smarted, but then the saliva acted as a balm, and the smarting eased a little. She felt for the source of the pain and irritation, parting the folded curtain of flesh with her left hand, feeling with the fingers of her right, slowly, like a blind person discovering a new face.

It was like a soft, strange sea-creature, or a dark, unexplored cave world of mystery, and somehow untold promise. She touched the pain, winced, let her fingers wander.

This was from where the water came. Her finger traced upwards. And this? A tiny spot no bigger than a Braille dot. She circled it with the tip of her finger, frightened lest it hurt, lest this too be something the men had caused.

As she did so strange feelings whirled in her head like dancing ghosts. The men, their looks as they feasted their eyes on her, their smell, the things they had done to her. Their need of her.

And magically the spot seemed to grow beneath her finger, and she knew it had some connection with the men. There was a strange sensation in her breasts. She brought up her left hand, and felt her young nipples, now curiously hard.

She closed her eyes, going into a deeper, second darkness, and her finger seemed to trace an automatic circle.

There was something far off like the distant roaring of thunder, did it come from within her or from the dark world outside? Her finger moved faster, propelled by a hidden force, and the spot at which she touched felt red hot, she imagined it must glow in the dark like a hot coal.

Faster and faster now, and the girl began to give off small, spontaneous cries of pleasure and fright as the crescendo built.

Then the storm broke, and her back arched. The typhoon crashed across her in colossal waves, a water weight of new, unknown, impossible pleasure.

At last it slowed, subsided, and she drifted off into bemused sleep, her hand between her legs like the redundant guardian of a conquered city.

Bianca remembered it all, she could smell the crisp linen of the sheet, the slightly musty air of the house, the scent of woodsmoke that filtered like country perfume into the house.

She remembered, then she laid down the photograph, so the ghosts could not see what she was about to do.

A ghost in New York City had once whispered to her 'Angelita', and for a moment she had looked into the eyes of the past.

But it was banished, for she knew there was just the ditch, the gunfire, and the flat, one-dimensional images of who they had been.

She slipped a hand beneath the top of her panties now, her long nails parting the luxuriant hot-house flower of her sex, and without guilt or shame she found the place she had discovered that night in her parents' bed.

She closed her eyes and let her finger circle the spot. She was back in the big bed with her solo anthem of pleasure. Her refuge from the awful need of men-money, from the wasteland of detachment.

Slowly she moved, like a conductor with a familiar, well-rehearsed symphony, waiting for the climax and the pleasure. And the inevitable tears that would follow.

Chapter Five

Nick registered in his own name, giving a fictional address in Hong Kong, listing his occupation as banker, and his last port of call as Hong Kong.

False names were more trouble than they were worth. They led to slip-ups and embarrassments. It was too easy to forget a false name – especially a first one. The chances of Bianca linking Nick's name with the newspaper were thousands to one against, even though his name was read by millions each week.

It was a conceit of journalists that their names on a story – the longed for by-line – meant that they were household names. The reality was otherwise. A public opinion poll once asked people to name five journalists. Ninety-five per cent couldn't name more than one.

And keeping his name also meant that Nick could pay with his own credit card instead of having his company travel agent meet the bill with a voucher. If Bianca checked, that could be important.

It was a calculated gamble. Bianca worked in and around the media, but the media was stratified, and Nick worked at a level she would never be involved with.

He and Jessica doubted too if Bianca would ever read the tabloids – especially the Sundays – and if she did whether she could possibly remember such a nondescript name (Jessica's words) and link it with her rich banker from Hong Kong.

His American Express Gold Card was sufficiently international for it not to attract attention as to country of issue. Jessica and Paddy had checked in the day before and it was discreetly confirmed that Miss Vasquez had a reservation for the night in question, and for two nights afterwards.

It seemed to be going almost *too* well.

Jenny had driven Nick to the airport in the Volvo, and they spoke very little during the 25 minute journey from Richmond, but as they skirted the Northern airport perimeter road on the short-cut route, she said:

'You still haven't told me exactly what this is you're doing. I mean, three of you, in Paris! Someone must be getting generous with expenses.'

Nick stared sullenly out of the rain-soaked window. Now it was all actually happening he felt more and more apprehensive about it. He was supposed to be a journalist, for God's sake, not an actor. How had he ended up doing something like this?

It wasn't even as if they were exposing an international gun runner, or drugs smuggler. Just a tart – if she was one – albeit a famous one.

He turned to her: 'Need to know Jen, I told you that. Some famous lady who's up to no good. I'm basically along as back-up.'

She flicked him a sideways glance: 'Need to *know*, Nick? I'm your wife for God's sake. Who am I likely to tell? I could have ruined half the showbusiness reputations in London with some of the stuff you've let slip to me before.'

He put a hand on her leg and stroked it, sensing a slight flinch on her part as he did: 'Look, I was told no-one, and no-one includes you. Suppose you said something by mistake, and it got out, you'd never forgive yourself – and neither would I.'

But he knew he was lying. He discussed everything with Jenny, no matter how private or secret, personal or business, and she must know that, and wonder why this was an exception.

90

Well, she would learn soon enough if it all went according to plan. Then she'd know that the reason he hadn't discussed it was because he was ashamed to. Ashamed to tell her that his role was that of sexual tethered goat, and that if he *had* dared tell her, she might have said: Me or that. Choose. And he couldn't have faced that.

She rarely read the Enquirer, she hated it, but she would read that particular issue, and it would not take her long to deduce just why he'd gone to Paris, and what his role was.

Worse than that she would know that their friends knew, other parents at Rebecca's school; neighbours, shopkeepers, acquaintances at coffee mornings. She would become The Woman Whose Husband was in The Bedroom with Bianca.

She would have to take the sneers, the knowing smiles and the constant whispers. The whispers that said: well, he *said* he made his excuse and left but . . .

And the question would hang unanswered and heavy with innuendo. Coming, as it would, on top of everything else that plagued their marriage, Nick wondered just how it would affect them.

He wondered and he dreaded, and he wished he had the courage to tell her there and then. But he didn't. For he still clung to some silly hope that it would all go wrong.

So much about these sting operations was imponderable. There were so many possible slips twixt cup and lip. In fact, the majority did not work out. Only in the movies did people fall expertly into traps set for them. When humans stepped down from celluloid they rarely spoke the lines assigned to them.

But this seemed to have a destiny to it, a kind of inevitability. When Nick had been a kid at school, he'd dreamed up all kind of scenarios to imagine why a lesson he hated would be cancelled, or a teacher or bully who plagued him might fail to make it to school that day.

He had once prayed absurdly and dangerously that the school bus would not make it to the top of the steep hill that approached his school. He prayed it would falter, that the brakes would fail to hold it, and it would roll backwards, gathering momentum, toppling over on the bend, spilling its human cargo into the road. He would survive, of course, with a neat bandageable, photogenic injury that would keep him off school for months.

And now his hopes appeared as childish and unrealistic. Normally the future seemed like an unrolling carpet, but now he had the distinct feeling that the next couple of days were completed, written like acts from a play, and he was merely allocated to live through them, playing his allotted part.

It would all happen, just as Jessica had planned it, Nick knew it would. Then he would be part of a little bit of contemporary newsmaking, and he sensed that somehow he would be changed by it.

He kissed her goodbye at the airport. She said: 'Remember us in Paris?'

'Yeh. Magical, wasn't it?'

'Don't do anything we didn't do.'

'What?' He gave her a quizzical look.

'Just a joke. Will you call me?'

'Call you when I'm leaving, OK?'

She squeezed his hand: 'Don't look so worried. It may never happen.'

Oh yes, Nick thought: Oh yes it would.

Sony Walkman it wasn't. Effective it was. Paddy showed Nick the projecting piece of steel that acted as the on/off switch, then he started the tape which slithered smoothly around and over the tiny cogwheels and the metal spools.

'It'll give you ninety minutes, and that's more than you need. Try not to turn on any heating equipment. It tends to be noisy, and it could very easily spoil your sound quality. I'll put a mike and lead on it, and then you're flying.'

Nick nodded.

'When she knocks on the door of your suite, push in the switch and it'll start. Say your name and the date and time into the mike then cover the tape with the shirt and leave it. Try to make sure that the mike can see air. That way you'll get good sound.'

'What's the name and date stuff for?'

'For the courts if it comes to that. Then you can swear on oath that it is your voice and that's a true date.'

Nick shivered. That was their deepest dread. That Bianca would sue and they'd all end up in the witness box at the Royal Courts of Justice in the Strand, known to all as the High Court.

'Then close the cupboard door.'

So simple, Nick thought. Wonder why he had to come all this way just to do this?

'It rarely fails, can stick occasionally, but it's just been serviced so there'll be no problems with this one. We've had a crop of right villains off it. Should have notches on it, like those World War Two fighter planes.'

'Yeh,' Nick said, with deep sarcasm, 'if it works perhaps we can paint a picture of Bianca on the side of it.'

For the sake of security the three of them did not dine at the hotel. Bianca was not due until the next day, but Jessica believed that if she was at all suspicious she might arrive early, or send an envoy.

If Mr. Lonely and Frustrated from Hong Kong was drinking and eating with a man and a woman with whom he was clearly on good terms, then a rat might be smelled.

But in the taxi to the Latin Quarter there was a little

good natured moaning from Paddy: 'First and probably the last time I'll stay at the Crillon and I can't even eat in the dining room.'

Jessica smothered a yawn, of tiredness not boredom. Nick knew she was tired, and she looked drawn and white. She had a lot riding on this story, a great exclusive if it worked, probably her credibility if it failed.

She'd been on it for four weeks, doing other stuff as well, and tomorrow was the night it would either come off for her and cover her with glory (and himself, he conceded) or shatter at her feet.

She looked as though she wasn't sleeping at nights from worry.

Nick put a confidential hand across in the darkness of the cab's interior and touched her arm, withdrawing it as quickly. He did not want Paddy seeing that, because one lunch was an affair in Fleet Street, and he had already been spending a lot of time – necessarily – with Jessica, over the last couple of weeks.

She looked up at his touch.

He said: 'Relax, it'll be OK.'

'Sure. I know, I'm a bit knackered, that's all.'

Paddy said, with enthusiasm: 'I feel like getting rat-arsed tonight.'

'We can get pissed *tomorrow* night, once we've got Bianca in the bag.'

'Sorry mein Führer, I hadn't realised you were in the Temperance Movement.'

'Oh fuck off Paddy, why don't you take this a bit more seriously. We've got you a free trip to Paris, what more do you bloody want? No sweat to you if it fails; me and Nick look like prize dickheads.'

'Hey, hey, children.' Nick put his hands up like a referee separating warring contestants: 'Let's all be friends. We're in Paris, we have money. Better still, we have other *people's* money.'

'Yeh, sorry Paddy. You know us girlies.'

Paddy didn't see the sarcasm, but took it as a gesture of peace: 'Yeh, sorry too. Just orange juice for me tonight.'

It was an uneasy dinner. They ended at a Moroccan tourist dive in the cobbled streets of the Latin Quarter, eating cous-cous. Nick had little appetite, because he could not take his mind off the events that would follow the next night, and clearly neither could Jessica.

Sullenly they picked at the food, and three times Paddy said: 'I wish I'd had steak frites.' Although they had vowed not to get rat-arsed they ordered litre jugs of red wine.

Slowly the wine improved their spirits, and when the two jugs were empty they ordered more. Anecdotes began to unfold; of legendary wild men and drunks, of reporters interviewing other reporters by mistake, of stories they'd been on, of malice and mayhem, and of photographers.

All the best anecdotes seemed to be about photographers, who were regarded – mostly unfairly – as having the tact and sensitivity of the Waffen SS.

Paddy had the floor: 'So there's this bloke, right, snapper for the Express, scruffy bastard, breath like a horse.'

'The one who puked up at the Guildhall, nearly got on News at Ten?'

'Him,' Paddy said, 'Ike something. Once got nicked at Newquay on that trawler thing for pinching a policewoman's tits, swore the crowd had pushed him against her. Mega-piss artist. So anyway, he's sent to photograph this model up at Manor House, she'd won the pools or something . .'

'No, no, she screwed the Hollywood bloke, met him in Stringfellows, o-d'd on heroin about two years later,' Jessica corrected.

'Whatever. Anyway, so this bird has got this incredible

dog as it happens, mega-expensive, Lord Fauntleroy the Fifth, you know, pedigree long as your arm, peke or something.'

'Afghan,' Jessica interrupted.

'Whatever. She lets him in, dog's upstairs, and she says whatever he does he mustn't open the front door and let the dog out, busy road, the Seven Sisters. So he says of course he won't, anyway, he says can he back his car into the space in front of her house, and she says OK, so he goes out – only he leaves the door open, doesn't he . . .'

'And the dog –' Nick tried, but Paddy wasn't yielding this anecdote.

'So the bloody dog goes bounding out, Ike's reversing his car into the drive and squashes the fucking thing flat!'

He put his hand up, horizontal: 'Flat.'

Nick said, because he knew this anecdote backwards,: 'So the model, Jess, she comes screaming out . . .'

'Yeh, screaming out,' Paddy took over again, determined not to yield the punchline, 'because she hears the thing yelp, sees the door open, and by the time she gets out there, Ike – who has never set eyes on this bloody dog, remember – has scooped up the remains of Lord Barking Mad the Third of Tiptree or whateveritsnamewas, and is holding the thing up, all dripping and squashed.'

'And he says –' Nick was cut off.

'And he says to the model, "This yours love?"' Paddy was triumphant: 'This yours love? He's just killed her fucking dog. Would you Adam and Eve it.'

Nick choked on his wine, couldn't help it, he always did. This yours?

'What did she do?' Jessica asked.

'Sued him,' Paddy said, 'him and the Express. As God is my witness, this dog was worth more than some cars.'

'Get to court?'

'Naw, settled it.'

'Was Ike in the shit, with the Express I mean?'

'Naw, they all thought it was hilarious. They called him Kennomeat for about a year.'

Nick said: 'What's he doing now?'

'Had a bit of a stroke,' Jessica said, 'took redundo, running a boarding house on the Isle of Wight. He'll make Basil Fawlty look like Egon Ronay.'

'Is this YOURS?' Paddy kept holding up the imaginary squashed dog, re-living it: 'he's just run over her fucking dog and he says, "This yours?" Jesus.'

'Ike was nothing,' Nick said, 'not compared with that Scottish bloke, remember him Jess, when the planeload of Argentinian girl hockey teams was diverted to Gatwick?'

She choked: 'They charged him! Four counts of indecent assault . . .'

And so the punctured night leaked away, squandered like so many before in the same manner. Because there was no other way in which to dispose of it. It was valueless, it could not be saved or used properly, it was simply a waiting day, and it begged to be frittered.

They divided up the bill and ludicrously over-tipped the complaisant waiter. On the return trip Jessica stopped the cab over half a mile away from the hotel.

Nick was annoyed, he didn't want to walk the rest of the way: 'Come on, Jessica, this is paranoia.'

'No it's not, it's common sense. Suppose she, or someone else she knows, sees you turning up in a taxi with us. What the fuck did you think we went out to eat for?'

'Yeh, you're right. Can *I* keep the cab?'

'Sure. We'll see you tomorrow.'

Nick went to his suite alone, and lay down on the bed fully-clothed. He planned to think, but he was actually a little drunk, and he fell into a troubled doze.

He awoke at three with minor drink-induced palpitations, went to the bathroom, cleaned his teeth, undressed and got into bed.

But it was only as dawn touched the high Paris rooftops that he finally slept again. He dreamed of Jennifer, and Bianca, and somehow they became one.

And still he felt no desire.

Chapter Six

The familiar ball of something knotted and tight lodged deep within Nick's stomach, and he felt the strange hot-cold of fear as his hands turned icy and his armpits soaked with sweat.

He couldn't keep still, couldn't settle, he had to move, pacing up and down, washing and re-washing his hands. It was his third shirt, he had only brought four, and the Nagra had to go beneath the last.

As he washed his hands once more he looked into the gilded mirror and thought: Who *am* I? It was always the same at such moments, though in truth there had never been *quite* such a moment for Nick.

Confrontation, showdown, the fronting, whatever newspaper jargon was in vogue at the time, meant the moment you approached the subject of your story and asked he or she for comment.

It could range from the innocuous question to a minor star about some TV row, or the heavier stuff with a crook or bent holiday operator.

But you were always frightened, most probably of physical assault, as policemen or bailiffs must be. Yet there was some other fear that was in the mind, and had nothing to do with the corporal. It was the fear of yourself, of knowing that whatever moral courage was required in such a situation it had no equal moral authority.

You could pretend so, especially when dealing with the crooked of the world, but you didn't really believe it. You were *not* a policeman, or a bailiff. No-one, certainly not the law, had invested you with any authority to do what you were doing.

By what right did you do it? The simplest, the least moral. By the right that you could do it, *would* do it, that you got paid a lot of money to do it. And that it was too late to change your life and do something differently.

And that if you did not do it, there were others queueing behind you, who would happily take the money you earned and do it. And do it worse than you, do it without the sensitivity and tact you fondly believed you brought to it.

So you rationalised it, as those who do the sometimes unjustifiable can do. And that was how the evil reproduced itself, minor in your case, major in others, but working from the rationale. If I don't someone else will.

And this, tonight, to prove that a famous model, an international celebrity, was a harlot? By what right did you do that?

Nick observed the face that stared back at him from the mirror. And the same answer came dumbly back. Because she's there, like the fabled mountain. Because it's all part of some inexorable, impossible to halt process, and you are a part of it, and it is too late to stop now.

For you are the professional, and in truth this is the only way you know how to make your living. And if, in a year's time, there is another such occasion, though you protest now, you will be there, looking at yourself as you do know, wondering why, and knowing all along.

Bianca had already checked into her suite. From her vantage point in the lobby, Jessica had seen her arrive and had telephoned Nick's suite to tell him.

The Enquirer had a photographer in the lobby too, and he had taken a secret shot of her as she checked in. Now all she had to do was telephone. He was scared shitless like an actor before an important first night performance, which in some respects is what it was.

He looked at himself again in the mirror. He would do it, and the fact that he would scared him beyond measure.

The set was ready. A two-day old copy of the South China Morning Post was folded on the dressing table, Cathay Pacific labels on his luggage.

The Nagra was in place beneath the remaining clean shirt, and the neat stacks of US dollars, still with their paper bands, were in Nick's briefcase.

He had divested himself of drivers' licence, Press card and private membership cards for everything from clubs to video shops. It was now down to his ability to act the part, and to the gullibility and greed – or sheer carelessness – of Bianca Vasquez.

He looked out of the window at Paris. Jennifer had said at the airport: 'Remember us in Paris?' He had. They had come here for their honeymoon, watching their francs, staying in a cheap hotel in Montmartre off the Rue des Martyrs, amused by the whores on the corner, their hotel room overlooking a tiny square with a non-functioning fountain. They'd lunched on baguettes and pâté and pâtisserie, drinking from a bottle of red wine sitting on the steps near the Sacré Coeur.

Paris would always be something special to Nick, but now it failed to touch him. It was like drinking champagne at a funeral. He wished it had been another city, something Gothic and heavy, something suitably Wagnerian for this götterdämmerung of the spirits.

The telephone rang, and he started, his heart racing. He answered it: 'Hello, Nick Carter.'

'It's Bianca. You were expecting my call.'

Lights, camera, action. Nick was going, adrenalin surging through him. Acting, hating himself, but the devil part of him thrilling at his ability at deceit.

'Yes, I was. How are you? I have some champagne on ice, I love champagne, don't you?' Trying to judge it. Being a nervous man, but cocky too, immature and unsure, the kind of man who would be vain and stupid enough to buy seconds of love with a beautiful woman. She must believe his cover.

Eventually he replaced the receiver, and stood perfectly still. He had a wild thought. He could ruin it, he could say something when she knocked on the door of his suite, enough to make her shy away in suspicion, and Jessica would never know, the Enquirer would never know. Nick could sabotage it.

He banished the thought instantly. How many paces from Bianca's to his? He went to the telephone, dialled Jessica's room, and said: 'It's happening.' Then he replaced the receiver.

There was a small rap on the door. He went to the concealed Nagra, pressed the switch and breathed his name and the date and time into the mike. Then he closed the cupboard door.

When he opened the door she was there. It was Bianca without a doubt. It was the face and figure of a thousand pictures in magazines and on television.

And there was something else too, something that almost robbed him of breath. Not just that she was beautiful, stunning, her dark skin almost translucent. But that she was *real*, a real person, a living thing, not some one-dimensional object, some name, a subject under discussion.

He felt an overwhelming desire to touch her now, as she stood, to experience the texture of her skin. Nick suddenly felt, like a rush of blood, a feeling that could only be described as: She *lives*.

He invited her into the suite, walking provocatively straight into the bedroom.

If she was to protest it would be now. In a suite the bedroom had extra significance. She took a chair, and a glass of champagne.

And they talked. Bianca questioned him gently in the

102

guise of conversation. About himself, his job, about Hong Kong, a place she knew well.

Luckily he had been there many times too, and he had read and rehearsed, but he was disconcerted to see that on a couple of occasions she deliberately tried to trap him by referring to incorrect locations. He corrected her with all the unsubtle insouciance of the man he now felt he was.

And the Nagra ran unseen like a long and silent snake. At length he said: 'Look, I'm jolly embarrassed about this, but Annabelle said, well, you know, she hinted.'

He tailed off as though bashful and nervous. She got out of her chair and came over to where he was sitting: 'You're quite sweet.' She paused: 'Have you slept with many women?' She leaned over and put her arms around his neck.

'Enough.' He hoped it had the right amount of lying male bravado. She said, with disarming candour: 'I doubt it. Enough is a great deal.'

This was the moment. And Nick knew he would not flinch from it. It was the article of his faith. He took the money, he took the perks, this was the moment he earned them. He said: 'I would like to sleep with you. If that's possible.'

'It is possible, my dear Nick, but you will have to give me ten thousand pounds sterling or its equivalent in hard currency.' Crazy, Nick thought, 'or its equivalent'. It was like some banking transaction. As she spoke he had detected a tiny tremor in her left hand.

And he could not believe it was all so simple. Tapes were notoriously bad at recording the real sense of events and conversations. Most conversations were repetitive, unclear, with interruptions, prone to double meanings when they were transcribed into cold print.

Yet he had not even had to mention money, she

had done that for him, virtually without prompting and in the most unequivocal way in terms of meaning.

He said: 'I have the money, but it seems a fortune.'

'You know who I am?'

'Yes. You're Bianca Vasquez.' This for the tape. It would be invaluable if she said nothing that could contradict that, or bring it into any doubt – even if she said it as a joke. But there was no possible reason she should contradict him, and to his relief she did not.

'Then you know that you are getting something precious, something that normally a man like you could never have.'

'Yes.'

'Ten thousand.'

'I have US dollars. Eighteen thousand.'

She smiled: 'A generous exchange rate, I should give you a reduction.' He stood up, her arms still around him, and as he did his body brushed against hers, and he felt the smell of her catch in his throat. It was like some intoxicating wild maquis,

Bianca followed him to the briefcase, and watched as he retrieved the new notes. He said: 'Do you want to count it?'

'No.' She picked up the bundles as though weighing fruit. 'I think you are a man of honour.' She looked him straight in the eyes, hers piercing his. He met them: 'Yes, I am a man of honour. I wouldn't cheat you.'

And Nick knew that now he was someone else. He was the man from Hong Kong, the stupid, shy, vain man who would give eighteen thousand American dollars to possess the body of a famous woman.

So Nick was not a man of honour any more, he was *that* man, the man from Hong Kong who was not bound by truth.

He asked: 'Have there been others – like this I mean?' Perhaps this would spoil it, now that he had his evidence.

Perhaps this fishing for information would make her sense the trap.

She said: 'For a shy man you talk a great deal. You have paid your money and I shall sleep with you. You can do all the things of which you have ever dreamed with the most beautiful woman you will ever know.'

'I had no wish to insult you.'

She took a step closer to him: 'Haven't you dreamed of sleeping with Bianca? Surely every man has.'

He nodded dumbly: 'Yes, I have longed for you.'

'Now I am here. And for your money you can realise your dream.'

Some distant part of Nick, the professional deep within the disguise of his new role, realised now that the tape had damning evidence.

She was cold, dead, crucified. All that remained was for him to extricate himself. And yet he wanted the absurd charade to go on, if only for a few moments longer. Some spell had been cast in the room, something bewitching, and he found he did not want it to be lifted.

'Thank you.'

She smiled at his politeness, and there was almost a flash of electricity in the room. She was close to him now and he felt a tremor of fear run through his body.

He must act soon. 'Sit down.' He did, somehow powerless to disobey, and she sat astride him. Nick knew that if he didn't act soon it would all go out of control.

She took his hands: 'You're cold.'

'I'm sorry.'

'I'll warm you.' She slid his hands under the hem of the short, black dress she wore. Up beneath her thighs, up to her buttocks which were naked.

Nick said, anxiously: 'Please, may I just say something.'

The buttocks were muscled, free of fat, and the skin

105

was like the surface of a peach. She got off his lap suddenly, and Nick felt a stab of disappointment as his hands left the delicious skin. He was torn between the deep relief that perhaps he now might escape, and the sensation of bitter disappointment that he had somehow angered her and would lose something precious.

She stepped out of her dress in one movement, and stood naked before him. Her beauty filled the room, and Nick felt it was like standing before some work of art.

He felt as though he was choking. There had never been a sensation in him like this in his life before. She dominated the room, filled it, she *was* the room, there was nothing else, no other point of focus.

She took a bundle of dollars and rasped the sharp edges down the front of her body, across one breast and then the other. The incredible spears of her nipples were proud and erect.

Bianca took the bundle and drew it slowly and tantalisingly down past her navel into the edge of her pubic hair. It was as though the air was being drawn from the room, as though her presence was devouring the oxygen.

Nick felt heady, intoxicated, light-headed from her beauty. He was losing his balance, the whole world was tilting and then some tiny warning bell sounded.

If he did not act now, there was nothing, no going back. To his amazement he heard a voice, the voice of a man he knew was Nick Carter, coming from a long, long way away, and it was saying:

'Look, I'm sorry, but I don't think I can do this.'

Chapter Seven

Jessica lifted her glass of champagne, tilted it in Nick's direction, and said: 'Megastar.' He saw something in her eyes; mockery perhaps – admiration? – envy?

It was *her* story, but he was the one everyone was talking about, the one of whom they asked the question, What was she like? And, of course, Did you?

Nick didn't want it that way, but that was the way it was becoming, and she knew it. He lifted his own glass, and toasted her, without irony: 'Any stars about they're called Jessica.'

'Thanks.' They touched glasses. It was the symbolic bottle they'd promised themselves after they'd left Paris, the token of what they'd achieved, but now, as they drank, it seemed to have no meaning.

The story had been the splash, the main front page story, and then every other paper picked it up when the first editions of the Enquirer came in. By late evening it was on the TV news bulletins, local and national.

By Monday morning the newspapers were having a field day, and the foreign newspapers and magazines were working overtime on Bianca Vasquez.

Bianca herself had vanished within hours of being confronted by Jessica with the news that her secret life was no secret anymore. There wasn't a sighting of her anywhere, certainly not at her homes in London, New York or St. Paul de Vence.

It could only be a matter of time before she was discovered, because the hideous price of fame was that, in the words of a famous boxer, they can run but they can't hide.

Now Nick and Jess were bone weary from the late nights, the concentrated work, and the sheer nervous effort of coping with the Bianca story. The adrenalin that sustained them had gone, and it was like coming down from a drug high.

And it was out of their hands now, for the greater part. The juggernaut was up and moving, as every media outlet hunted for Bianca stories and for Bianca herself.

He and Jess would write more, of course, but the momentum had passed from their hands, as the chronology of media production demanded it must when a story is broken by a newspaper that appears only once a week.

As though reading Nick's thoughts, Jessica said:

'We broke it Nick, don't forget that. Whatever the others turn up, we got it rolling.'

'You actually, Jess. Your story.'

'Well, thanks, but remember, the boy done good. You was brilliant out there on the park, my son.' Nick laughed at her mock sportspeak, and lifted his glass again. 'Well, to the dynamic duo.'

'Batman and Robin. Gotham City.'

They drank. Nick said: 'Do you know what Gotham means – really, I mean?'

'Nope.'

'City of fools.'

'Very apt.'

The pub was half empty, it was gone nine, and the after-work drinkers had headed off for Waterloo, Victoria, Liverpool Street and the daily grind home.

'Just between mates, Nick, did you give her one?'

He felt the unhealthy heat creep like a slow and poisoned tide into his cheeks. 'Leave it out Jess, for God's sake. I expect that from the others, not from you.'

She pulled a funny little face: 'Blow job?'

'You're a classic.'

'Won't tell a soul, cross my heart and hope to die.'

He pulled a rueful face: 'As you well know, she was in and out in three quarters of an hour. I mean, come on.'

'That'd be a marathon to some of the men I've bonked.'

'Tough. You shouldn't screw journalists, they're all too pissed.

Nick felt irritable, and he suspected that beneath the banter from Jessica there was a slightly barbed irritation with him. But neither wished to go home, Nick because he wanted to postpone whatever lay ahead between him and Jenny; Jessica, presumably, because she had nothing to go home to since her marriage had ended.

Not even the bizarre promise of conflict; just the dead zone of the single life, the sterile world of choice, wine, TV and the unfilled bed.

He pretended to look around the pub, as though searching for someone. She said, with waning interest: 'Well, did you?'

Nick looked back at her: 'Sorry? Oh, did I screw Bianca? Would you feel better if I had? Would it confirm your worst suspicions of males in general and me in particular? Or would it invest me with whatever dose of machismo I lack to make me the successful Fleet Street male?'

A sub-editor from a rival newspaper, a man they both knew, came in and joined them, thankfully putting an end to the bitchiness.

Nick thought Jessica looked tired, and somehow inexplicably sad. She should be elated. Her name was first on the story, and she'd done several TV and radio interviews, including a live link-up with one of the American big three.

But he realised he didn't know her, not really; couldn't understand her – that would never be possible, because she was a woman and he was a man, and he had the most deadening, dawning realisation that the two sexes were from different planets.

It didn't matter whether you liked women, or sympathised with them, or knew all the technical, physiological details of their complex biological make-up. It didn't even help to have an imagination. Because you couldn't *know*. You couldn't *know* what it was like not to have a cock between your legs, but to be a receptacle.

You couldn't have that sense or that knowledge, of a body programmed for reproduction, to have your insides torment you every twenty-eight days with cramp and pain. To know you were a walking biological time-bomb, programmed to need things you might not want, to want things maybe you couldn't have.

And all in the certain sure knowledge that your prime was short. That even if you possessed the looks society prized so much, there would be an end to it.

Nick looked carefully at Jessica. What would it like to be inside her head now? To think what she was thinking, about him, about the man who had joined them. To *be* her?

Deep down they hate us he thought. They hate what we are, how we regard them, how we use them, how the dice are loaded in our favour. They hate their sometime need for us.

When the man left, Jessica turned, cruelly: 'Christ but he's boring. Anyway, what was I saying? Oh yes, did you and Bianca get it together?'

Nick downed his warm champagne. It had been beyond the wit or capability of the over-priced pub to provide an ice-bucket.

He said: 'I'm off, I've had a bellyful.'

'Sorry Mister sensitive. It was just that you were damned quick to hang on to the tape.'

Nick grabbed his folded overcoat from an adjoining stool: 'You got what you wanted, didn't you? She incriminated herself out of her own mouth.'

'Sure, but that was five minutes and then you were on

110

me like a flash, and off with the tape. What's wrong, didn't you trust me? And what about the rest?'

'No business of yours Jess – or anyone's. If you think for one minute that I'm letting anyone get their hands on that tape so they can hawk it round Fleet Street, you must think I'm crazy. I had to make an idiot of myself in there to get her to leave, and I'm not going to be made a laughing stock of.'

'Well, Lordy, Lordy, Massah, I'm mighty sorry, I'm shuh.' The tape was in Nick's briefcase, nestled against his leg at the foot of the table, and it seemed to glow through the fabric like threatening Kryptonite.

'And if you think I'm being over sensitive you want to spend a few nights chez moi.'

'Wifey still got the hump?'

'I think hump is the wrong word. She has retreated into a dignified, hurt silence. Rebecca's been packed off to her Gran's leaving Jenny to have her migraines.'

'Migraine is real, Nick.'

'Yeh,' Nick stabbed a finger at his own chest, 'and so am *I*. And just for once it would be nice to walk through the door to a woman who *welcomed* you, who *supported* you, who realised that the reason she can fuck about all day at coffee mornings is because I jump in this cess-pit five days a week.'

Jessica grabbed her coat: 'Is she pissed off because you didn't tell her exactly what was going to happen in Paris?'

'Yeh. I mean, I couldn't know it was going to work. I didn't expect it to. But I should have given her a hint.'

'Has she cut off your tap?' Jessica said it innocently, pulling on her coat. As they got up to go, Nick shook his head:

'Why are you so fascinated with what Jenny and I do – or don't do – in bed, Jess?'

'Not do? She *has* cut off your tap.'

111

'You're impossible – and you bloody do it to wind me up.'

'Works though,' she gave him a playful jab, and smiled at him. The old Jess. He smiled back. He *cared* for this woman.

'Your potentiality for evil is unlimited.'

'Don't underestimate your own. You get a little message from the chairman?'

'Bottle of Scotch, and I *hate* Scotch. You?'

'Flowers, I'm a girlie see. I love Scotch.'

The wind was whipping up dust, dirt, and old newspapers the familiar London tumbleweed slipping down the pavement. There wasn't a cab in sight, so they started to walk, leaning into the wind and the man-made onslaught.

She said: 'Best story for ten years, I thought the chairman said something about expressing their gratitude in material terms.'

'He did – but it's not the 14th for another ten days, who knows?'

'Fat chance – hoi!' A black cab with its For Hire sign off was scurrying in the opposite direction. He slowed, looked at them, and drove on.

'Bastard!' said Jessica, with feeling. 'Paddy asked me today if you and I were screwing.'

'I hope you told him it was the red hot affair of the century?'

'Bloody right – hey, there's one. Taxi! Taxi!' The black cab slowed next to them. 'I said we'd been bonking for years. Wife swapping before my old man ran off, threesomes down at your place now I'm a single girl again.'

'Thank God. If you hadn't it would become Rumour of the Week, I can do without that in view of all this Bianca crap.'

'Paddy's an arsehole.' She opened the cab door.

'Notting Hill Gate, please.' Nick said, in through the

112

open door, 'grab the Tube for God's sake, you'll be home quicker.'

She winked: 'Naw, the lady likes her luxury. Take care.'
'Yeh, you too.'

She pulled down the window of the now closed door. 'No problem Nick. Just go home and fuck her blue.'

He said aloud to the disappearing taxi: 'Chance would be a fine thing.'

It was the pit of the night; the darkest, deadest, emptiest hour. The luminous digits of the clock mocked Nick as he willed them to advance.

He had been awake for over an hour, mind racing, the fragments of the Bianca story whirling around his head. He was at the centre of something big, and took an inner pride in that, but something was missing, some triumph he felt should be present and wasn't.

And above all he should be comfortable here, for this was his kingdom, his house, his home – his and Jenny's – the place they had created with their energy, their drive, their skill and the money that had stemmed from all these things.

No-one had given them this, not the furniture they sat on, the pictures they gazed at, the clothes they wore. No-one had given them anything, they had achieved all this.

There had been compromises along the line, things he would rather not have done, or said, people he might have been kinder to and about, under other circumstances.

But he was here, he had arrived here, and he had been there, so he knew the difference, knew what this meant. He felt Jennifer shift in the bed next to him.

And this woman had shared it with him. He would not give that up without a fight, any of it, the job, their marriage, none of it.

Nothing was insurmountable, dammit it all, hadn't he

113

had that lesson hammered into him the hard way? Nothing was insoluble if you worked hard enough at it – not even this . . . he could not bring himself to form the word in his mind . . . not this thing, between him and Jenny.

He would solve it. He and his wife would be lovers again. He thought about earlier, about the dream, about the half-awakening, and banished it. Dreams are like odours, bad ones eventually go away.

It was Jennifer he loved, Jennifer he wanted, no-one else. He felt a rush of strange, youthful affection for the woman next to him.

At that moment the telephone rang.

The clock said 4.30. He moved quickly, anxious to kill the clamour that had invaded the sleeping room, and he felt his wife shift uneasily in her deep sleep.

He freed a cramped arm that was clumsy with pins and needles: 'Yes.'

'Nicholas Carter?'

'Yes, this is Nick Carter.' No-one ever called him Nicholas except his mother. Something about the man's accent? What was it, Russian? French? More like Spanish, but a joke Spanish, heavily accented.

'It's four-thirty in the morning, who is this?'

'You have only scratched the surface of the Bianca story.' Nick heard Jenny mutter something in her sleep, and he lowered his voice to a hissed whisper: 'Who is this?' Could it be one of the lads out on the piss, having a wind-up. The accent sounded phoney, just ludicrous. The man had said 'Neekolars'.

Well, let him commit himself first, Nick thought, because I'm damned if I am. I'm not making a fool of myself. But he never *once* thought of replacing the receiver. You could never be sure. Out of a thousand cranks, fakes, loonies, there could always be the one with the genuinely *great* story. 'A friend.'

'Really?'

114

'Get a pen and paper now and make some notes.' There was the tone of command in the man's voice, and Nick felt somehow – rebuked.

'Look, who are you?'

'It doesn't matter. Get the pen. *Please*.' The please seemed less like a plea than a concession, a conciliatory gesture, some move of diplomacy towards a man to whom the caller might feel he had been hasty and dictatorial.

Nick got out of bed, and saw Jenny turn to her own side, curling into a foetal like ball. With pen poised he said, wearily:

'Go ahead.'

Jenny said: 'Who is it?' Nick shushed her: 'Go ahead.'

'Bianca has consorted with the Grey Wolves of Jaffa in Tripoli, Libya.'

'We know that,' Nick said icily.

'Then why didn't you use it?'

'Because we can't prove it. There is no hard evidence to connect her, just hearsay.' The man gave a slight exhalation, almost of relief.

'Then you don't know about her meeting in Paris?'

'With whom?'

The man with the Spanish accent gave a name, then a date, and the name of a hotel in Paris. The man said certain names would be in the register. He gave a flight number, and an airline for Bianca. He gave the date a private jet had landed at Le Bourget, and who could prove that fact, and the plane's originating airport.

'You will be able to prove all this. It will not be hard.'

'This man is the head of the Grey Wolves front organisation, you know this?'

'Yes.'

'Then if everything you say is true you must work for some intelligence organisation. No-one else could get information like this. Either that . . .' Nick paused,

115

and suddenly felt a hint of fear . . . 'or some rival terror group.'

'I work for no-one. I have friends.'

Nick tried to persuade the man to meet on a strictly confidential basis at a place and time of the man's choice. The caller declined. Nick casually mentioned the possibility of money. The man was not interested.

'I'm not seeking money.'

'Then why? Why call me? Who are you? Has Bianca harmed you in some way?'

'Because I wish to see *justicia*.' The man said it in Spanish, as though the word was so important it could only have the right emphasis in his own language.

Nick said: 'You're from Spain.'

'I'm from nowhere. I shall telephone you again.' The line went dead, and Nick looked down at his notes, then turned off the bedside light and slipped back beneath the duvet. Jenny was facing the other way, and he heard her say: 'Who calls you at this time in the morning?'

'I dunno. A nut, probably.'

'It was about Bianca, though, wasn't it?' She said the name as though she was a former lover of her husband's, or a rival of her.

'Well, yes. He was giving me some background. If what he says is true, it's a bloody good story.' He put his arm around his wife's waist, sensed her immediate rigidity, and removed it.

'I think I'll get up. I won't be able to sleep now. I'll watch a video or something.'

'Not too loud.'

'It's OK, Becky's at your Mum's, remember?'

'I'm not, so not too loud. *Please*.' He felt her hostility like an odour, and said: 'Don't worry, I won't disturb you.'

He put Annie Hall on the video. He loved the scene where Woody's character Alvy is in the kitchen of the

116

seaside place with a new girlfriend, and the lobsters are loose. With Annie it had been fun. But the girl can't understand why he's so upset. And he says something like: 'I'm tense since I quit smoking.' And she asks: 'When did you quit smoking?' And he says: 'Sixteen years ago.' And she looks at him blankly, and says: 'I don't understand,' and then, 'Is that a joke, or what?' And you see the look on Alvy's face, and you know that what has just happened is vital, because he knows that there is absolutely nothing between he and the girl, and never, ever could be.

Nick thanked God he and Jenny had never played such a scene. He was confident there had been no such pivotal moment in their relationship, when either or both had realised there was nothing, nothing at all between them, or left for them.

So there was still hope – wasn't there?

Earlier that night he had thought, for a few brief, sleep-confused minutes, that they had been on the edge of re-birth. He had been in a half-sleeping, half-waking fever of desire, utterly hard, and his subconscious registered the triumph of return.

He and Jenny had grappled in sleep, his tongue searching for her's, her mouth parting instinctively for him, his body hot against her.

But as the urgency of the long-vanished need brought him back to wakefulness, he became aware that he was grappling with a phantom of his dreams made carnate.

For the object of his lust, the mover of his revival, was not his wife. It was Bianca. And that knowledge and the revealing physical truth that Jenny was not Bianca, and that it was not his wife he desired, but Bianca, with a power he had never experienced, killed his desire almost instantly.

And Jenny, half aroused, herself waking, felt it happen so whatever she sensed might be happening in Nick's

117

mind, she could feel the evidence of his suddenly waned desire.

She shrank from him in disgust and disappointment, putting a no-man's land between them.

At six-thirty Nick was showered and dressed. He telephoned Jessica, and after quelling her initial annoyance, told her about the early hours telephone call, and arranged to pick her up at seven.

He went to the bedroom to say goodbye to Jenny, but she was sleeping, and when he knelt on the bed and kissed her head, she didn't stir.

No sleeper had ever been so rigid and unwilling.

Chapter Eight

Bianca felt an enormous sensation of floating; a narcotic of weightlessness. She had never felt so free, so unfettered – so *light*.

It was as though if she released her grip on the arm of the sun lounger, the gentle Hawaiian breeze would lift her, and float her like a balloon over the palms and the surf.

It was like the physically pleasurable symptoms of some strange illness.

She had read a story once of a wealthy man who had decided to give away everything he possessed. He had simply walked off into the countryside with just a few cooking utensils, a little food, materials for shelter and the clothes he wore.

The rest of the inhabitants of the town thought him mad, and Bianca, when she'd read it, tried to imagine why someone would wish to do that. Now she understood. It was for the most immense sense of freedom.

As soon as she had seen the girl and the man approach her – the female confident, almost cocky, the male nervous and uneasy – she knew they were reporters. They had that *look*, that shop soiled air of aggression. And as soon as the woman spoke, it all fitted.

The call from the girl Annabelle, then the nervous man from Hong Kong in the Paris suite. Bianca had become the athlete who runs one race too many, the boxer who succumbs to the lure of another big payoff.

The bridge too far, the risk of humiliation in discovery, but the addiction too strong, the thrill of the game too deep and too necessary.

So there was little surprise, more a kind of resignation, all hidden, as the reporters went through their routine, the man embarrassed, obviously, at being present.

And as the woman spoke, Bianca felt that inside herself, something was being peeled back, layer by layer, the skin of years. She felt exposed, and somehow scoured.

There had only been one such moment in Bianca's life, and that recently. In a room, a voice – such as that one – speaking to her, saying the unthinkable. So now, in the road, the female reporter reciting the litany of Bianca's crimes, Bianca felt giddy, as though she was listening to her life replayed.

She had told the woman: 'It's totally absurd. Print one word and you'll hear from my lawyers.' But she could see from the look on the reporter's face, a kind of vicious determination, that they had evidence. The man in Paris had obviously been a reporter too.

Bianca did not return home. In a white haze, she drove straight to Heathrow, ignoring her previous appointment, and with her Gold Card bought a First Class ticket to San Francisco; suddenly feeling the blind panic of the hunted.

In San Francisco she took a cab into the city, and checked into an anonymous hotel, using a false name. No-one seemed to recognise her. It was the logic of association. If you saw Paul McCartney, without luggage, checking into a Holiday Inn, alone, you'd think. 'Well, it's not Paul McCartney, because he'd be staying at the biggest joint in town.'

She bought a new set of clothes, anonymous stuff, jeans, T-shirts, simple summer dresses. In a nondescript hair salon she had her hair cropped short. The stylist said, kindly: 'Anyone ever tell you you look like Bianca?'

'All the time.'

At the American Express office Bianca drew 3,000 dollars in cash, and bought a Coach seat on a United

Airlines flight to Honolulu. On arrival she took an inter-island flight to Molokai and a month's rent on a Jeep from Dollar, before heading away from the airport.

Here, she felt, there might be some breathing space not allowed to her on Oahu, or the celebs, island, Maui. She'd done a modelling session here once, and she loved the island.

They called it the 'friendly island' now, but she knew that was a public relations device. Molokai had been the 'lepers' island', a place of death for thousands of leprosy sufferers.

Out on the isolated North coast peninsula called Makanalua, a young Belgian priest, Father Damien De Veuster had organised the leper colony into a proper community, with houses, a church and a makeshift hospital.

The lepers cleared land and farmed it, living on the crops they grew. Makanalua meant, 'The given grave.' Bianca took the Kalae Highway, cutting across the neck of the island, towards the village of Kalaupapa, where a few score of lepers still remained, then turned South-East towards Haupu Bay.

She found a Fifties apartment block, run by an elderly Japanese man, and paid cash for a month's rental on a one-bedroomed apartment overlooking a long green lawn before the palm fronted beach.

That night she watched the US network news on the small Sony TV in the living area, and saw for the first time her own face peering back at her from the frozen black and white of a British newspaper.

It was an eerie sensation, used as she was to her face being on the cover of a hundred magazines. It was as though someone had taken her face and turned it inside out, so that her evil showed like the seams of a reversed garment.

The next day she donned a swimsuit, went down to the

121

water's edge, and after a moment's hesitation, plunged in. The water was cold and it seemed to revive her after the lethargy of a broken night's sleep.

The surf was up and the locals were out, way beyond the breaking waves, lolling like porpoises, resting on their boards waiting for suitable waves, enjoying the water and the sun.

Bianca swam hard, diving under the crushing breakers, submerged in a weight of green, then surfacing, ploughing through the water, breasting the moving peaks of wave, until she was almost half a mile offshore, among the basking surfers.

She could feel the cold seeping into her bones now, and she could see that the surfers were eyeing her strangely because she wore no wetsuit, and had no board.

Bianca felt the tiny tug of current, turning her in the water like a parent's playful hand, gentle fingertips that she knew could punish her if they wished.

She was rich, and she was famous – infamous now – worth everything, and worth nothing. And out here she was simply a minute organism of a form of life. And the sea could chill her and kill her, pull her away, drag her under, and she would be powerless to stop it.

And it would be so easy to assist it. Swim a little further, perhaps, until she was too exhausted to make the return journey. To lie back in the water, and feel the gentle roar in her ears, to let the cold do its insidious work. So easy.

There was movement in the water near her, the splash of hands, and she looked up into a broad, Islands face above a green wetsuit on a shocking-pink surfboard.

The boy said: 'You OK?'

'Yeh. I'm OK.'

'It's kinda cold out here without a suit. Wanna lift in?'

There was no guile or deception in the young teenage face. And no guilt. When had she last seen such a face?

'Yes, thanks.'

122

'Climb up.'

He slid forward on the board, and put a hand out to Bianca, she took it, and it was like being hauled onto the saddle of a horse.

The two rode in together, using their hands as paddles, gently riding waves the boy had clearly chosen for their lack of power. In the hiss of the flattened surf, she slid off and shouted:

'Thanks.'

'No problem.' The boy spun his board, skated it on the film of water, then dived flat out on it, into the breaking surf. Chilled, Bianca ran back into her apartment, streaming water, reflecting on what a strange feeling it was to be alive.

Now, in the warmth of the afternoon sun, she lounged, feather-light, in the chair. How soon would they come, and who would deliver the Judas kiss?

She had nothing now, was nothing. She was the bull in the ring, like the hapless creature she had once seen in Madrid.

How they tormented it, thrusting in the spears, hurling the barbs that hung like cruel jewellery as it launched its menacing, yet pathetic attacks, on the coiffed dandy with the elegant shoes.

She had sat, rigid with something approaching contempt, transfixed by the bull's agony, until the creature staggered under the blood loss and the pain of its injuries.

Bianca had seen the massive head go down, the weight of its own pride now unbearable, as the man-mannequin thrust his tiny sword deep into the defenceless neck.

The bull had staggered back, but had not fallen. For a few seconds the bull and the matador eyed each other with a kind of bafflement, the matador embarrassed at his inadequacy, the bull puzzled by the expectation.

The innocent monster stood with the instrument of death protruding from his bulk, and then it registered.

The legs went, the big eyes glazed, and he crumpled. Bianca had watched the bull for a long time, until they towed it ignominiously across the bloodied sand.

When would the matadors come? The bull had had no choice, it was bred for its purpose. Had she been bred for hers? Had she as little choice as the bull?

Was that what some women were bred for, the amusement of the male matadors? To be disposed of when they were too old, too weak, to slow to lunge on cue at the wielded cape?

She would not die like the bull. She would take the dandied sequined matadors with her.

Impaled upon their own swords.

Jessica went to Paris, Nick stayed in London, and they got the splash once again. 'Bianca's Night with Terror Boss'. The man they had dubbed Spanish Voice, from his accent, had got it all correct.

They had proved that the front man for the Grey Wolves of Jaffa had landed at Le Bourget in a private jet that had started its journey at Tripoli, Libya. Jessica got the landing and take-off records, plus a passenger and cargo manifest to prove it had been him on the plane.

What she didn't tell the office, or Nick for that matter, was that she stole them when someone's attention was diverted. Breaking the law never seemed as serious in a foreign country, she felt.

Then she and the photographer went into the centre of Paris, checked in at the hotel and in four hours had proved that the passenger had also stayed there at the same time as Bianca.

Her name was in the computer files. The photographer discovered that by chatting up a receptionist, and adding a dash of well-concealed bribery in the form of an Hermes scarf, a bottle of champagne and what seemed like a tub of expensive Balenciaga perfume.

The man's name was not in the computer files, but he had been there. Jessica discreetly showed his picture around, and the staff confirmed it, showed her the suite, gave her little vignettes to colour in the overall picture.

It was less co-operation than venality. Jessica loved France, loved-hated the French, but knew their tremendous practicality when it came to putting wads of folding stuff with Banque de France on it, in their back pockets.

And she spoke reasonable French so she chatted up the hotel staff, and confirmed also that Bianca and the Arab had eaten dinner in his room. It was enough. You didn't need to prove sex – in fact, the lawyer would have insisted that both parties sign an affidavit saying it happened before he would have allowed the allegations.

It was enough that she had flown to Paris on the same day as the terror boss, had stayed in the same hotel, and had dined with him. Everyone knew what Bianca was now, let them draw their own conclusions.

When Nick arrived at Annabelle's flat, she was reading the story. He noticed a dark, wet ring where a coffee cup had rested on Page One. None of it mattered a toss. Sensation today, coffee-cups later, fish and chips tomorrow.

He took the envelope and handed it to her. She slit it with a tomato-red thumb nail, viewed the cheque, and gave a small pursed-lip look of gratitude.

'You kept your word.'

'I said we'd pay up, on publication. You delivered, so have we?'

She gave him a peck on the cheek: 'Thanks. Will I have to tell the tax people about this?'

Nick sat down, unbidden: 'Fraid so. Any payment of over £500 in a tax year, our accounts people are obliged to tell the revenue.'

She folded the cheque: 'Pity. Still, let them try and collect from Spain.'

'That where you're off too?'

'More or less.'

'We didn't name you, you could stay.'

She came over to where he was sitting, and ruffled his hair: 'For a big boy, you're naive. it won't stay secret for long.'

'Known only to Jess and me, the Editor and the chairman.'

'And their secretaries, and the accounts department, who will not be able to resist boasting that they just bunged twenty grand to that old slag who used to be on Page Three. Come on, Nick.'

'I suppose you're right. Any chance of a coffee?'

'Sure.' She went through to the ivory coloured kitchen and rummaged in the cupboards.

'Would you like real?'

'Thanks. That would be great.' He remembered the taste of the appalling instant coffee he'd had on a previous visit. Nick felt a touch of pity for her, and tried to kill it. She was a hooker, she took cocaine, and sold it to others. She'd probably never done a decent day's work in her life, and now he'd handed her twenty thousand pounds.

He went into the kitchen as she poured the grains into the automatic coffee maker. As she put the blue foil bag back into the cupboard, he said: 'Nicaraguan, that's unusual.'

'Isn't it. Saw it in my local Oxfam shop first, and now I buy it all the time, it's delicious.' He tasted it later and agreed it was. Nicaragua, Oxfam shops. Perhaps Annabelle was not quite the dumb ex-Page Three girl. He wondered if she actually did read the Guardian.

Over the coffee he said: 'Did you have any idea it would get this big?'

She shook her head: 'Nope. But no regrets, as Edith Piaf said. But . . .' she paused.

'What?'

126

'I had a funny phone call this morning. Not obscene, more – menacing.'

'What did he say – I assume it was a he?'

'He said, 'We'll get you for this,' that's all.'

'Accent?' Nick felt a tingle of fear.

'Neutral, mid-Atlantic. Like a bad DJ.'

'You scared?' She seemed remarkably calm under the circumstances.

'The day a punter scares me . . .'

'Perhaps it was the CIA. You shouldn't drink Nicaraguan coffee.'

'Maybe. Not yet – so don't look so worried – but I'm leaving the country. Nothing in my contract says I have to stay, but I won't do a runner on you. I'll let you know.'

He got up: 'Ah well, no peace for the wicked.'

'And how wicked *were* you, superman?' Annabelle had a wicked gleam in her eye. He smelled the perfume, suddenly, as though someone had switched on a perfumed fan.

'That's like hearing an Irish joke for the fifty millionth time. Useless first time around, and downhill from there.'

'Come on, you can't blame me for being curious. Did you make an excuse and leave like you said?'

He headed for the door, turned and winked: 'Actually, I told a little whopper there.'

'Oh yeh?' Her face brightened.

'Yeh. Actually *I* made the excuse, and *she* left.' Her face fell.

'You wicked little bugger.'

'Keep in touch Annabelle.'

When he got home he played his messages from the telephone answering machine. Message one was from Jenny. She was at her mother's 'for a couple of days'. Two was from Annabelle. It asked him to remember what she'd said before he met Bianca. In Annabelle's case, if *he* didn't make the excuse, she wouldn't leave. It was hard to detect if she was joking or not.

Message three was from Spanish Voice, naming names. Nick made careful notes, then re-recorded the voice onto his pocket tape recorder. If it was true, it was sensational.

The telephone rang, and he picked it up expecting Jenny and getting Jessica.

'Nick?' Her voice was high and urgent.

'Jess, great you called. Spanish Voice has been on and –

'Listen! I'm on a payphone at Heathrow and my flight's closing. I don't have much time.

'Heathrow?'

'Yeh. We've found Bianca!'

Chapter Nine

Nick left the cavernous rough-brick and gingham basement of Joe Allens, the calves liver and red wine suffusing him with a feeling of well-being.

Jessica was in Hawaii, carrying a verbal promise of a quarter of a million pounds sterling if Bianca would come onside. It was breathtakingly audacious, that the very newspaper that had exposed Bianca should ask to tell her story.

But a coup if it worked, and Nick felt the answer would be money. He doubted if anyone could – or would wish to – top a quarter of a million.

And now that the game was up for Bianca, perhaps she might feel that sum would justify telling the full story. The Enquirer could only offer so much because of its other media and business outlets; TV, magazines, even movie studios.

Syndicating the story to newspapers all over the world would recoup a lot of it, too.

And Nick felt, smugly, that money would clinch it for Bianca. It was where she lived, her shrine. Anyone who would screw for ten grand would talk for twenty-five times that.

But so far she was holed up on some obscure Hawaiian island where half the population were leprous, acting like a cornered terrorist.

But if anyone could get her onside, Jessica could. Nick didn't begrudge her the trip, he felt she'd earned it. And, anyway, these foreign jobs were over-rated, especially the long-haul ones.

Everyone thought you were on some kind of holiday, even

your colleagues, and they knew better. The reality was you sat for 12 or 14 hours on a 747 – not Business Class anymore either, those days were over.

You sat with the punters, and were just as shattered by the time you arrived. But instead of jumping into a hot shower and bed you had to work.

Then you were jet-lagged for days, working flat out, and the minute it was over no-one said, 'Relax for a couple of days out there, mate,' instead you were on the next Jumbo home to cope with jet-lag at the other end.

He thought this one sounded like the recipe for a heart-attack. Spanish Voice had not called, but Nick had his work cut out anyway, dealing with the rest of the story.

Spanish Voice had given three names, each of which, the caller alleged, had had sexual relations with Bianca – and for money. The first was a member of Parliament, the second, not only an MP but the Cabinet Minister who had been on Jessica's original list. Nick had some new information on him, something Annabelle remembered Bianca telling her. The third name also set Nick's pulse running, and exercised his attention and imagination. The man was a royal, albeit a junior one by marriage.

It would take an impossible series of multiple, coincidental heart attacks, plane crashes or traffic pile-ups – the felling of the equivalent of two soccer teams – before the wife of this particular chinless wonder ever clambered incredulously onto the throne.

But he *was* a royal. He had been up there on the balcony at the Palace on at least one occasion, joining in the royal group wave-fest to the adoring Royalites clogging the Mall on a wedding day.

According to the caller, Royal had met Bianca at a celebrity clay-pigeon shooting contest in East Anglia the previous year.

There, at a country house where they were guests of an aristocratic host, the royal – so the caller said – had a

130

sexual liaison with the girl. Their early dalliance had been so obvious, the caller said, that at least half-a-dozen guests remarked upon it.

But in the end, like all of them, he paid. So tomorrow, Nick and editor Miles Rimmer would go to Buckingham Palace for a private, secret and off-the-record meeting with the head of the Palace Press Office.

It had taken some persuading before Miles agreed to make the official request by letter. But Nick knew that a telephone call from a journalist – particularly one from the despised tabloids – would be brushed aside like some regal animal brushing away a bothersome fly.

They could not as easily dismiss a request from a Fleet Street editor with millions of loyal royalite readers. And they would, Nick felt sure, be bloody curious.

Nick turned into Kingsway, hoping there'd be a spare cab outside the Waldorf. In the old days it was a five-minute walk back to Fleet Street, with perhaps a stop off for a port at the Wig and Pen.

Now there was the jungle of cab-hunting for the long trip back to Kensington. A black limousine with smoked windows cruised up to the kerb, and Nick unconsciously stepped back to let the occupant out. Instead, a window slid silently down, and a voice from the interior said:

'Mr. Carter?' Nick peered into the dark insides of the limousine, feeling faintly threatened and not knowing why.

'Yeh, I'm Nick Carter. Who's that?'

He saw a distinguished, aquiline face, framed by stylishly cut grey hair which, despite the fact that the man was obviously in his late Sixties or early Seventies, was only faintly receding at the temples. The man said: 'May I give you a lift?'

'Do I know you?' Nick hesitated.

'We haven't met, but please get in. I won't bite, and you'll take an age to get a cab.'

The voice, like the face, carried authority. To disobey it

would be like standing upright against a gale-force wind. Nick got in and the car moved slickly into the Kingsway traffic.

'A good lunch, I hope.'

'Yes, good.'

'Joe Allen, wasn't it? Not a restaurant I know, unfortunately.'

Nick leaned back in his seat. 'No, the Athenaeum or the Garrick would be you, wouldn't it?' The man smiled.

'Just who *are* you?

'I'm a patriot.'

'Why does that word make my flesh creep?' Nick said.

'Don't worry, not that kind of patriot, I have no wish to launch any coups against legally elected democratic governments of whatever political hue.'

'Glad to hear it.' Mandarin clothes, the slightly old-fashioned but well cut suit – genuine Savile Row probably – white shirt, starched collar, club tie – which one? – Nick didn't have the faintest, but he'd try and remember the design and check it somewhere.

'I was a civil servant, now retired.'

'Nice pension perks,' Nick's nod encompassed the car and chauffeur. The man smiled showing expensive teeth, still his own. He had ice-blue eyes that looked hard, but not cruel.

'I have independent means, and my pension is generous.' Pity my Dad hasn't, and his isn't, Nick thought with a stab of jealousy.

'I shall get to the point. Miss Bianca Vasquez.'

'Rings a bell.'

'You've stirred up the proverbial hornet's nest. And now you're getting calls –'

'What?!' Nick was incredulous, 'how do you know –'

'I know.'

'If my telephone's tapped I promise you the Enquirer will kick up a stink. You bastards have got a nerve.'

The man placed a calming hand on Nick's, and the hand

132

was soft and quite cold: 'Don't jump to ludicrous conclusions. I have no governmental authority whatsoever. I doubt if anyone would tap your telephone Mr. Carter. With great respect, you are not important enough.'

'But you *think* someone is calling me.'

'Yes. Ignore his information. He has an axe to grind. He is a sick man. He seeks to take revenge by linking people with Miss Vasquez, people who are totally innocent of any wrongdoing.'

'People like – who, for example?'

The man smiled his bland mandarin smile: 'Ah, well now.'

'You people are embarrassed shitless, aren't you? That a hooker should have a House of Commons pass. Boy oh boy, she could have walked a bomb in there, or some hitman.'

The man played at adjusting his exclusive tie: 'I will agree that everyone in government was *highly* embarrassed. But it has all gone too far now. Decent men smeared – that is what would happen if you pursued the crazy fantasies of your caller.'

'He's been right before.'

'A lucky guess.'

'More than that – and you know it. And if my telephone is not being tapped, how come you know about this?' Nick tried a shot: 'Is it you? Is this some kind of double bluff?'

Again the assured laugh, and Nick felt off balance. This man was the headmaster allowing the insubordinations of a precocious but rebellious pupil in whom he sees promise.

'You *know* it isn't me. And neither have I had any sexual relations with Miss Vasquez.'

'What's the message? That's why I'm in here, isn't it? There's some deeper message – perhaps something to do with the national interest?' The cynicism was like phlegm

133

in Nick's throat. They sickened him, the whole mess of microbes that crawled over that dead, decomposing thing they called The Establishment.

The man's face went hard: 'You were right about Miss Vasquez, and for that you and your female colleague are to be congratulated.'

'But . . . there's always a but.'

'It is a plot to discredit the United Kingdom, our institutions, our government, our system, our royal family –'

Nick was cold:

'First time I've heard royalty mentioned in this little package.'

'You're being used Mr. Carter. Be very careful. Be sure of your facts.'

'Stop the car.' He rapped on the glass partition, but the car continued until the man leaned forward, rapped on the glass and said: 'Victor, pull in here will you.'

Nick flipped the door catch and stepped out of the Whitehall-on-wheels: 'Some other time, perhaps.'

'Of course. A pleasure to meet you. I'm sure you're a decent man.' The door closed with a luxurious squish and the car purred quietly away. Nick took out a pen and made a note of the registration number. He enjoyed the remainder of the journey on foot.

Back in the office he spent the rest of the afternoon in the picture library, sifting through hundreds of black and white newspaper stills. Senior civil servants, members of previous governments, industrialists, high-ranking Army, Navy and Royal Air Force officers.

After two hours he found himself staring into the face of the man in the limousine. It was Sir Percival Bellamy, the man once believed to be – because in the British way such things were never formally acknowledged – head of the British Security Services, the man immortalised in fiction as 'M', James Bond's boss.

Nick was very frightened. Bellamy had retired years

previously. What was his involvement in this? How did he know Nick was receiving calls giving information? Was that just spot-on speculation, given that the Enquirer clearly had a good contact?

Back at his desk there was a message to call Jenny, and he looked at his watch – Christ, nearly eight. He dialled his home number, she answered, and there was a lightness in her tone that cheered him.

'Are we going to see you at some civilised hour, you workaholic?'

'Actually, I lost track a bit. I'm on my way. I'll try for the eight-seventeen, but be on the safe side expect me about nine-twenty. Can we still eat?'

'Sure. Snack, some paté, bottle of wine. Did you lunch today?'

'Mmmm . . . I'm dehydrated.'

'Anyway, rush off. That was a kind thought of yours today, Rebecca loved it.'

'What, Jenny?'

'The limo – it was great.'

Nick's skin was cold and clammy: 'What limo, what the hell are you talking about Jen?'

'Oh come on, Nick, you should take more water with it. The film company limousine you diverted for us.'

'Just a second Jenny.' Nick put the telephone receiver on the desk, and his head in his hands. His heart was beating wildly, and he was having difficulty breathing. He knew what had happened.

At length he picked up the receiver: 'Sorry, love, I got something trapped in my throat. Chauffeur job, was the grey-haired bloke there?'

'Yes, Rebecca thought he was sweet – what film company is he boss of?' Nick quickly named an imaginary distribution company. Jenny would never know or check.

'He seemed quite taken with you,' Jenny said, 'good to see you're doing proper stories again.'

135

'They drove you straight home – no detours?' Nick held his breath.

'Nope. Straight home. It was incredible that he was going past Janet's wasn't it? – I'm surprised you asked him, you don't normally mix business with pleasure.'

Nick ran a tongue over dry lips: 'He offered, actually – I mentioned you were down there, he was passing that way. 'Thought you'd both like the treat, not to mention the lift.'

'You're a sweety. It was thoughtful after all the pressure you've been under lately.'

After the call, Nick went to the lavatory, lowered the seat and sat, his head in his hands. Whatever Bellamy was doing now, whether he still had some role in government, or represented some outside people – he clearly knew just about everything he needed to know about Nick.

He – they? – knew Jenny's friend Janet's address in Surrey, that she and Rebecca were there, that Jenny's car was in the garage for a service – even the approximate time she might be returning.

It was crude, but no doubt Bellamy thought it would be effective. Strike at a man through his family. He felt a rage, incredibly not at Bellamy, he somehow *understood* that, but at his wife, for being so *stupid*. How could she have got in a stranger's car, a car containing two men, *however* plausible the excuse. At the very least she should have checked with him at the office.

In some casual and seemingly unconnected way he would have to impress upon Jenny *and* Rebecca that from that point onwards they would both have to be careful of such behaviour. But how could he do that without alarming them, and discussing what had happened, with Jenny?

He didn't even know if he was close enough to her now, whether she would just dismiss what was happening as fantasy. Could he tell her in detail about Spanish Voice,

136

about the limo – no! That would terrify her. He resolved to leave it.

In Hawaii it was just turned ten a.m. the same day. He'd call Jessica, tell her about the man in the limo, about what had happened to Jenny, about tomorrow's trip to the Palace.

Then he would ask if she'd made any progress getting through to Bianca. He knew it was a long shot, that she was facing tough opposition, and that Bianca herself might never entertain the idea. The odds against it were long, although Nick believed, as he always did, that in the end money would have its usual final say.

He would never admit it, but he was mentally betting against his own side. He didn't want Bianca to go with the Enquirer, because if she did, it would mean Nick Carter as well as Jessica, who would have to work with her.

And he knew he could not bear to face the woman he had betrayed. He dialled the fourteen-digit number and was rewarded with the first, long American ringing tone.

Forgive me, Jess. But fail, please. Fail!

Chapter Ten

Nick said: 'Miles, with the greatest respect to our esteemed noble house, the Palace are lying their balls off.'

His editor gave him a searching look: 'And why would they do that, Nick? Why would they lie – to me, I mean . . .' his voice trailed off. Clearly he could not conceive of the representatives of Britain's royal family lying to Miles Rimmer.

'Why? Because that's what they're paid to do – and they get the nod right from the top. They lied about Anne and Mark – that they were getting married, that they were splitting. They lied about Charles and Di . . .'

'Some prevarication, perhaps . . .'

Nick was pacing up and down the room: 'When he was lined up for Marie-Astrid of Luxembourg, before he decided if he was going to have to be faithful for the rest of his life he might as well have a wife who was at least beautiful – the Palace officially – *officially* – denied that he'd been more than twice to Luxembourg that particular year.'

The Editor smiled benignly and examined some documents while Nick continued.

'I went to Luxembourg and was told, *officially* by the Grand Duke's office that actually Charles and Philip had been there, on private visits, *six* times. Basically so he and Marie-Astrid could get on.'

'Didn't she go to work in a leper colony, or something – eventually I mean?'

Nick gritted his teeth: 'My point being, Miles, that they lie all the time.'

The Editor motioned irritably for Nick to sit down, and

the reporter did. 'The head of the Buckingham Palace Press office, a man knighted by the Queen herself, *personally* gave me his categorical assurance that the individual concerned had *not* spent the night in the same house as Miss Vasquez, and had denied totally any impropriety with the lady at any time.'

'Only,' Nick said, 'after getting your *personal* assurance that the whole conversation was off the record.'

Miles gave Nick a patronising smile: 'And do you think the conversation would have taken place *at all*, had I *not* given that assurance?'

Nick ground a fist into his palm out of sheer frustration: 'Perhaps not, Miles. But that's my point. That's what they do. I've had twenty-odd years of them and people like them, in government, out of government. The Palace, the big banks, industry, football clubs. They lure newspaper people into their cosy, little conspiracy. They try to make you one of them, part of it, playing to *their* rules. And when they do that they've cut your balls off, you can't function effectively.'

Miles looked irritated. He didn't like being lectured by one of his inferiors, and anyway, he had his own reasons for not wanting to upset the Palace.

'However, our royal assures the Palace Press office that he was back in London by midnight, and at no time was alone with Bianca Vasquez. I hardly think he would lie.'

'Why? They lie all the time. Their whole raison d'être is based on lies.'

'Save me the republicanism. Perhaps your anonymous caller over-extended himself. He meant well, but he got the facts wrong. By the way, has he asked for money yet?'

Nick could see the doubt, the cynicism. 'No. I think he's straight. He has other motives, but I'm buggered if I know what they are.'

Miles wagged a finger: 'It sounds like revenge to me. Revenge on Bianca, perhaps on the royal. Beware of

revenge, the basest of motives.' Nick remembered what
the ex-Intelligence boss had said to him in the limousine.
Could it be revenge?

Miles' secretary brought in some tea. Miles had asked
Nick if he wanted a drink, and Nick, who would have killed
for a gin and tonic, had eagerly said yes.

Miles poured.

'I think he's got it right,' Nick said, doggedly. But there
was little but dogged defiance in what he said now. One of
the men who had been named was a Member of Parliament.
He had simply denied the allegation. He also said if they
used an unsubstantiated allegation along with his denial, he
would regard it as libel, and he would sue.

The office lawyer said the man would win. The story was
not carried. The Minister's office had issued a likewise total
and categorical denial. The Minister let it be known that he
would also sue if the allegation was used. The office lawyer
said ditto.

Anyway, everyone in the office said the Minister was
such a raving queen that the Enquirer would look stupid
if they even *suggested* he had been to bed with Bianca.

But there was something Nick knew, something he had not
told Miles. Something he believed implicated the Minister,
but that would not convince Miles or the lawyer.

It was something that had to be put to the Minister's face,
and without warning too. Something that would knock him
off balance, something for which he could not possibly have
an answer.

The Minister had refused to grant them an interview,
so there was no opportunity to put it, and to merely
submit it tamely in writing would ruin it. The Minister
would then have time and space to think up an excuse,
even to seek injunctions preventing publication if all
else failed.

Nick had an appalling sense of stupidity, as though
something was there but hidden, and he was too dense

to see it. They had tiny clues to a vast puzzle, and they could not make a picture out of it.

And Nick sensed – *knew* – that what they had got hold of was being strangled by the appalling civilities and conventions of secrecy that haunted British public life.

In America there would be – God, there would be *something*. Some way of getting at this; but Americans actually believed they were free, Britons only thought it.

What would they do if it was a villain, a pop star, some soap hero with suspected AIDS. Knock on his bloody door, that's what. But, no, it was a Minister of the Crown, and you couldn't knock on his, could you?

'One way of *really* finding out about the Minister.'

'Yes?' said Miles, wearily.

'Knock on his door.'

'Very good,' said Miles, assuming Nick was joking, 'oh, very good,' But Nick wasn't joking.

The address was on the files and in Who's Who, it was hardly a secret. The Minister lived in one of the discreet old town houses in a quiet square in Knightbsridge, just a stone's throw from Harrods.

It was the kind of house you couldn't buy simply on a minister's salary.

Nick had the gin and tonic of which Miles had cheated him, and then, several more. After all, it was a crazy idea, and he wouldn't do it. You couldn't knock on a Secretary of State's door, like he was – what, Nick thought? Like he was an ordinary Englishman? Could you?

The sun was a molten ball of orange flame, dipping slowly into a sheet of quicksilver, flooding it with fire and blood as Bianca watched from her balcony.

The owner of the apartment block had called unexpectedly two days previously – a courtesy call, he said, something he did with all his tenants.

The Judas kiss turned out to be an insincere shake of

the hand. Six hours later the first TV men arrived. As she drove out of the parking area, the TV truck blocked her way. There was a reporter with a microphone and a man with an expensive mini-cam.

She drove slowly but insistently towards them and eventually they moved, the reporter hurling questions, the cameraman panning with professional detachment.

Bianca had planned only to go to a nearby beach, she had just a few dollars and the clothes she wore. So it was impossible to flee further.

After an hour, she returned, went through the thickening media blockade, and back to her apartment. She remembered the parable her father had once told her, about the servant of the rich family whom Death touched in Baghdad market place. He fled back to the house in terror and told his master he must take the fastest horse and flee to another city, Samara.

That same day the master spotted Death in the market-place and asked him why he had scared the master's servant so. And Death replied: 'I had no wish to frighten him, I just wanted to remind him that we have an appointment tonight in Samara.'

There was nowhere left to flee. That night she watched herself on television, thinking how ugly she looked now, with her short hair.

The next day would bring more journalists, from the big city papers and TV stations in Honolulu, and from Los Angeles and San Francisco – including the West Coast correspondents of the British newspapers.

Then, like waves of fighter planes more media people, the harder men and women from London and New York, who would not observe such civilities as were still being observed by the local Press.

And now that she *was* found, how soon would the others try to silence her, the ones who knew what she knew? The fastest horse could not save her now, Death had touched her, and she could only meet him at the appointed hour.

She sat down at the cheap dining table and started to write. Several hours later, she put the contents into two envelopes addressed them, and rang for the concierge, the elderly Japanese man from whom she had originally rented the room.

At the door he bowed and Bianca said: 'I would like you to mail these for me – it's very important.'

'Yes – is no problem.' He paused, dipping his head slightly: 'I no tell them – I no tell the TV people.'

She was a foot taller than he was, and she put her hand on his shoulder: 'I know – don't worry it's OK.' She handed him the envelopes 'I have written out dates, Please do not mail them before then.'

He took them: 'You have my word.'

'It's Mr. Yakamoto, isn't it?'

'Yes. I make sure. Don't worry, the reporters not see them. I keep them in my quarters.'

'Are you married Mr. Yakamoto?' The old man shook his head. Then, for the first time, Bianca saw his left hand, or what would have been his left hand, but where only the leprous stump remained.

'I'm sorry.'

'No. No sorry. Life is good.'

'Yes, life is good.' She handed him another small envelope, containing five one-hundred dollar bills. 'This is for you – for the task I have set you.'

The sad eyes looked at her. How long had he been here as a leper? Had he been born here, a child of leprous parents? A plain of vast, infinitesimal sadness stretched away in his gaze.

'I no need money.'

'For friendship.'

'Friendship.' He took the extra envelope reluctantly.

She remained in the apartment for 48 hours, thinking,

144

not eating, knowing that at least the reporters could not knock on her door.

A burly local policeman guarded the foot of the stairs like a Pacific sentinel. But once, during the day, Bianca heard her name called, went out onto the balcony – foolishly – for who else could it be but a reporter or photographer – and saw the English woman, the reporter from the Sunday newspaper who had first confronted her in the London street.

She was standing on the grass in front of the beach, somehow having eluded the security. There was a man beside her, firing shots from a camera. She heard the familiar clack-clack of the motorised Nikon.

Bianca allowed them their small triumph, then went back inside, without replying to the shouted questions. As dusk fell she sat just inside from the balcony with the screen doors open.

The fragrance of the tropical night was a pot pourri of sea, coconut, frangipani and bougainvillea, and the sun took a generation before, once again, it poured into the sea. Bianca watched until her world turned black, then telephoned Mr. Yakamoto at his tiny cubicle.

She asked if he would come to her apartment at eight the next morning, not before, and let himself in with his pass key. The man said he would.

Nick rapped three times on the large door, using the lion's head brass knocker – nothing so vulgar as a door bell here.

After about a minute there was the turning of several locks, and a thin, swarthy faced man in a black, single breasted jacket and striped trousers opened the door.

'I'd like to see the Minister, please.'

'Your name sir?'

'Nick Carter of the Sunday Enquirer.' He handed the servant a business card, and the man said: 'The Minister does not receive journalists at his home.'

'Just hand him the card.' The servant gave him a long, evil look, then closed the door. Nick waited, not even knowing if the man would return.

The servant's accent, Nick noted, was Mediterranean, similar to Spanish Voice. Nick was regretting the alcohol now, he had the growing awareness that he shouldn't be there, that what he was doing was foolish.

And somehow that made him even more determined to see it through. He had to throw these people off balance. The door opened again, and the servant handed back the business card:

'I regret that you must direct your enquiries to the department press office.'

'It's *important*! Tell him I *have* to see him.'

The servant seemed to blanch at such an informal reference to the Minister, and said firmly: 'I'm sorry, sir.'

Nick stabbed in the dark: 'Was it you? Have you telephoned my home?'

'I beg your pardon?'

'You've given me information haven't you – over the telephone. About the Minister – "Nick lowered his voice, "this is your chance, you fool.'

The man's eyes were widening: 'Sir, you must leave, otherwise –'

But Nick jumped for the door, colliding with the man, smelling garlic pushing him aside, and all the time thinking, *knowing* – this is madness.

The corridor was short, sprouting into an octagonal tiled reception area, with three doors leading off – where would he go, and what would he say? Behind him the servant was shouting.

Slam! The breath left Nick's body in a whoosh as something hit him with incredible force in the solar plexus. Something human and hard crashed into his head and the force of the blow cracked him into the wall with a noise that sickened him.

146

He saw black and purple, and then a cascade of lights and stars. Two ramrod piston punches hit him one-two in the ribs and Nick cried out in pain.

He staggered upright, was aware of two faces, two men, two light blue suits, counterpointed with the flashes in his eyes, and harsh metal driving into the skin of his temple like a drill.

'One move, I blow your brains out. Frisk him.'

Nick felt rough hands going over his clothes, in his pockets, under his armpits, into his socks, up to his crotch and around his privates – it was like a crude medical.

A second voice said: 'It's OK, he's clean.'

'Lean against the wall, fingertips out, and spread your legs.' Nick did so – utterly scared. He heard the rustle of paper and realised from the lack of bulge against his heart that they had his wallet.

'He's a bloody journalist.' one voice said.

'The . . . Enquirer . . .' Nick mumbled.

'Shut up!'

'My Met. Police card's in there.'

'Shut *up*' A foot hooked his ankle and spread his legs even wider. Nick felt he might split. His head was clearing, and into the empty space recently filled with pain and fear, came the awful awareness that he was now in serious trouble. This was arrest, this was police cells, a charge and a Magistrates' Court appearance tomorrow morning. Shit!' Nick said to himself with feeling. Never make a decision when you're pissed.

Someone was speaking into a walkie-talkie and Nick concentrated on the expensive wallpaper. They wouldn't fire him for this, surely?

'Turn. Turn!' Nick forced himself up, and winced as the pain in his ribs hit. 'What was all this about?' Nick was facing two nondescript men in light blue polyester suits. They were in their thirties, both had would-be Zapata moustaches and short hair.

147

Whichever one had pulled the gun had put it away now.

'I wanted to see the minister,' Nick said, absurdly.

'So do the Provos,' said the man directly opposite, the same man who had spoken before, 'You're very lucky you weren't shot just now. If you'd looked like a typical Mick you'd be on the carpet with half a dozen rounds in you, you daft sod.'

'Yeh – sorry.'

Both men gave the little resigned, police-issue shake of the heads. The clearly-senior man nodded to the second: 'Tell the Minister it's OK, just an over enthusiastic member of the scumpack.'

The second detective disappeared through one of the doors, and returned after about a minute, during which Nick tried to meet the other policeman's eyes, and couldn't. Daft sod, that just about summed up how he felt.

'He says to send him in.'

'You're joking?'

The detective shrugged: 'That's what he said.'

'He should be on his way to the nearest nick.'

'He's the boss.'

The detective reached over and pulled Nick roughly towards the door: 'You're a lucky lad. Get in there – be polite, and if we hear one peep, just *one* – your feet won't touch the ground.'

The Minister was seated behind a venerable desk at the edge of the room, his back to the window. Standing next to the desk was a man of about twenty-five, slim and dark, and dressed in sweater and slacks that positively reeked of money, of South Molton Street and famous designer names.

The young man did not speak, he just looked at Nick, and Nick could sense his contempt. The Minister was ostensibly working on some papers, and it was over half a minute before he looked up. It had the look

148

of the old busy-man-working-on-important-documents-will-look-up-when-absolutely-finished, trick.

'Mr. Carter. How can I help you? And what exactly do you mean by bursting into my house like that? One would expect *you*, of all people – a *journalist* (Nick felt there were inverted commas around the word) to understand the danger of what you just did. You *are* aware of the security situation – terrorists and the like?'

'Yes Minister. I apologise, sincerely. I had to see you.'

And the point was gone now, the impact, the whole purpose of the exercise, which was to do what the Minister least expected, and take him by surprise.

Now Nick was the naughty boy, and nothing he said now could have any impact. Standing on the carpet, suit ruffled, a bloody great bruise coming up on his face, probably a few more on his ribs, half pissed, half prepared, no tape. It was a gigantic balls-up, all of it.

'Well, you're here now. Pull up a chair.' Nick did, and groaned as he sat down and his ribs hurt. 'This is Jonathan Petty, he's one of my principal researchers in my capacity as a humble Member.'

The young man nodded: 'Mr. Carter.'

'You *are* aware,' the Minister said, 'that my Press office gave a full, categorical and unequivocal reply to your absurd suggestions, after full consultation with me.'

'Yes, but –'

'Then . . .' the Minister spread his hands 'your incursion seems all the less justified. I am afraid I shall have to telephone your Editor tomorrow. However, I shall spare you the indignity of arrest.'

The room was half lit, and the Minister's face was partly in shadow. He's lying, Nick thought. Remember that, *believe* that, he's a deceitful lying bastard. He thinks he can do what he wants, he's like all his type, he believes the country exists for them, that they run it how they see fit, use it for their own ends, but worse – that they've got the right to do so.

149

Nick said: 'There was something I didn't tell your Press office. Something too personal.'

'Really? We're fascinated, aren't we Jonathan?'

'Absolutely,' the young man added.

Nick trembled slightly. This was not some crooked Sportsman, a car dealer, an actor, it was a member of Her Majesty's government. He couldn't escape the inbred fear of that, and worse the instinctive Pavlovian sensation of *respect*.

'She was here . . .'

'She?'

'Bianca Vasquez visited your home.'

'Utterly untrue.'

'She has described your house in detail.'

'Don't be preposterous, I entertain literally thousands of visitors in any one year.'

'In your bedroom – your private bathroom, your private quarters? How many people visit those, Minister?'

Something hardened in the two men facing Nick, and Nick felt it. Don't forget, they're not soft, not effete, they're *steel*.

'Well, pray continue.'

'You have an English master on one wall of your bedroom, a Constable, I think. There is a small collection of antique snuff boxes on a Chinese lacquered cabinet. There is an opium pipe from Turkey –'

'It's called a hookah, Mr. Carter.' He realised the Minister was making fun of him, and that the play on words was deliberate and taunting. Come and get me – if you can.

Nick ploughed on: 'By the bedside there is a framed picture of your wife and children. On one pillow is an old teddy bear you have had since you were a child – you call it Buffy.'

It wasn't working, Nick knew. The man should be shocked devastated, exposed, and there was nothing coming back, no fear, just *steel*.

150

'. . . the bed has an ornately carved headpiece and is partly canopied. It is French, 19th century. The bath in your bathroom is un-enclosed and has eagle claw-and-ball legs.'

The Minister started to applaud, slowly, bringing his hands together, derisively.

'That's enough Mr. Carter, that really is enough.'

'Bianca Vasquez was in your bedroom, and knew enough about you, to know all these things. She told someone else and that person told me. How do you account for that, Minister?'

'Dear, dear, dear . . . dear oh dear.' The Minister said, wearily to the young man: 'Get the magazine Jonathan.' Jonathan went to a drawer, rummaged, pulled out a magazine and tossed it carelessly towards Nick, who caught it.

It was a copy of House and Garden. The Minister said:

'Page thirty-eight, I think – and onwards of course.'

Nick flicked through the pages, still not quite understanding, through the fog of alcohol, the point that was being made. Then he found the page. It was a five-page photographic spread on the Minister's London home. Every room was featured, even the bedroom and bathroom, and a glimpse at the accompanying text showed some of the references to the Minister's teddy bear.

Nick could feel the blood rushing out of him to his feet, like a G-force, weighing him down as though with divers' boots.

'I . . . I . . .' he could only stutter.

'*I* think you owe me an apology.'

'Yes . . . yes, I do . . . I am most terribly sorry. Bitterly sorry, really, I have made a total fool of myself. I hope you can forgive me.'

'You should read your cuttings more carefully.'

'I thought I had,' Nick replied, glumly, 'clearly our library don't cut House and Garden.'

'They should,' the young man Jonathan said.

'Will you call my Editor?'

'Wait and see.'

'I didn't get his permission to come here.'

'Pity,' said the Minister, without any, 'show Mr. Carter out, would you Jonathan.'

Nick walked for a long time, as though he could physically distance himself from his humiliation. At Earls Court he got a battered mini-cab, and asked to be taken home.

Outside he noticed that every light in the house seemed to be on, and when he opened the front door, Rebecca came dashing along the corridor, leaping into his arms, squeezing him tight.

'Lovely to see you back, darling, big kiss –'

'Daddy, oh Daddy.' His daughter was sobbing. 'Becky, what's wrong?' Jennifer came out into the hall: 'Thank God you're back.'

'What's wrong Jen?' He pulled his wife and daughter into him, very close.

'There was a telephone call tonight, unfortunately Becky took it. It was someone saying something – well, horrible – about you. You and this Bianca woman.'

'Sorry, Beck, love, sorry, sorry, sorry.'

'An hour later, another call. I got it this time.' Nick could feel Jenny shaking: 'What? What did they say?'

'He had a funny accent, said . . .' she took a deep breath.

'Jen, *what*?!'

'That you'd be harmed, *we'd* be harmed, all of us, you know if this all didn't stop, this writing about Bianca.'

'My God!'

'Nick, what happened to your face . . .' she put up her hand, and gingerly touched the livid bruising.

152

'Ow! Some stupid sod at the office opened a door right in my face – are you two OK?'

Rebecca hung onto him, clinging to his clothes, pressing her crying face into his overcoat, and the three of them hobbled together into the living room like that, like some absurd trio in a garden fête race.

None wished to break the bond, and they sat on the sofa, holding, linked like that for a long time. Nick kissed his daughter's head, cooing, whispering re-assurances, stroking her hair, and with his other hand, squeezing Jenny's hand, and giving her rueful but what he hoped were encouraging glances.

And inside he felt just cold fear. When he had settled Rebecca into bed, talking with her for a long time, stroking her to sleep, agreeing to leave the landing light on and the door ajar, he went into his study.

There in the book-lined room in which he had planned to one day write the Great Novel, he switched on the anglepoise and rummaged in the top drawer of his desk.

Under sheets of paper, snapshot holders and old envelopes, he found the cardboard sleeve containing the reel-to-reel Nagra tape. On the sleeve he saw the blue felt-tip penned words: 'Bianca Vasquez', and the date.

He held the tape like a talisman now, pressing it into his palm like a small ikon, feeling it burn as though red hot. Downstairs he noticed the living-room was in semi-darkness, and he knew what that meant. Jenny was lying with a wet flannel over her face.

Nick said softly: 'Migraine? Are you OK.'

'Mmm-mm, I'll be fine.' She lifted the flannel off her eyes: 'What's going on Nick? Are we all in danger – *really*, I mean? Shouldn't you tell the police.'

'People playing silly games, that's all – well, I think that's all it is.' He saw the agony in her eyes. From the pain of the migraine, from the fear, from . . . *because* of him, he

153

couldn't know which. 'And anyway, I don't see what the police could do.'

'Well, the telephone people then. They could intercept the calls, they do it all the time. Remember when Marjorie got those obscene calls.'

'Yes, I suppose so – no!' He remembered Spanish Voice. If he called, they'd intercept, and that would scare him off. But suppose it *was* Spanish Voice who'd made the obscene call, who'd threatened his wife. Suppose it was all some gigantic game of bluff, and double bluff: of misinformation.

Perhaps Bellamy the ex-M had been right. Perhaps it was some gigantic campaign to discredit Britain, and perhaps Nick *was* being used. Jenny had said the man had an accent. So did Spanish Voice, so did the Minister's servant – so did half of bloody London.

'No, let's give it a while. Rebecca'll be fine. We'll leave the answering machine on most of the time, especially if I'm not here, then we can listen in to see if it's OK.'

Nick poured himself a drink and sat in the gloom listening to his wife's harsh breathing. You could witness pain, experience it, remember it, but it all became academic. When you were in pain it dominated you – and when you weren't, you could only imagine.

A month ago he had been a middle-of-the-road feature writer with a career trundling along to middle-age. His marriage had problems, but maybe they would have sorted themselves out.

Now everything was at risk. His job, after that foolhardy visit to the Minister's house, his marriage, because he wondered if it could survive this as well as his impotence – but things a lot more important than that.

The safety, perhaps the lives of Jenny, Rebecca and himself.

Jenny groaned from under the flannel: 'Darling, sorry,

154

can you call Jessica urgently in Hawaii. I just forgot about it, you know, with the phone calls and everything.'

'Yeh, OK.' He sipped his drink.

'I think it's urgent, love, after what's happened.'

He put his drink down: '*What's* happened?' He felt the first faint tremor of alarm: 'Have we got her? Has Jess bought Bianca up?'

Jenny sat up; closed her eyes quickly, then opened them again as the migraine rocked her: 'Didn't you see the news tonight, TV, or the radio?'

'No . . . I've been on a job, then stuck in a mini-cab playing the Bangladeshi Top Ten, what the hell's going on Jen?'

She came and put her arms around him:

'Oh darling, I'm sorry. You don't know, do you?'

*   *   *

Bianca looked out once more at the velvet Pacific night. The apartment was in darkness, and the sky with its diamond carpet of stars seemed to merge into the ebony of earth and sea.

She could hear the pounding of the surf, and the counterpointed sigh of the wind in the palms. She was naked, standing perfectly still, her arms at her side, merged with the night.

The balcony doors were open and she could feel the touch of the slight breeze against her skin like friendly fingertips. The fragrance of the night smells excited something in her, it was like being present at the moment before the dawn of creation.

It was wondrous, magical, and she stood like that for a long time, silent and still as a statue.

There was a noise in the night, human voices somewhere out in the darkness, perhaps the words of lovers on the beach, carrying on the night air, and suddenly the spell was broken.

155

She turned, walked to the bathroom, closed the door behind her and turned on the light. It was as she had prepared it, the tub high with foam on the hot water, the tiny object in its film of paper, resting on the side of the tub.

Bianca slid into the silk-like luxurious embrace of the water, lifted a leg and rested it on the side of the bath, examining the texture and colour of herself, drawing with her nails, gently from ankle to calf.

She added more water until it was so hot her body almost recoiled, then she reached out, took the razor blade, unwrapped it, and placed the edge against the raised veins on the inside of her left wrist.

We arrive and we depart. It is, Bianca thought, nothing.

She closed her eyes, pressed down with the blade and felt just the dullest of sensations. Her eyes still closed, she transferred the blade into her left hand, already experiencing a sensation of numbness, sought out the veins of her right wrist, and pressed once more.

After a while she opened her eyes and marvelled at how red her blood was, and how much of it soaked the bubbles and discoloured the water.

It seemed hardly possible for there to be so much blood in a human body. She closed her eyes again, at last feeling the throb from her wrists beneath the water, like an extra heart pumping out her lifeblood.

She thought of the big bed in Managua, squashed securely between her Mama and Papa. She felt so weary now, so weary of it all. She decided that she would sleep, and in the morning, when she was rested, when the terrible tiredness had gone, she would play with her brothers.

Life was good now, and the awful detachment was leaving Bianca at last.

Her legacy would remain.

*　　*　　*

156

Mr. Yakamoto took the note and let himself into the bathroom. He put on a rubber-glove she had left for him, and after rinsing away the blood he folded her arms across her chest, closed his eyes, and said a Christian prayer he had been taught at the leper school. Then he wept.

Chapter Eleven

Nick and Jenny sat across the sterile dinner table as intimate as rival champion chess players.

'You *didn't* kill her Nick, she killed herself, it's not your fault.'

'No, of course not . . .' Nick toyed with his food, 'I didn't, she did. Simple, really.'

'So stop it. I know you're blaming yourself.'

Nick swigged some of the wine, and it tasted like medicine in his dry, poisoned mouth: 'If I hadn't done my job with that *precision* and *efficiency* . . .' he bit into the words, 'for which I am so well known, our little dark-skinned hooker would be alive and well and still turning tricks.'

'Don't, love.' Jenny's fingers skirted the wine glass, came forward cautiously like emissaries, and touched his, 'if it's anybody's fault it's Jessica's and that other girl – you know, the . . .'

'Tart?'

'If the caps fits. That's what she is, isn't it?'

'They also serve who only stand and wait.'

She gripped his fingers: 'For God's sake Nick, you were only doing your job.'

'So were the SS.'

'That's absurd and you *know* it!'

'Seems a fair parallel to me.'

'Nick, *love* . . .' she gripped both his hands and lifted them above the glasses, squeezing them, and he let her . . . 'you didn't make her *kill* herself. Perhaps there was some other factor, perhaps she was frightened of some of the people she'd slept with.

159

Perhaps she was ill – God knows. Don't blame yourself.'

Nick freed a hand and drank some more wine, viciously, feeling acid meet acid in his throat: 'Well, actually, we *did*. We pulled the props out of her life. Maybe she was frightened of these other people, and maybe that's *why* she killed herself, but if we hadn't – me and Jess, the Enquirer – if we *hadn't* . . .' he stopped, unable to go on.

Jenny removed her hand and looked off sullenly into the distance: 'She chose to be a prostitute.'

'Is that a capital offence now?'

'Don't imply I'm a prude, or that I'm narrow minded. I'm not. You know my view and you always have. There wouldn't be prostitutes if there weren't men to pay them. I'm just saying that it can have its consequences, and in this day and age they don't have to do it.'

'No?' He gave her a sour look, 'for some of them it's survival.'

'We're talking about Bianca. She didn't have to do it, she chose that way of life, and . . .' she let the inevitable moral decay that was implicit, hang between them unspoken but understood.

'Actually the world is full of people enjoying "that way of life", one way or the other. Politicians sticking their snouts in the trough, girls screwing for a dinner or a weekend in Paris.'

'Oh yes?' Jennifer said bitterly.

'Oh yes. Some screw cash-on-the-nail like Bianca. Others want more, diamonds, furs, a holiday, a house or kids.' He tried to bite the words off, but they were out.

He knew there was a world of difference, but he wanted to take it out on Jennifer, all of it, Bianca's death, his guilt, his confusion and his sorrow.

Nick wanted to goad her and wound her, to prod the creature in her that stayed snug and smug in its protective carapace. He wanted to force her out into the light of the real and filthy world as he saw it. He wanted her to see it for what it was, with its compromises, its betrayals, its lies and its dashed dreams.

But instead all he saw in her eyes now was the predictable hurt, and the empty, unbridgeable canyon of incomprehension.

She said, calmly: 'I'm enlightened. Is that how you see me? Is it? A kind of . . .' she looked around, as though physically searching for the word . . . 'a suburban Xavier Hollander. The happy hooker with a Hoover, swopping sex for security.'

'I didn't say that.'

'Because I had a career before I met you, and after.'

'Yes, and I always supported you in it, always, even when I hardly knew you and you had that chance to go to Uganda.'

'My point being that I could work full time if I wished.'

'The choice is yours.' He stared sullenly into his wine as she took an exaggerated draught of hers.

'I don't work full time because we chose it, didn't we Nick? Because of Rebecca, someone being home for her after school, the house, dinners . . .'

He shrugged: 'If you don't want to be here for Rebecca . . .' it was like scratching his own wound. He felt wretched.

'Nick that's vile. You and she are my life. I'm saying, I had a career, could still have one.'

'We don't need the money.'

'Really?' She gave him a cruel smile. Beyond a certain point she could be vicious. He could see it coming.

'Don't need the money, or is it don't need the competition?'

'As in what?'

'As in better to have the little woman at home, hoovering the carpets than out there competing, perhaps

161

meeting other men. That's how I met you after all, darling, gallant Scoop Carter turning on the charm in Casualty.'

'Save it, I'm tired.'

Her words came out like a snarl from between gritted teeth: 'Do you say that to Jessica? Do you? Are you too tired when Jessica is talking? Oh no, I bet it's Yes sir, three-bags-bloody-full-sir to Miss Bossyboots isn't it? Jessica calls, Nick comes running.'

'Crap. She's a colleague.'

He got up and crossed to the drinks cabinet, going for the cognac.

She said: 'You spend an awful lot of time with her for someone who is just a colleague. And you can pour me one of those – a very large one. I feel like getting rat-arsed . . . oh, sorry Nick, was that crude? Can wives not say rat-arsed like colleagues?'

'Are you seriously suggesting – Jessica and me?'

Her eyes were like laser beams.

'Because if you are it's the most utter balls. Go on, pick up the phone, call her?'

'You said her name once, in your sleep.'

'I don't believe this.'

'You had a hard on too.' She paused for effect. 'It was a while ago.'

'You bloody bitch.'

'You haven't answered my question.'

'Sorry, I must have missed it.' He handed her an absurdly full crystal glass of cognac: 'Hope you make it to the bathroom before you puke tonight.'

'Are you having an affair with her?'

'No.'

'Are you sure?' She took a big swallow of cognac.

'You're getting pissed.'

'Good. Are you?'

'I'm quite sober, actually.'

'I meant, are you sure? Don't deliberately misunderstand me.'

'Yes, I'm sure.'

'And what about me, don't you want to ask me if I've ever cheated?' She saw, like the bitter fruits of an unwanted victory, the expression of shock and disbelief in his eyes.

'There's no need for this, Jen.'

'Because who knows,' she drank more cognac, 'the happy hooker with the Hoover might have had better offers.'

'Stop calling yourself that for Christ's sake.'

'Oh, I rather like it. It's an interesting concept. I hadn't really thought of it before. The housewife as tart, the wife as harlot. New cooker please, hubby?' She put on a gruff voice: 'That'll be forty-three and a half screws.'

'Jen . . .'

'That'll do nicely sir, never leave home without it . . .' she giggled, but it had a hysterical edge to it.

'I did not say, for a second . . .'

She cut across him: 'If your little suburban tart is so expensive to keep in clothes and the like, why don't you make more use of what you're paying for?'

'Christ but you can be an out-and-out bitch when you want.'

She walked to the door and looked over her shoulder in a parody of flirtation: 'I haven't turned a trick in a long time – that's what we hookers say isn't it?'

'Go to bed, Jen.'

'Sure. Why not come up and see me sometime, big boy?' She slammed the door behind her, and Nick felt as though he had been stabbed through the heart.

He sat in his study fingering the Bianca tape, turning it over and over in his hands, knowing that the voice on the tape was stilled now.

The door opened without a knock, and his daughter came in before he could slip the tape back into the drawer. He held it now, furtively, like a kid caught with a dirty magazine.

'Hello, cherub, you should be asleep.'

'Daddy?' she came hesitantly towards him, 'have you and Mummy had a row?'

He scooped an arm around her and pulled her into his side: 'Just a bit of one. It happens – it's called being old, and grown-up and boring. Where is Mummy?'

'Lying down. I heard your voices.'

'Oh . . . did you hear what we said?'

'No, but I could tell, because you both had those funny purple voices you have when you row.'

'Purple?'

'Yes, purple for angry, brown for when you're talking to me, but not concentrating . . .'

He hugged her: 'You're a crazy sausage.'

'At school . . . at school they had a magazine they showed me . . .' Nick knew what was coming and dreaded it . . . 'it said you had sex with Bianca, the model who killed herself.'

Nick tried to act shocked, and in truth, *was* a little:

'My darling, you are too young to be reading magazines and talking about people having sex.' he tried to put quotes around the word.

'Don't be silly, Daddy, I know all about that kind of thing!'

'Do you indeed . . .' When had his daughter grown up, where had he been, and why hadn't he realised it?

'It said in the magazine, you *did*.'

'Look,' he stroked her hair, thinking how much it felt like Jenny's when his wife was younger – when he and she had both been younger: 'That magazine, is *satirical*, do you know what that means?'

'No, but the other girls said –'

164

'Never mind what the other girls said, Daddy *knows*. It's a magazine that makes fun of people, including journalists. They get it wrong all the time. What they don't know they make up.'

'That's what the girls say about the Enquirer.' Touché, thought Nick.

'Well, I didn't –' Nick coughed and tried to make the following two words as technical and antiseptic as possible, 'have sex with Bianca. The only woman I love is your Mum.'

'You don't have to love someone to do sex, that's what the girls said.' Nick blanched. Was this his *little* girl?

'Well, look love. This is not something you and the other girls should be discussing – does your teacher know you talk like this?'

'Miss Blincow? She's *stupid*.'

'You tell those girls your Dad didn't do anything wrong with Bianca. And tell them it's bad manners to speak ill of the dead.'

'OK.' She kissed him, 'I love you Dad.'

'I love you too Becky.'

'What's on the tape?' Nick slid it back into the drawer: 'Oh, you know, an interview.'

'With Bianca? Her name was on it?'

'Yes, with Bianca. Go to bed now, love.'

'I'm sorry she died, she was beautiful.'

'Not a patch on your Mum.'

'Oh Mum's OK, but Bianca was *beautiful*. You must be very sorry she's dead.'

'Yes, I am, very sorry.' And he thought, this is unbearable. He wanted to weep.

Rebecca suddenly threw her arms round his neck, squeezing hard: 'You won't die, will you Dad? Please say you won't die.' He could feel her tears on his face.

'No, chicken, I won't die. Promise-promise.'

* * *

Jessica was jet-lagged and bleary, deeply depressed from recent events, and battling an eye infection she'd picked up in Hawaii. Everyone wondered why she'd bothered to come straight into the office after a journey of over twenty hours.

Nick knew. She wanted to remind herself who she was, and what she was. She wanted to reconnect to that energy which is place and purpose.

But mostly, Nick suspected, it was because Bianca had died by her own hand, and Jessica was deeply struck by that. Had she caused it by her intrusion into the complex, by the shouted questions – had that been the trigger?

There had been too much time to brood; in her hotel room with only the contents of the refrigerated mini-bar for solace, then on the long flights home via Los Angeles.

Miles told Nick he had personally telephoned Jessica and told her she could stay there and have a week off – hotel paid for by the company – but Jessica had declined.

Nick understood. Anyone would give their right arm for a free week in Hawaii, but not under these circumstances. You just wanted to head for home, to the familiar. She wanted to be near Nick, because Nick held the other bloodied dagger, and she wanted the comfortable lies of a fellow conspirator.

Wearily she handed him a plastic bag with a bottle of Scotch in it: 'Greetings from Hawaii and don't say I shouldn't have bothered it's cheaper at ASDA.' She mocked Nick's favourite phrase.

'Well it is, and you shouldn't, and I'm gin not Scotch, remember? But thanks anyway.'

'You're welcome, have-a-nice-day, and how sick I am of hearing that.'

'You look knackered.'

'Utterly cream-crackered.' She ran the heel of her hand

over her bloodshot eyes: 'Think I'm getting conjuncti-
vitis . . .' but Nick saw the tears too.

'Come on Jess, you're whacked . . .'

'I never thought it would come to this, Nick, as God is
my witness. If I'd thought this, I mean,' she waved a hand,
'they could have stuffed the whole story, all of it.'

'Yeh, me too. It's not our fault. Blame all the politicians
and the terrorists, all those bastards who used her.'

She gave him a cynical bloodshot look: 'Don't chat *me*
up, Nick, I'm not one of the punters. *We* killed her,
you, me, Annabelle, Miles, the chairman, the fucking
lot of us.'

'That how you feel? Really, I mean?'

'Sure do.'

'Nothing we can do about it.'

'There is. The story's not over yet. Let's get all the
other lying scumbags who screwed her and now think
they're safe because she's six-feet under.'

Nick collared a messenger and gave him some coins
for the drinks machine. 'Chocolate?' Jessica said, 'I hate
chocolate.'

'The sugar boost'll do you good. Story's all bogged
down. Nothing moves. Not a word from Spanish Voice.
Annabelle's gone to ground.'

'We've got her number though?'

'Natch, but she's running scared.' Nick wrote down
the new number for Jessica. She put it in her pocket
and said: 'No more funny-farm calls at Dunroamin?' He
shook his head.

'Admire your balls in going for the Minister.' Nick smiled
ruefully: 'I was *that* far . . .' he left a tiny gap between
finger and thumb, 'from getting the bullet. Miles nearly
had a coronary. I think in the end he didn't feel he could
fire the man –'

'who'd-been-in-the-bedroom-with-Bianca. You've got a
job for life here, my old son.'

'He's still lying though.'

'How can you be sure, Nick?'

The messenger brought the drinks and the change, and Jessica grimaced at the sweet powdered chocolate.

'Because he's a politician and I saw his lips move. But we're going to fix him, you and me. And the rest of them, including that little chinless wonder Hanoverian fart-face.'

'It's good to be back Nick.'

'Mighty nice to have you back Mam.'

'I'm feeling good, I'm feeling gay, I've ruined another life today.'

'Not heard the company motto for a while. Go home, Jess, take a tranq – and sleep.'

*   *   *

At first Nick thought the caller was Spanish Voice, then he realised it was a different foreign accent, and the male voice said: 'It has all gone too far. Let her rest.'

'If we don't?'

'Then look to your life and your family.'

'If you touch – *anyone*, I'll fucking crucify you.'

The man laughed, and the line went dead.

The flat Annabelle had chosen was in that anonymous land behind the Post Office tower, with Tottenham Court Road to the East. It was in a pre-war block in a drab, backwater street.

She let him in and paced ahead of him into the postage-stamp living room: 'OK, what happened?' She turned and handed him a piece of paper. He read it and felt his mouth go dry.

'Someone put that through the letter-box *here*?'

'No. I went back to my place in Epping to get the mail, and I found this. No stamp on it. They knew where to find me.' Annabelle lit her Pavlov cigarette: 'I'm scared – I can tell you.'

'Go to the police?' Nick said it without enthusiasm, knowing as he had told his wife, that there was nothing, in reality, that the police could do.

'How do you know it *isn't* the *police*?'

She was scared and deadly serious. He said lightly: 'Give it a break. I'm as paranoid as the next man, but I don't think the Old Bill would stoop to this.'

Annabelle drew deeply on the cigarette until it glowed bright red: 'Not PC Plod, you prat, the other lot, Special Branch, MI5, the secret lot.'

'But why? You, I mean, you and me? –'

She looked up sharply: 'You had one of these?'

'Something on the same lines.'

'Bianca was up to all sorts, Nick. Most of it's out, and isn't that enough? Middle East terrorists, Arab princes, a senator . . .'

'Not all proved,' said Nick, wagging his finger, 'pure speculation.'

She stubbed out the cigarette, barely smoked: 'I *know*. And so do you. People are scared.'

'She's dead for God's sake.'

'Diaries! Letters! Who knows what she left.'

'The police in Hawaii found nothing.'

'People are scared. I know what those people are capable of, all of them.' And Nick knew it was true, knew what they could do. Men of untold wealth, corporations bigger than countries, intelligence and police services that acted first and sought justification afterwards.

He'd thought Britain might be different, but he'd learned it wasn't. He'd learned what the secret police – call them MI5, call them Special Branch or Intelligence, that was what they were – secret police; he'd learned what they could be capable of. The dirty tricks in Ireland, against CND, the Greenham Common women, the trades unions.

The British people had no conception of what could

169

be done for them, or to them, in their own name. And the knowledge was made all the worse because if you voiced the fears, you sounded paranoid, a nutter out on the fringe.

Ulster, Gibraltar, over Sellafield, and no-one seemed to care, or if they cared, could do anything about it, could bring anyone to account.

Nick had no doubt, from his experience, and from what he had been told by those who knew, that if someone *seriously* threatened the security of the state, and no other method could be found to silence that person or make he or she desist, then that individual would, after no doubt careful consideration, be killed.

And it would be so easy. A car crash, a 'suicide', a city centre stabbing. You would read it, and turn the page, muttering about violent societies, the state of the roads, of secrets in closets enough to make a person take their own life.

Nick was terribly afraid for himself and his family, for Jessica and Annabelle, for all of them. But who were *they*? Was it some organisation with whom they could treat, with whom they could say: 'Right, if we stop now, will it be OK?'

If the threat itself was real, it was Kafka-esque, and unspecified in its source, vague and shadowy, and all the worse for that.

'Are your wife and daughter at home?'

'No . . . no . . .' Nick came out of his reverie, 'Rebecca's in France ski-ing with the school. Jenny's gone to her sister's in Grantham.'

'You couldn't have been followed back from Epping?' The thought that they knew her new address, may even be *watching* at that very moment, terrified him.

'In *this* traffic? You've got to be joking . . .' she lit another cigarette, 'Anyway, I did all the back doubles

170

once I got into town, and I stuck the car in an NCP up at Farringdon, and took a Tube.'

'Brilliant.'

'I've seen all the movies. Want a drink? I've only got gin.'

'Thanks, plenty of ice and tonic.' He took the gin and tonic, and quaffed half an inch off the top. 'It hurts how much I need this stuff at the moment.'

'Cheers.' She sat down on the sofa next to him, as he re-read the note. 'Couldn't they, you know, check the typeface or something, to see what make the typewriter is, then check all the makes that . . . ?'

His withering glance stopped her: '*Too* many movies, Annabelle.'

STOP CO-OPERATING WITH THE NEWSPAPERS OR WE'LL HARM YOU.

He leaned back and closed his eyes. Just what did you do when this happened? He couldn't buy a gun, the law didn't allow it, and he wouldn't really know what to do with it. A knife? – Absurd. It wasn't *fair*, it just wasn't *fair*.

'You're shaking.' She had her hand on his arm.

'Because I'm scared bloody shitless.' He kept his eyes closed. 'Me too.'

'I wish to Christ I'd never set eyes on you or Bianca.'

'Thanks.' she said it without malice.

'You know what I mean.' He found her hand with his, and stroked it. Strange hand. Different hand. He kept his eyes tightly closed. That way it could all be shut out and he could live in this dark world, with just the hand on his arm, the touch of strange skin, the feel and smell of a different woman next to him.

He felt her breath on his cheek, and her lips on his cheek, his ear, her breath on his eyes, the overpowering scent of her. Nick stayed frozen, not wanting it to stop, not wanting to break the spell by bringing in the spoiling power of words.

Her lips found his, the faint taste of tobacco, strangely not unpleasant, just *different*. Her body was against him, he could feel the press of the big breasts.

Immobile as she worked around him, his lips pressed against her in a virgin kiss, he let it all happen, thinking, 'I can stop any time I want,' and knowing that the lie was part of the enjoyment.

Like some uninvited but absurdly welcome stranger, he recognised the appearance of desire, and it shocked and thrilled him.

He opened his eyes, and her face was very close to his. Hers was the face of the messenger bringing the news of reprieve, the news that there is to be life after the siege.

He said: 'It's not possible.'

She was puzzled: 'You're kind of crazy, do you know that about yourself, Nick?'

She kissed him again, and her tongue went deep into his mouth without preamble, and it was like an invasion and an occupation, and he was the traitorous welcomer, the waver of the forbidden flag, and the eager collaborator.

He knew it was – what, wrong? But her strong, muscled tongue forced life into him, grappling with his like the rough and tumble of wrestlers in the mud.

And it was so *sensual*, like being in the back row of the cinema when one had been a teenager and kissing was the only sexual pleasure you got.

Their heads rocked to and fro, two faces circling clockwise and anti-clockwise, and Nick realised with a sense of disbelief: This isn't kissing, this is *necking*.

He was hard, priapic to the point of some sense of embarrassment, his desire and physical manhood obvious and evident. His erection threatened to burst out of his trousers, it was physically excruciating and delicious at the same time.

His eyes were closed and his mind conjured up images

172

of caverns and moisture and tongues, and all the time the very real and different smell of this *other* woman, this woman, who was not the same as Jenny.

And he knew the meaning of infidelity, and why it was so easy, and why – because of that – it had taken so long for him to succumb. Because it was a drug he could not afford, the drug he needed, and therefore could not allow himself.

But there was an echo of something he was denying in himself and mentally he turned away, as from a cry of conscience. Her tongue left him: 'Nick, I can't believe I'm saying something so corny, but I hadn't actually planned this. For some reason it's important that you know that.'

'Me neither,' he shook his head, 'Scout's honour.'

'God, you're not even my type. You're so different.'

'I'm nobody's type, it's OK.' He could only concentrate on her lips which at that moment were the most desirable things he felt he had ever known. They were fleshy, rouged, and the middle of her upper lip seemed to hang and quiver.

It was like a taste of ripe fruit you cannot get fast enough, so that you bite and suck and feel the juice on your throat, until it is not just taste, it is pure sensation.

He kissed her, tongue hidden, closing his eyes like a frightened schoolboy, wanting her to go on and on kissing him and not to stop until he was exhausted from the taste and feel of her mouth.

Nick felt whole and rounded and liquid, mobile like some computer drawn character who can move across the screen without the angular lift of joints.

Yet up there, like some tiny, triangular warning on a risqué TV movie, up there on the screen of his mind sat the tiny St. Christopher medal size images of his wife and daughter like an admonishing symbol.

173

She said: 'Can I have one more cliché, please? We'd be more comfortable in the bedroom.'

And the words creaked out of him as stilted and worthless as Neville Chamberlain waving his useless, lying piece of paper and promising peace for our time. Nick said: 'You do realise I can't go through with this?'

And like a man straddling some compromise line between good and evil, he knew both that he could not, and yet that he would. And even more strangely, that in the incredible world he now inhabited such things were not impossible, nor contradictory.

Annabelle stood up, unbuttoned the small red dress she was wearing, and stepped out of it. She said with a kind of sexual menace: 'Oh, you can Nick. I assure you that you can.'

And beneath the discarded dress, was a cotton slip, and her breasts were very big and very full. She said: 'It may be wrong, but it's not a crime.'

He could feel his blood pounding; he was alive with male sexual desire, nothing more, but certainly nothing less, and the detached part of him knew it was both inevitable – and given moral suspension – natural.

Nick stood and crushed his body against hers, kissing her furiously, his hand between them on her breast feeling the hard nipple, and aware that his cock was hard against her pubis through their clothes, and that she felt it, registered it, and let loose a small moan either at the sensation or the prospect.

She broke from his lips, and spoke into his ear: 'You see? It's impossible for you to go now.'

'Yes,' he said it simply, the affirmative that would propel him into some other world. And there was suddenly nothing of him but his cock, his lips, his hands, and this fabulous woman body in front of him, now on him, locking, intertwined, their clothes coming off in a kind of frenzy, tearing, ripping, and neither

174

caring, and the Beast had returned with a vengeance of triumph.

No Jenny, no Rebecca, no job, no world, and whatever she was, or he was, at that moment Annabelle and he were intimate and loving, and *honest*, and there was so little honesty left in his life anymore.

She came behind him and he felt the wet cushion of her pubis against his buttocks. Her hand, with the stealth of a pickpocket, crept between his buttocks and cupped his balls with infinite care and gentleness.

And his fear of that – the male instinctual fear that few women could ever understand, of putting the treasure in foreign hands – vanished. To give up the centre of the citadel to control, and what could be captured, required the most incredible trust.

But her touch was instinctive, and she slowly withdrew her hand, brought it round him and slid it along the length of his cock. He could feel her breath on his ear, her hair on his shoulders, and the crush of her breasts against the wet skin of his back.

And then she turned him, held his hand, led him to the bedroom, and lay down next to him. He said: 'I care for you Annabelle. I didn't even know it, but I do.'

And Nick knew it was the intoxication of the moment, that the words were the gabble of fever, and he was not offended, when she laughed, kindly, and said: 'Lovely man you're speaking a foreign language. None of that is necessary. It is simply necessary to know who we are.'

Yes, Nick thought. Who we are. And who are *we*, she and I? And does our being two make us different? He said: '*Who* am I?'

'A fool, well, a little bit of one.' She kissed him and it was the lingering Upper-Circle-of-the Odeon kiss, and he felt, *ecstatic*!

'Don't you know?' Nick remembered that Jessica had asked him that. Did he?

He shook his head, dumbly, thinking that beyond all the odds, she might have the answer. And she did, but it was not the one he could have expected.

She laughed: 'You're a man, my son.' she kissed him, 'Kipling.'

And Nick found he was laughing too. Could it all have been so simple? Was that what he had been denying, that he was a man?

She said: 'Nick would you please fuck me as hard as you can for as long as you can, and when you can't stop yourself, please come inside me. Will you do that?'

He said he would, and he did, for longer than he dreamed possible, and then his face was alarmed, ecstatic, control going, and hers excited, triumphant, almost demonic, and then his limbs were water, his muscles vibrating like a tuning fork, and all the passion was pouring from him.

It alarmed him, overjoyed him, this was not an explosion, it was a dam burst, a massive, unstoppable release, and he cried out to her, clung to her, buried his face in her hair, as she wailed and grunted in triumph and perhaps ecstasy, he did not know, or care, or ever want to know.

And when he had finished the convulsive shuddering, and they had lain still for a few deceptive seconds, he saw once again the lips, the fleshy lips he had wanted so much, and some inherited knowledge of experience pre-warned him that now he might find them repulsive, but he did not; instead he wanted to kiss them, and did, slipping his tongue into her warm mouth, and feeling her respond.

Then for a while he couldn't speak, but simply breathed deeply like an athlete, and kept his eyes closed, sleeping, not realising it, and then waking and knowing, and saying: 'I'm sorry.'

She shushed him with a finger on his lips: 'Don't spoil

it.' And astonishingly, he immediately slept again, and when he awoke for the second time, she was looking at him: 'Hi.'

'Hi.'

'Nick that was a gorgeous mega-fuck, and I am not lying to you, cross-my-heart-and-hope-to-die.' She crossed her heart with her finger, which meant drawing a red fingernail across her breast, and Nick thought. This is delicious.

She said:

'And this is where you normally say, 'And didya, huh, didya?'

Nick laughed: 'You did or you didn't, *you* know. And maybe if you felt I needed to think you had, then you might lie about it, so . . .'

'Joe cool.'

'Well,' Nick said, 'didya, huh, didya?'

'Loads and loads of times superman. But the show ain't over 'til the fat lady sings' . . . A memory twitched like a nerve.

'I thought the fat lady had?'

'Don't interrupt . . . until the fat lady sings until her throat hurts.'

'You're outrageous,' Nick was grinning with pure happiness.

And then they both slept, conjoined like that as the light faded in the room, and Nick dreamed about nothing, just wallpaper inconsequential dreams like a TV interlude, of streams and meadows and waterfalls and clouds, a kid's Easter dreams.

When he awoke, her eyes were still closed, but when he kissed her she opened them, and it was clear she had been awake. She kissed him back, generously, luxuriously, and he marvelled at how different she was from Jenny, how the kisses were different, Jenny's small and fluttery, a ballet of lips and tongues, hers wide and sensual, a steamy Latin waltz of kissing.

177

He had been used to the curve of Jenny's small breasts, cupping neatly in his hand like a ripening fruit. Annabelle's were larger, and he could feel the swell of them now against his chest, skin glued by the grip of their bodies' sweat.

'You're a nice guy when you loosen up.' She kissed him again, and there was the wet suck of their lips, a suck-smack sound that made him think; why, even the sounds of love are different.

He pulled a hand around the back of her head, and brought her face into his again: 'You're OK yourself.'

'Well, I'm not a monster, I think there was a time you thought I was.'

'I didn't think you were a monster.'

'You fancied me?'

'I must have.'

'It's only sex.'

'Yes, only sex. And I'm a man.'

'Feeling guilty?'

'I suppose I must be. Tell the truth, Jenny and I haven't made love for months. Not her fault – *I* couldn't, wanted to but couldn't.'

Annabelle moved in the bed, getting comfortable, and for an instant it was as though Jenny was there in the bed with him.

'Lucky you were doing it at all, after all those years.'

He grimaced: 'It wasn't her, it was me. I was impotent.' He had said it, spoken the forbidden word, and it was like releasing some poison, the word seemed to leave him like an excised growth, and he felt immeasurably lighter, healthier.

'Who brought the cure?'

'That's obvious.' He was talking to the darkness, feeling liberated and free.

'Is it . . . ?' she traced a hand down to his pubic hair, 'go again?'

He laughed, relaxed: 'More recuperation – sorry. I'll be there.'

'If you knew how tired we get of men who *perform*, instead of make love, *fuck*. It's not a concert, and we're not an orchestra, bring in the first strings, bass here . . . ah, crescendo.'

'Must have read the wrong books.'

What do the books know?'

He suddenly smiled in the darkness. It was crazy. He said, with a kind of joy: 'You know when I said I needed more recuperation, well . . .'

He felt her vaginal muscles tighten on him: She said: 'The boy is back with a vengeance.'

'God but this is wonderful. 'He kissed her, rolling her onto her back, still inside her, but hard now.

'Thanks, Annabelle. Just thanks.'

He started to thrust into her, savouring it as though it might be the last time, and he felt her bottom rock in response. She said,: 'Don't thank me, Nick, thank . . .' and then her voice was a distracted moan.

Spanish Voice called the office, and there was something in his manner, an abruptness, that Nick couldn't decipher. The man was different – changed somehow.

'You're doing nothing. Why?'

'Bianca's dead.'

A hesitation: 'I know that. You must press on.'

'I did, and bloody near lost my job, because your evidence was bollocks.'

'I know what happened at the Minister's house, I regret that you were embarrassed.'

'No,' Nick said, viciously 'You *can't* know, because there were just three of us in that room.'

'Why do you think he let the magazine do a feature on

179

his home, go into his bedroom? Why? Because Bianca had been in there, and he had to have some way of discrediting her if she ever told.'

Nick was sweating, nervous, angry, the man continuously put him off balance: 'Who is telling you this? Who are you?'

'I'm your friend – your country's friend!'

'Don't give me that country crap, I'm sick of hearing that from all directions. I'm being threatened, my *family* is being threatened, everyone involved in the story is being got at.'

Except, Nick thought, disloyally – except Jessica.

'. . . who's doing it?'

'I don't know.'

'Ah . . . well, the one I really need to know, and you don't know. You get it right, you get it wrong –'

'I was never wrong –'

'Well I'm not Bob Woodward and this is not the Washington Post. There are other stories, and the public's had a bellyful of Bianca, and terrorists, and . . .'

'Do you take lifts in limousines, Mr.Carter?'

'Who the *fuck* are you?!'

'Someone who *knows*, someone who wants to see justicia.'

Again, he said it justicia, and Nick realised that the something in the tone was other than passion or anger. Sorrow?

'Go to East Anglia, check out the story of this royal personage. He lies.'

'There are *other* stories we have to do.'

'*Please* . . .' the word shocked Nick.

'I'll see what I can do.' The telephone went dead, and Nick unhooked the rubber earpiece connected to his personal tape-recorder and called over to Jessica: 'Jess – have a word.'

* * *

They got nowhere. The locals were used to big-league royals visiting Lord Manham's place – Charles and Di frequently shot there – so they were equally used to reporters, and had learned to keep their mouths shut.

Lord Manham owned the village, supplied the jobs, his writ ran. Jessica summed it up in the hotel that night: 'It's feudal. They're all scared stiff of him. I wonder if he has droit de seigneur?'

They ate dinner and talked, drinking their appalling wine with a kind of dogged determination: 'We had to try.' Nick speared some hardly-thawed boil-in-the-bag duck a l'orange.

'Don't these places realise there's more to life than prawn cocktail, steak and bloody duck?' He called over the waitress. 'Do us a favour, love, stick that back in the microwave for a few more minutes – number nine.'

'All right.' Nick looked at Jessica: 'Would you believe it?'

'Worth our while having another go in the morning?'

'Can't see the point – top you up?' Nick emptied the last of the claret, 'he's got them all onside. If royal *was* there all night, none of those straw-suckers will tell us – *if* they knew anyway.'

They missed breakfast, coming down after food curfew which was at nine sharp, paid their bills and left. Eight miles out of the market town where they'd stayed, they spotted a Little Chef and a petrol station.

'Fancy the all day?'

Nick grunted assent: 'They'll have a pay-phone, we can check in, it's almost ten.'

Jessica pulled her VW Golf off the road and into the parking area to drop Nick off: 'Order me the all day breakfast, coffee, extra toast, and I'll fill up.'

By the time Jessica had walked in, Nick had called the office, ordered, and the food was actually arriving.

'What kept you –?', then he saw her face, and she was

ablaze. She sat down and pushed the breakfast, extra toast and all, to one side.

'They lied, baby, the Palace lied.'

'He *did* stay the night – who told you?'

Jessica jerked a thumb over her shoulder: 'The girl in the cash desk at the service station does the early shift. Royal drove in here in his Aston Martin, filled up and paid with cash.'

'What time?'

'Eight-ish. She's definite.'

'What exactly did you ask her – drink your coffee.'

Jessica cursed as she fumbled with the plastic cream carton, then spurted it across her hand: 'Stupid things . . . just an on-spec conversation, you know, do they get many royals in here, Manham's place being up the road; that kind of thing.'

'You bugger – you never stop.'

'How much I loved our Queen, not sure about some of the other bloody hangers-on, just to see if she'd bite.'

'Brilliant.' Nick felt gloriously hungry, and he carved out a little pile of egg, sausage, fried bread and bacon, and crammed it in his mouth . . . 'Gog onnh . . .'

'You're disgusting. Told her I didn't like Anne and Eddie and everybody lowering themselves appearing on It's a Knockout.'

'Tog geth her roundg toth charity thingth . . . ?'

'Christ, Nick, you can't be that hungry? She rambled on about the charity shoot up there, and I mentioned our friend, and bingo – she remembered him.'

'And she was sure it was October 7th?' Nick picked a bit of inedible bacon from his teeth . . .' Sorry, Jess.'

'If I was your wife I'd divorce you – October 7th, she was absolutely sure. No question.'

'Hang on a minute. She's a petrol attendant, right? Why would she be so sure of the date. It could have been the next day, the previous week.'

'What date don't you forget?'

'It was her *birthday*!'

'Eighteenth, key of the door now. She was eighteen on the 7th. She was working the early shift so she could get home early, go out and party-party.' Jessica gave a small, in-chair wiggle of triumph. 'She's eighteen, and she meets a royal on the same day. One for the grand-kiddies, that.'

She tucked into her breakfast.

Nick said: 'Then they *did* lie to us. Officially and in front of a Fleet Street editor. He must have spent the night there, and they must suspect, or *know*, that he screwed Bianca. Why would they lie to us, why else, unless . . . ?'

'Unless the podgy faced little git did get his leg over and is now running scared.'

'Breakfast's on me Jess.'

'I thought I ordered extra toast.'

'I got it – look – one, two – that's extra toast.'

'No, Nick, I'll show you what extra toast is. Miss – can I have five rounds of toast please – extra butter?'

'This is heart-attack-on-a-plate.'

'Yeh, good innit.' She attacked the fry-up.

'Wait . . .' Nick said, 'until Miles hears this.'

The Editor of the Enquirer said: 'Completely and utterly out of the question.'

Nick said, in disbelief: 'Sir Anthony lied to us!'

'And your proof is an 18 year old petrol attendant? Really!'

'She's speaking the truth, Miles,' Jessica said, doggedly, 'she didn't even know who I was. Why should she lie? It was her birthday, and she remembered.'

'And you tape-recorded her statement, then got her to swear an affidavit, of course.'

His eyes went from one to another: 'No, of course you didn't.'

183

'Miles if she'd thought we were reporters she'd have run a mile. She's a kid, a kid from Suffolk, give us a break. Half the people we speak to don't know we're reporters when we first talk to them, if they did we'd never get anyone to talk.'

'But you went back to her – asked her to put this on the record?' Jessica looked at the floor. Nick said: 'Like Jess said, Miles, the kid is eighteen. It's feudal up there. Her Dad probably works on some local estate. She'd be terrified *she'd* get in trouble. Good God, it's not London!'

'I'm aware of that. Corroboration, then.'

'Royals don't eat breakfast in Little Chefs. He bought petrol, he left – she was the only one there.'

'Pity.'

'It's true,' Nick said, 'he was there, and he spent the night, and the Palace said he didn't – categorically. They lied to the editor of a national newspaper.'

Miles shook his head, splayed his hands, looked through the nave of fingers: 'That is not even prima facie evidence of impropriety with Miss Vasquez – even if he *did* spend the night there, and even if they *did* lie.'

'They did!' Nick could see the anger on Jessica's face.

'The word of an eighteen year old who would most probably not back it up. She could be mistaken, it could be a boast.'

'We can go back to them, back to the Palace,' Nick said desperately, 'prod them – tell them we're not satisfied . . .'

'NO!' Miles Rimmer's fist crashed down on the table: '*I* am sick and fed up of Bianca's name – so is the public. Perhaps it's time to let her rest in peace.'

He stood up to indicate the audience was over. Nick saw Jessica eyeing the editor dangerously, put out a hand and signalled her to leave. She stood her ground.

'You've lost interest in this all of a sudden, Miles.'

184

'Miss Alexander, I think you're forgetting *who* you are and *where* you are. This is not a democracy and not a workers' co-operative. My door is always open, and you and Nick have had a great deal of my time lately. Good morning.'

'How long to the knighthood, Miles? What did they promise you? Five, or keep your nose clean and it's three? You know those scumbag motherfuckers are lying to us.'

Miles Rimmer's face was parchment:

'You will leave my office NOW – or I will call security and have you ejected. Your colleague was within an ace of losing his job recently. At this moment you stand in the same jeopardy.'

Jessica rocked on her heels, her hands knotted into fists.

'Leave it, Jess,' Nick said, gently, then: 'I'm sorry Miles, we've both been working very hard. We're tired.'

'Of course.'

'Come on, Jess . . .' he led her out, like a blind woman, because she could see nothing for the cold rage that consumed her.

In the corridor she looked up at Nick, and he had rarely seen such outrage: 'They've bought him, Nick – they've bought him on a promise. So simple. Sir Miles Rimmer. It's what the little bastard has wanted all along.'

Chapter Twelve

Jennifer Carter thumbed the Yellow Pages, reached Electrical Retailers, found a number and dialled it. She told them that she wished to buy a tape recorder, and gave the name of the make.

The man said it was not a standard make, that it was used for specialist work, mainly secret surveillance.

'Can you get me one?'

'No, your best place is London.'

'Well, I live there, I'm just visiting.'

'OK, that's your best bet. If you'll hold on I'll give you the name of a stockist.' Jennifer wrote down the number, and dialled it, long-distance from her sister's Lincolnshire home.

'They're expensive,' the man at the other end, said, 'what do you want one of those for? You a private detective or something?'

She laughed, hating her deceit. Was this something she was learning now, how to lie convincingly? 'Actually my sister in . . . Canada . . . sent me this tape, and apparently it only fits a Nagra . . .'

'Oh well, don't buy one, you'd be crazy. Bring it in, I'll lend you one of ours, I'll loop the tape up, give you an earpiece, and you can sit in the stock room and listen to your hearts content. When do you want to come in?'

'I'm not sure, I'm in Lincolnshire at the moment.'

'Well, when you do, ask for me – Dave – I'm here every day.' She wrote down the address in Soho, and replaced the receiver. Her sister came up and said: 'Calling Rebecca in France?'

'No . . . no . . . just trying to get hold of Nick at the

187

office. I transferred the charge.' The silly, inconsequential lie came so easily. The tape was like a germ that had come into the home and infected them all with its cargo of deception.

But she had to know. Had to!

* * *

It was nine when Nick left the old Fleet Street pub where he'd poured a couple of gin and tonics down Jessica's throat to calm her down, drinking nothing himself because he was driving.

When he was thirty he'd been breathalysed and banned for a year, and had tormented himself ever since about the remorse he would have felt if he'd killed or injured someone.

The night was clear and crisp as he drove down the Embankment, and the city glittered. He could see across the river, the tide was high, the river full and swelling, a lustrous sheen on the surface, which was dotted with pleasure boats.

Waterloo Bridge was still alive with traffic, double-decker buses crawling across like illuminated Dinky toys. Further down, where the Thames swept left, he could just glimpse the House of Commons and Big Ben. It was rare that he felt any deep affinity for his adopted city. Mostly it was drab and dirty, a city without a heart, more a collection of cliquey villages than a vibrant capital.

Except for moments like this, when it looked like every tourist poster. It glittered and throbbed, seemed alive and welcoming, a place that millions crossed oceans to visit.

It was like a beautiful woman in sleek black hung around with expensive jewellery. After the Embankment Underground station, he turned right, planning to cut across the bottom end of Trafalgar Square, go down the Mall, past the Palace, up Constitution Hill, and then west, through Belgravia.

He was in no hurry. Jenny was still in Grantham,

Rebecca in France, and for the moment there was just the peaceful security of the car and old pop hits on Capital Gold on the radio.

The feeling of danger had receded, even if some of his guilt at sleeping with Annabelle hadn't.

He couldn't rationalise it, excuse it, apologise for it, he simply knew that what had happened was unstoppable.

She had not called him, and he had not called her. He felt they both understood it was a once only thing, and that neither minded.

There had been no more threats, and Nick couldn't help but feel that was because there had been no more stories, and the part of him he didn't like, the cowardly, unprofessional, don't-rock-the-boat part, was secretly glad.

Perhaps if it did die with Bianca, then there would be no more calls. Not Spanish Voice, not the threatener. And after a while thing would return to normal, and he and Jenny could pick up the pieces.

And what did he care, *really*, if the royal got away with it, or the Minister, or any of them? He couldn't sustain his anger or his outrage at what they'd done. Ten years ago perhaps, but not now – he was – God, what an admission – too old to be a crusader. He just wanted peace. He knew Jess would hate him, but in the end, what did he care about that, either.

Why should he dance his life to someone else's tune, to another's outrage? He'd swung closer than he'd ever been to danger and intrigue, and now he felt there was a chance to get away from it, to curve up and away, up towards normality.

One dead person was enough.

He first noticed the car behind him as he passed the front of the Palace, and turned up Constitution Hill towards Hyde Park corner. It was directly behind him, even though there was little traffic and plenty of room for it to pass in the outside lane.

Nick caressed his brakes to make the lights come on as a hint to the other driver to pass. Nick was damned if he'd rush. The lights in his interior rear view mirror remained, and Nick swore under his breath.

As he eased his car into the whirlpool of cars around Hyde Park corner, the following vehicle stayed with him as though attached, and Nick felt the first flutter of anxiety.

Was it the police? Well, at least he had not been drinking if they *did* stop him. He took the first left off the corner for the back doubles through Belgravia, heading for the West German Embassy, the Belgravia Sheraton, and eventually up through Beauchamp Place, cutting out the Knightsbridge bottle-neck.

The car was still following, and Nick slowed, trying to make out if it *was* a police car. It was difficult to tell, but it looked a dark colour, not white, the normal Metropolitan Police colour, and there appeared to be nothing on the roof like spotlights or a sign that would illuminate and flash while revolving.

Nick eased his foot down on the accelerator as he swept around Belgrave Square. His follower kept station, and Nick felt his hands grip the wheel tighter.

This wasn't accidental, he was being followed; and by someone who didn't care if Nick knew it. He felt that familiar pit in his stomach, his heart beginning to pound.

At the lights near the Sheraton, he deliberately slowed, although they were green, then at the last second as they turned first amber, then red – he shot through.

He heard a protesting blare of horns, and headlights flashed, but he was through, and the other car stayed, faithfully, at the lights.

He wondered what to do. Whether to turn off, continue or try another route. Did they know where he was heading? What did people do in the movies?

At the next lights he made sure all the doors were locked.

He grabbed the short time span lights at Beauchamp Place and turned into the main Knightsbridge traffic flow, left, going West. Traffic was thick but moving quickly, and he used his chance, moving in and out of the lanes like an 18 year old with his first Ford Escort, gaining whatever distance he could.

By the time he reached the site of the former Cromwell Road air terminal, he was confident he had lost the car. But he couldn't relax. If it was so desperate to follow him, why didn't it jump the red light?

London motorists were notorious for crossing two, even three seconds after the light had gone against them. Anyone serious enough to follow him would surely not hesitate at a minor traffic infraction.

He drove past the Earls Court junction down to Talgarth Road, past the Baron's Court turn off, then swept up onto the Hammersmith fly-over.

Nick was sweating with the tension, but there was a kind of relief too. Perhaps it had just been a mild touch of paranoia; perhaps he'd cut up the other driver earlier and not realised it; there were always nutters prepared to drive on your tail to frighten you and prove a point.

Then he saw a car three car-lengths behind, headlights on full and dazzling. It swept out into the fast lane, causing others to brake hard and flash their lights.

Nick's heart jolted like the kick from a drug intake. He tried to accelerate himself, and to pull out, But his way was blocked.

He was coming off the flyover, fast, in a seemingly unstoppable river of cars, and the following vehicle was now in his blindspot, but the glaring headlights lit up the interior of his car.

There was nothing they could do, was there? Surely to God? They couldn't force him off the road here, not in front of all these people, they'd cause a collision, people would see, they'd intervene, stop it, help him, call the police . . . And all the time Nick knew his wild litany of hopes were false.

It was London. He could be lynched from the nearest lamp-post and people would walk past looking the other way.

He bit his lip and flashed a glance at the petrol gauge. It was over half-full. Right you bastards. He'd ignore the turn off for Richmond at the Chiswick roundabout, he'd go for the Chiswick fly-over and the M4. He'd put his foot to the floor and go like the clappers for Heathrow Airport.

There he'd jump out of his car and grab the nearest policeman he saw. They wouldn't *dare* try anything there, not with cops in flak jackets carrying Smith and Wessons and Heckler and Koch sub-machine guns.

It never came to that. Suddenly the car was level – Nick registered ludicrously that it was a Ford Sierra, then it swerved, and he was forced into the inside lane to avoid a collision.

Nick was braking hard, the tyres protesting, trying to avoid the car in the front half of the space he'd squeezed into. And unbelievably the Sierra was squeezing into the gap, forcing the front car to accelerate, and braking itself.

Nick knew he was inches and seconds from a collision. He was fleeing for what could easily be his life, at least his liberty. He should have used his car as a battering ram, smashing into the offending car, trying to disable the occupants so he could make good his escape.

But he was civilised New Man acting on instincts he had developed all his life, and he didn't. Instead he braked, desperately, trying to avoid that awful tearing metal-crunch sound of collision.

He heard a medley of horns and a light show of flicked

on-off full beam headlights. Then his car slithered to a halt, and he was thrown forward by the suddenness of the stop, and pulled up sharp by his seat belt.

He slammed the gear lever into reverse, looking backwards, frantic to escape. But he was trapped, a line of cars backed-up in the slow lane behind him, honking horns furiously at what they thought was vehicular horse-play.

To his astonishment he was shouting: 'Help me, help me!'

But there was no help, it was the isolation and separation of the car, he had no human relationship with anyone around him, despite their proximity. Each lived in his precious piece of metal territory.

Two men were jumping from the car that had trapped him, and they were heading for the driver's and passenger door. Stay in, or try to run? He flicked the door unlocked, ready to run.

He had seconds, or fractions of them, before he could in practicality flee. And he hesitated, hanging in a terrible limbo of indecision, his eyes wild and terrified.

And suddenly his window was obscured by a dark shape, and then a face, white and indistinct, leaning and peering into the window. No weapon, no courage, no . . . no escape.

They can't, Nick thought, they CAN'T! Not here, I can't die in full view of hundreds. Please God help me.

The door opened and Nick screamed – or he tried – but there was just a silent hoarse rattle, the fear paralysing his vocal chords. A hand was on his arm, a gloved hand, Nick noted it with clinical detachment, and he was mouthing, rasping: 'No . . . no . . .'

And then he saw the uniform, and the arm that was pulling him out became a body, a face, a peaked cap. He gave a pathetic sob of choked relief.

It was a policeman. It was incredible, they were

policemen! And the relief became shame, became anger in a cocktail of choking fury.

'You fucking bastards . . . you bastards . . .' Nick struck out, and the policeman parried the feeble blow, pushing Nick up against the side of the car. 'What the *fuck* were you doing, you could have *killed* me, caused a crash. You *fuckers*!'

One of the policeman was directing the traffic around Nick's halted vehicle, and the other one put up a hand: 'All right sunshine, calm down or you're in serious trouble. Shut it.' Nick had tried to speak, but the words chocked on a ball of spit.

'One more word and you're nicked, and that's a promise my son.' The policeman had a leather gloved finger an inch-jab away from Nick's face.

The second policeman put out some traffic cones then came round to join his companion: 'Well, well, well . . . what have we got here?'

Nick regained his voice, trying to be calm, outraged, middle-class of Richmond who knew how to deal with, and was not intimidated by, policemen: 'What you just did was *outrageous*!'

'Been trying to catch up with you since Knightsbridge, where's the fire?'

'Knightsbridge? You've been following me since Buckingham Palace.' The two of them laughed and shook their heads.

'You're imagining things. You jumped a red light near the Sheraton in Belgravia, and then you must have been going some because we didn't find you until just now, been flashing our lights at you for a full minute.'

'Well, you bastards scared the living daylights out of me.'

'Mind your language, sir –' a gloved finger prodded his chest, 'Have you been drinking tonight?'

Nick exhaled, trying to calm himself: 'No I have not

been drinking. Look, don't you realise that what you did was frightening? Don't you *understand* that?'

'Who else would follow you – sir? Do you owe money to the Mafia?' Both policemen laughed. 'Driving licence please.' Nick produced it from his wallet: 'Actually, I'm a journalist.'

'How nice for you? Do you own this vehicle?'

'Yes, I do. I have a Metropolitan Police Press card.' The second policeman said: 'Won't be necessary on this occasion. May we see your insurance certificate and vehicle registration.'

'They're at home,' Nick said sullenly.

'Right. You'll have to produce them at a police station within the next seventy-two hours.'

Nick was calming now, and began to take in the police vehicle. Why was it different? Why had he not realised they were police officers?

Christ, the car was *red*, and it had no lights or any other paraphernalia on the roof, just as he had thought. Red. There was only one branch of the police that drove red Ford Sierra saloons, and that was the Diplomatic Protection Squad, armed officers who guarded the foreign embassies.

He glanced down at the policeman's tunic, saw the slight bulge at the hip, and the tiny tip of a dark leather holster.

Why would members of the DPS chase a traffic light jumper? The second policeman was kicking the tyres – a useless exercise as any car salesman would tell you – but it looked knowledgeable and in this case, authoritarian.

'Any problems?'

'Nah, not really. His near offside could do with a couple of whiffs, but we'll let it go this time.'

'All right Mr. Carter, you can be on your way, and next time, remember – amber means slow down and stop.'

The man had a pig-white face, scarred with acne and

poor diet, and his breath was sour. His uniform smelled of cheap frying pan fat.

Nick said, suspiciously: 'You're not going to breathalyse me, then?'

'We'll take your word for it. Off you pop.'

'How did you know my name?'

'Because . . .' the policeman leaned his face into Nick's until Nick could feel the reek of the sour breath . . . 'it's on your licence.'

'Yes . . .' Nick said, feeling foolish, 'of course.'

The policeman saluted, and Nick knew he was being mocked: 'Mind how you go sir.'

'You're Diplomatic Protection Squad, aren't you?'

'We never comment on operational matters sir.'

'Do you normally chase motorists – armed I mean?'

'All part of the job sir, and the Metropolitan Police never comment on operational matters.'

'Armed?' Nick was still frightened, but he couldn't resist it. It was all . . . *wrong*, something was terribly wrong.

'In the nation's interest sir,' the dead-pig face said, and suddenly Nick was beyond fear, he was ice-cold. It would be a face like that that would be behind the pistol that shot you in the back of the neck and tumbled you into some reeking, corpse-filled pit in Eastern Europe.

'I thought your job was to protect the public. You know, "to protect and serve" – not decide what was in the nation's interest.'

'They're the same thing really, aren't they sir? Now drive your vehicle away from this spot. And *sharpish*!'

Nick got in his car, and watched the two policemen walk away and get in the Sierra. He started his car, signalled, and pulled out past the Sierra.

At the roundabout, he turned off for Richmond, but on a quiet stretch he stopped – opened the door, and vomited a sickly stream of bile.

He sat, window open, letting the cold air refresh him,

watching his rear-view mirror in case the police would trail him again, but there was no sign.

When he got back to his empty home, he poured himself a large cognac, took several swigs and sat down in the semi-darkness afforded by the illumination of a single table lamp.

Why would a DPS car follow him? And why had the policemen lied, because it was the same car that had tailed him from the bottom of Constitution Hill, he was sure of it?

They suspected him of drinking, they asked him if he had been, which in police minds was the same thing, but they had not breathalysed him. Why?

And HORTI! Nick sat upright, spilling some cognac. The routine was, if you didn't produce your registration and insurance documents at the scene, you had to produce them at a police station – any police station – within seventy-two hours. And for that they gave you a form HORT – I, known to policemen as HORTI.

And they hadn't. Why?

They were policemen, not imposters, he was sure of that, and they were armed. But there was something about them, something not *right*, and he couldn't put his finger on what it was.

Well, fuck them, because it wasn't going to work. He wasn't going to be intimidated by them, and he was going to make life as difficult for them as possible.

He dialled 213 1212

'Scotland Yard.'

'Press Bureau, please.'

'Are you Press?'

'Yes I am.'

At length Nick was connected to a Press officer, a woman he knew – one of the few helpful ones – and he told her what had happened, when, where, and how bloody furious he was about it.

'Diplomatic Protection Squad? Are you *sure*, Nick?!'

'Absolutely, and they were armed.'

'Doesn't sound like them to chase a traffic light jumper.'

'I've just explained, that wasn't it, they trailed me from Buck House.'

'OK, leave it with me. You at home now? You are, give me the number.' Nick did.

'OK, I'll check it. Did you manage to get their numbers, that would help?'

It hit Nick like a flash. That was it, that was the extra factor, the thing not *right* about them. Neither had numbers on the epaulettes of his uniform tunic. He was *sure* of it. It stood out like an obvious clue that takes hours to realise and solve.

They had taken their numbers off, *deliberately*, so they could not be identified. Whatever they had done was unauthorised, and Nick had no doubt that it would *not* be reported in their log of duty.

Why? Who could ask them, *tell* them, to do such a thing? They were policemen, for God's sake. There were rogue cops, corrupt cops, but two who would – on instruction, for how else would they know to follow and stop him – intimidate him like that?

It was bloody scary.

At nearly midnight the Press Bureau called back, a different voice this, the friendly woman off-duty now. There was no record of any Diplomatic Protection Squad officers stopping a motorist just off the Hammersmith flyover that evening – nor, for that matter, any *other* police vehicle doing that either.

'It happened,' Nick said, doggedly.

'Sure it wasn't a wild kissogram?' the Press officer said, good-naturedly, but Nick was already putting the telephone down. There was a damp smear where he had gripped the receiver, and he watched as it gradually evaporated. Could he disappear that easily? Vanish in a man-inspired chemical reaction?

His insides felt like they'd been microwaved; that internally he was a set of molecules dancing and jumping, prodded, disturbed until they no longer had their original structure.

He looked down and saw that his knees were rocking, shaking, *visibly*. He was breathing quickly, in gulping gasps that he felt powerless to control.

Had they just meant to scare him, or was it some forewarning of what would follow if he continued to . . . what? Had Miles told them he and Jessica had pursued the East Anglian royal connection – or was Jess right about Miles' burning desire for a knighthood, and even if she was, would he *inform* on his own staff?

And to whom? Was this some governmental conspiracy? And if so, who was behind it – Sir Percival Bellamy? The Minister? Or was it some sinister section of the intelligence community, angered by the Bianca revelations, anxious to spare the royal family any future embarrassment.

And the callers – Spanish Voice – the other foreigner with the threats? There was no pattern.

'Ah . . .' he let out a long breath, trying to steady himself, trying to find a foothold to stop this cliff-slide avalanche into panic.

He lay full length on the sofa, hearing – or was it simply feeling – the thud-thud of his heart. In a startling moment of self-revelation he became aware that he could never again be the man he had once thought he was.

The man who is strong in crisis, the man who will be resolute and determined to beat the odds once the putative moment of danger arrives.

He was not the potentially brave man he had fondly, quietly, modestly, believed it would be possible to be. He was coming apart at the seams, turning from what he'd thought was a whole being, into an assembly of parts, all terrified.

As he had once told Jessica in the newsroom, there had been a time when he knew who he was, and roughly speaking, for what he stood. Now he knew that he did *not* know, and couldn't remember what it was like to know.

He stood for nothing, against nothing, unless reactively and even then usually abstractly. He was not a man of action, probably never had been. Where others acted, he talked, wrote, compromised, dismissed, moved on.

Others simply *were*, Nick knew he always *promised* to be. His life was compromise; not the necessary compromise of life, but compromise as a life-style, a pattern, a design – unconscious though it might be. He was the chameleon, the all purpose, go anywhere new season new morality man.

He had an opinion to fit any company, with just enough roughage to make it credible. He was anybody, everybody, whatever anyone wanted him to be.

There had been one sheet anchor in his life, one – pathetic perhaps – but rugged and held to belief, that of fidelity to his wife. And he had cast that aside in an instant, swopping precious jewels for the fabled mess of pottage, for the brief joyless sensuality, change and release that is the adulterer's crown.

Nick lay for a long time, listening to the tattoo of his frightened heart.

He awoke groggily to the sound of the telephone, rolled off the sofa and lifted the receiver: 'Nick? It's Jess. I've had the police here. Plainclothes men, Special Branch I think – they scared me shitless.'

'What did they want?'

'It was all mumbo-jumbo about official secrets and stuff, said they were looking for tapes.'

'Of what?' Nick's heart visibly missed a beat.

'That's it, they wouldn't say, I mean not specifically anyway. I think it's the bird from the petrol station. This

200

is Miles' doing, Nick, that creepy fucker is behind this. He's so far up the Establishment's arse for a sword on his shoulder, he's invisible.'

Nick told her about the car, the policemen, his doubts and fears, and the Press Bureau response.

'Good God, Nick, you mean the police who came here tonight might be – phonies?'

'No, not phonies, just not doing their job, doing something else, I don't know what – for a reason. To scare us –'

'It's working, mate.' Nick knew Jessica was experiencing the terror he'd felt. She was, like him, at the centre of a story with all kind of potential dangers, and she had just let into her home two male strangers, who could have been . . . Nick shuddered himself. Could have *been* anyone, despite their identity cards. Or despite what they were, could have done *anything*, to her.

'Nick,' her voice sounded like a frightened child, 'I'm bloody scared.'

'Me too.'

'What can we *do*?'

'Buggered if I know.'

'But the *police*! I mean, this is *England*.'

'Barricade your door tonight – just in case.'

'Fuck, Nick, you're making it worse.'

'Do it!' I'll pick you up at seven.'

'Wish I had a gun.'

'Me too. See you at seven.'

Nick showered, wondered whether to call Jenny, decided against it, then lay in bed for a long time. Thinking and frightened. At last he dozed off, then woke with a start, dreaming that he had been falling from a high building.

He got up, and went to the study, like a man who needs to handle a lucky charm. He flipped on the anglepoise, and rummaged in the drawer, feeling for the familiar cardboard sleeve that contained the tape.

His fumbles became more panicky as his fingers failed to connect, and he turned the desk lamp directly on the drawer and started to throw out the contents.

The tape was gone.

His heart was pounding again, and he was shaking. He had put it there, and now it was gone, so that meant someone had moved it or – stolen it.

He felt a wave of dizziness and steadied himself. Maybe Jenny had moved it. A stab of fear hit him. She couldn't play it – no, it was a special tape, she couldn't pop it in the cassette player, if she had been able to do that he wouldn't have kept it in the house.

But the Special Branch people at Jess's flat said they were looking for tapes. Suppose they were looking for this one – suppose they had broken into his house – they could do that – and taken it?

He picked up the bedside phone and viciously punched out a series of numbers from memory. The number rang for a long time before a groggy voice answered.

'Eileen? It's Nick. Yes . . . yes! I'm sorry. No, I wouldn't unless it was important. No, Becky's fine, I need to speak to Jenny urgently. I *know* what time it is, will you *please* get Jenny for me. Please!'

Jenny's voice was thick with sleep, but anxious: 'Has something happened to Rebecca?'

'No, look . . .'

'I've been in bed for two hours, for God's sake . . .'

'Did you move the tape?'

'Tape? What are you talking about?'

'The tape from the office, you know the one. The Bianca Vasquez tape, it's missing from the study. Did you move it? Did you?' His voice was almost a scream.

'Nick for God's sake don't scream at me, it's one-thirty in the morning . . .'

He spoke with terrifying calmness: 'Jessica, did you move the tape – please, did you?'

'My name is Jennifer.'

'Christ, I'm sorry, it was a slip of the tongue Jen,' He was on the point of tears, 'have you moved the tape, love?'

'Your precious tape is in the top drawer of the bedside table – your side, about two bloody inches from your hand.'

Nick slid the drawer open with his free hand, saw the sleeve, pushed out the tape and exhaled air.

'Found it?'

'Yes . . . yes, thank Jen.'

'I tidied up the study before I left, I don't suppose you noticed.'

But he was like an addict with his fix now, he had the tape safe in his hands, and he was calmed, almost euphoric. His moist fingerprints left their imprint on the white of the card sleeve.

'God, I'm an idiot. I *did* notice, the study looks great. I should've put two and two together.'

'I thought it would be safer there – easier to find, actually.'

'Right – great idea.'

'I'm going back to bed now Nick.'

'Me too. Sorry I woke you, honest.'

'Sleep well, Nick.'

He paused: 'I love you Jenny.'

'Night 'night.'

She stood in the hallway of the Grantham bungalow. That was a clincher if she had needed one. She would go to Soho and visit the man called Dave.

She wanted to hear the tape – all of it.

Those who had followed her life, and chronicled it in words and pictures, now attended at her death with the same professional detachment.

The small cemetery on the sloping swathe of green overlooking the sand, the rocks and the pounding surf, was a jostle of photographers, TV cameramen and reporters, who pushed and shoved to get a better view. They trampled on headstones and flowers, and desecrated without malice or thought.

The county sheriff's office had ruled out foul play, the cause of death was established from exterior post-mortem, and the short note Bianca left made it clear she was taking her own life because she, in her own words, 'could not go on.'

The body had been found by the Japanese concierge, when he had entered on instruction, the following morning. He followed the instructions contained in the separate note, and drained the crimson water from the bath-tub, then hosed the body and tub using the detachable shower-head.

He then destroyed the note containing the instructions, as it requested, and left the second for the police after he had telephoned them.

No family member appeared to claim the body, after all, no-one knew if Bianca even *had* a family, so shrouded in mystery were her origins. Neither did any of the famous photographers, magazines or great fashion houses, who had been so close professionally to Bianca Vasquez, step forward to offer to pay for her burial.

Bianca was the outcast, the social leper who had died on lepers' island. It did not take long for the newspapers to make the connection.

The money and possessions she had left were impounded, and the almost incredible possibility of a pauper's funeral was fast becoming reality, until an anonymous man contacted the company handling the funeral, and deposited 5,000 dollars to cover the cost of the casket, the arrangements and the plot.

The newspapers tried in vain to trace him.

There was speculation, of course, that the mystery man was a long lost family member, a lover, a politician boyfriend, an Arab prince, a terrorist leader; but no-one knew.

The Enquirer was not represented at the funeral. As it was held mid-week, this was a TV and daily newspaper story. Neither Nick nor Jessica sent flowers, deeming it inappropriate.

So Bianca Vasquez was buried in Hawaii to the incongruous audible accompaniment of crashing surf and whirring motor-driven cameras.

The only sound louder was the world wide collective sigh of relief from the anonymous.

The two of them sat in the car like a couple in the throes of divorce, bound now only by the cobwebs of old love and habit, by sour memories that lay at their feet like empty wine bottles.

Nick sat hunched, staring blankly out through the rain streaked windscreen, while Jessica leaned her head on the side window, eyes closed, parodying sleep.

The story was now as dead as Bianca was. Spanish Voice hadn't called, the threats had ceased, and everyone yawned if Bianca's name was mentioned.

They had both been accused, more than once, of being obsessed with the story, and in their private conversations they admitted that it was true. They dreamed about it, they talked to each other of nothing else; it ate at them, consumed their waking thoughts; they held it between them like the once precious promises of a dying affair.

And it was no longer enough – the Siamese twins were being separated, not by surgery but by decay. Yet like the couple they had become, it was still Nick-and-Jess, Jess-and-Nick.

But the newspaper wanted no more Bianca stories, unless they were utterly new and could justify themselves, not on hungover Bianca nostalgia, but on merit.

Now they sat in a car outside the home of a TV actor suspected of having AIDS. A 'doorstep'. How, said the sniggerers, are the mighty fallen.

It wasn't that that upset them; a story was a story was a story, be it on a doorstep in West London or an apartment in Molokai.

It was that it wasn't a *Bianca* story.

They'd already spoken to the actor through his entry-phone, and he had said firmly he didn't wish to speak to them, *or* confirm or deny the story, or 'put the record straight' – the standard newspaper ploy. He did not want to have anything whatsoever to do with them.

They composed a neat little letter suggesting that he speak out for the sake of his legions of fans to either dispel the rumours or speak courageously of the truth, and they popped that through his letter-box and returned to the car.

They'd been sitting for an hour, as the rain lashed down. The inert mobile phone lay between them like some sick black cat unsure of who will get custody after the divorce.

Nick yawned: 'Give it another go?' he asked, without conviction. Jessica flicked her eyes open, and across to him:

'Under the new code of conduct I would imagine that's harassment – their rules, not ours – why should we knock ourselves out and get pissed wet through? If he comes out we'll front him, if he doesn't, why bother?'

Nick shrugged agreement, but Jessica had already closed her eyes again. The rain began to beat a ragged rhythmn on the roof.

'It's a cover-up, I mean, you know that don't you?' She sat up:

'Give it a break Nick, I'm on your side – but

conspiracies? It's simple. Miles wants his knighthood so he thinks we've done enough. So does everyone else – more importantly, so do the public. Bloody girl's dead for God's sake.'

'So what?' Nick rubbed his palm on the windscreen, clearing a porthole in the condensation: 'what about the Minister, the royal, all of them – do they get away with it now?'

'Who gives a toss any more?' Her voice had a dispirited tone to it, like a burnt-out soprano.

'You for one.'

'Do I?' She wound her window down, let in some air and driving rain, needing the oxygen, ignoring the rain. Nick shivered.

'I don't think I do anymore.'

'Enough to go back to Norfolk and try to get that girl at the petrol station to sign an affidavit.'

Jessica laughed wearily: 'She couldn't even pronounce it, let alone sign it. Ran a bloody mile. Denied it all.'

'Yeh, and doesn't that make you think, eh?'

She gave him a curious look: 'And Elvis is alive and living with JFK on that island in the Bahamas?'

'Am I that bad? Really?'

'Nah . . . not really,' she gave him a little punch in the arm, 'but it's getting to you. Worst thing you can do, that, get so involved in one story you forget there's others.'

'This isn't over.'

'Maybe.' She rewound the window and shivered at the cold.

'The DPS stopping me was *real*, the guys from Special Branch at your flat were *real*, but the Press Bureau utterly denied that either incident had happened.'

'London's full of bent cops.'

'Oh come on, that's not bent, that's fucking spooky, I mean, you've got a royal who . . .'

'Leave it!' Her voice was an angry shout.

'What's with you?'

'Just fucking leave it. Tell you the truth I'm sick and fed up of this story just like everyone else. We've *done* it, and we've done OK out of it. We both got a two grand rise ..'

'Peanuts!'

'Better than not having it. Name in lights for a while, and didn't do our reputations any harm across the Street. But we don't want to look like one-hit wonders. If something surfaces, fine, I'll go for it, but until then let's get some other stuff in the paper, and let's forget Bianca!'

He felt the most immense bitterness towards her.

'That your last word?'

'Oh stuff it, Nick, just stuff it.'

* * *

Jessica heard the buzz of the intercom, came out of the living room and lifted the receiver.

'Is that Jessica?'

'Who is it?' Her voice was suspicious.

'Jennifer.'

'Who?'

'Jennifer Carter, Nick's wife. I want to talk to you.'

Jessica pressed the entrance button, replaced the receiver, and cursed. A colleague's wife always meant trouble for a woman. Nick's wife, double trouble. They worked too closely together for a wife to understand.

She didn't like Jennifer, and the feeling was mutual. It didn't mean anything. They just seemed to occupy different worlds, and there was that chemical thing. Some people – fine, others, forget it.

The grim look on Jennifer's face seemed to confirm Jessica's suspicion that something was up, and after they'd gone grimly through the civilities, the offer of a drink, alcoholic, no, coffee, no, tea, no, do sit down, Jessica said:

'Not a social visit I presume?'

'No. I'd like to know if my husband slept with Bianca.'
Jessica noted the proprietorial 'my husband', the lack
of name.

She shrugged: 'Ask him.'

'I did. He said he didn't.'

'Then . . . ?'

'So I'm asking you.'

'I wasn't there.'

'Yes you were.'

'I wasn't in the room . . .' Jessica gritted her teeth.

'But you're . . . close . . . what did he tell you?'

'I didn't ask him Jennifer. But for the record, he's
a professional. You read the newspaper. He made an
excuse and left.'

'I'm not an Enquirer reader, don't patronise me.'

Jennifer stood up, and so did Jessica, and they were
like two animals mentally circling each other, looking for
weaknesses.

'Something is happening to him – or has happened
– something strange, and I'm going to get to the
bottom of it.'

'Good luck, but it's none of my business.'

'Isn't it?' Jennifer took a step closer, 'you and he are
like Siamese twins.'

Jessica bit her lip, hard: 'This is my home Jennifer, and
you're intruding. I like your husband, I like him a lot, as
a colleague, that's all. I actually respect him. Do you?'

Jennifer said: 'Is that it, then, just respect?'

'Well I don't sleep with him, if that's what this is all
about.'

'Don't? Did, perhaps?'

'Don't now, didn't ever, don't want to ever. Is that
enough for you? Actually Jennifer,' Jessica couldn't
resist it, 'he's not my type. I find Northern men, so
. . . provincial.'

Jennifer gave her a look from head to toe and back

again, stripping her like paint: 'Really? From what Nick has told me over the years I would have thought there was very little that wasn't your type.'

Jessica rode it, like a boxer a blow: 'Actually, he's not my type among other reasons, because I wouldn't ever fuck a man who'd take orders from you Nurse Nightingale.'

'You're a little bitch.'

'You're not in my league Jennifer, remember that.'

'He said your name once, in his sleep. He was . . . excited.'

'Spare me. We work together for God's sake, all day sometimes, five days a week. We go out of town together. Sometimes I am sick of the sight of his face, no wonder he says my name in his sleep.'

'He said it with . . . he said it like you and he . . .'

'You and I have the same initials, same syllables, and I dream about him too, sometimes, so what? Horny dreams too, sorry Jennifer, even though he isn't my type. I've also dreamt about Dan Quayle, Hitler, had a horny dream about Princess Anne once, what does it all mean – nothing is what it means.'

Jennifer sat down again, and Jessica said: 'I have someone coming here any second.'

'Don't worry, I'll go, but you're doing something to him, you, the Enquirer, this business with Bianca. It's affecting him. I wish he'd never gone to Paris on that story, he should have offered to resign first.'

Jessica could take it no longer. She waved a hand at the Jaeger skirt, the cashmere sweater, at the fading tan from the last Winter holiday.

'Did the National Health Service pay for all that?'

Jennifer didn't understand, and it threw her off balance.

'That stuff on your back and your feet, the tan. What did all that add up too, four grand if you count Antigua?'

210

Jennifer was on her feet again: 'None of your bloody business.'

'Well the Enquirer paid for that, and they paid for it because Nick is their gun for hire. This . . .' she waved her hand again at the expensive rig, 'the house, your daughter's horse, all of it is because Nick performs for the Enquirer. And sometimes what he does isn't nice . . .'

Jennifer was white.

'And if he starts to bottle out, and get precious, because of you, then you might as well buy three five-quid National Coach tickets back to the dark, Satanic mills, and leave the rest of us to fucking well get on with it! OK!?'

'You've got the gab, Jessica, I'll give you that, just like Nick, always the clever phrase to hand.'

'Oh no, Jennifer, not at all. We're ignorant, muckraking tabloid journalists without a brain in our collective heads. We can't write, can't read, can't spell, we're idiots in dirty macs, anyone can do our job, it's so easy. Ask anyone.' The sarcasm sprayed like cobra venom.

'Don't show me out I'll find my own way.'

'Be my guest.'

'But I'm going to get to the bottom of this if it's the last thing I do.'

'Do yourself a favour, leave well enough alone.'

'If I discover that you and he . . . that anything, if . . .' she exhaled and drew in breath, 'I'll do my best to ruin you.'

Jessica brushed past her, and down to the door, which she opened: 'It has been so pleasant, sorry you have to rush.'

'I mean it.'

'You two clowns deserve each other. I don't think either of you appreciate when you're well off.'

She banged the door hard, and with great satisfaction.

When he arrived at her home, Annabelle was packed and

211

ready to leave. Nick said: 'Why so soon? You could stick around now.'

'You're wrong. It's still dangerous.'

He sat down heavily on a parked Samsonite. He reckoned if it would take an elephant's weight it would take his. He said:

'Actually, I've just had a lecture from Jess on the subject of the late departed. Jessica tells me I'm becoming paranoid – then you tell me I should be worried.'

She gave him a concentrated, searching look:

'I'm not joking Nick. Look at the people she was involved with. What about those you can't prove, can't *know*. Suppose they want revenge?'

He looked down the corridor of the flat, trying to remember his night of love with Annabelle. Then thought: no, sex was all it was, simply sex. And it was just a faded dream now.

'Come on Annabelle. The threats have stopped. They know we've got nothing now.' She was biting on her thumb, and he noticed that the normally ever present cigarette was absent.

She said: 'They don't know what you might have up your sleeve. And suppose they don't even *care*?'

'Have you given up smoking?'

She met his eyes: 'I've given up the lot. Booze, cigarettes . . .'

'Coke?'

'Especially coke. And don't look at me like that. I can handle it. But it's you who has to worry. Christ, it's a sewer out there. It's rotten and it stinks. There are evil people, and they're protecting everything, wealth, privilege.'

'This sounds like a party political broadcast.'

'Don't patronise me. I'm entitled to my opinions.'

'Don't Socialists pay to go to bed with girls?'

'It has nothing to do with politics. Politicians don't run

212

the country. Not countries like this anyway. It has nothing
to do with me being Left wing, but I've seen who runs
the country, that's all. And deep in your heart you agree
with me.'

She had a way of getting under his skin, of unsettling
him. He changed the subject.

He jabbed at the Samsonite suitcase: 'Where'll you go,
Spain?'

'Further than that.'

'You can tell me.'

'French Resistance. If you don't know, the Gestapo
can't torture it out of you.' The familiar cold wave passed
over Nick, like a ghost walking through him.

'You're crazy.'

'I'm alive is what I am, and I intend to stay that way.
I shall disappear until this is *really* forgotten.'

'If there's anything I can ever do.' He got up from the
suitcase, wanting to embrace her, clumsily like a kid at
school. He did, kissing her cheek, feeling that familiar
smell of her in his nostrils and his throat.

'Anything . . .'

'Leave her Nick.' She was looking him straight in the
eyes. 'Leave her, because she doesn't love you, can't
love you. Come off with me, leave the Enquirer. I've
got money, we can start somewhere, anywhere, a new
life, the whole bit. Kids if you want.'

'You're stark, staring –'

'I've never been more serious. We understand each
other, we can be *good* for one another. After this we
don't have to pretend with each other, we know the
truth, we can be . . .' she struggled . . . 'we can be *us*.
We can be free. Christ, Nick, can you imagine what it
must be like to be really free?'

'No . . . no, I can't.' And he knew that he couldn't.
And that he wouldn't leave the prison – if that was
what it was – he simply did not have the courage to

213

walk beyond the gates, to look back and see if he really had been confined.

But he glimpsed it in the imagination, for a brief second, as though a door *had* been opened, and then closed again.

He said gently: 'You don't know how flattered I am. But it's not possible. I love Jenny – and then there's Rebecca.'

'One time offer only.' She moved back, holding his hands out, 'unrepeatable bargain.'

'You're something.'

'You were honourable Nick – and Jessica was too. Never thought I'd find myself saying that about journalists.'

'Shit, we blackmailed you.'

'*She* did. And I had it coming.'

'Annabelle, did we kill Bianca? Tell me the truth?' He was surprised to find tears pricking at his eyes.

She cradled him on her shoulder, like a child, and suddenly he was crying, big, big sobs, the tears falling on her bare shoulder. And he didn't care, wasn't ashamed, because Annabelle had seen inside him, scooped out his biggest secret.

'Just tell me the truth.'

She pulled his face up, nuzzled it with hers, kissing away the tears: 'We didn't kill her Nick. Bianca's been dead for years. The people who killed her are the people who used her.'

Chapter Thirteen

Bianca haunted him. Her image, her memory, her face, the smell and touch of her, haunted him like a ghost. By day he thought of little else, by night she was in his dreams, if not as a living, breathing, touchable thing, then as a fragrance, a feeling or an unspecified sense of unease.

The previous night he had dreamed she'd dined with him at the Crillon in Paris. Even in the dream he knew this was sensational because people did not come back from the dead.

So this was a great story, the greatest. But when he tried to call the Enquirer to tell them, the telephone began to come apart in his hands.

He rushed from telephone to telephone in the sweltering August heat of Paris, but each one crumbled as he tried to use it. At last he got through to Miles Rimmer, but when he consulted his notes there was only a gibberish scrawl with disconnected words like clues from a madman's crossword.

Miles called him a liar, and said Bianca was still dead. Nick got out his pocket tape so that Miles could hear Bianca, but instead of her satin voice and the luxurious restaurant background noise of silver cutlery and the ping of crystal, there was just a long, piercing scream like the agony of a lunatic asylum.

Then the recorder had vomited up the tape in an angry brown coil, and Nick had seen Bianca's face in a soundless scream disappearing in the rear mirror of a limousine.

He had woken with a start, and gone to the bathroom to shower. It was beginning to frighten him.

*   *   *

Nick was late and as he walked to his desk he saw the secretary holding his phone, saying: 'Well, I'm sorry but – no, hang on a minute, here he is'.

She handed him the telephone, her hand over the mouthpiece, and said: 'It's that bloke again, the one with the funny voice,' and Nick glared at her.

What she'd said could be heard. He knew because people did it to him all the time. They said things the caller shouldn't hear, feeling safe because their hand was over the telephone.

But the receivers were powerful today, and Nick knew that to be sure you couldn't be heard – and if the telephone did not possess a 'hold' or 'mute' button, it was necessary to put the mouthpiece under the armpit and then close the arm on it. That *was* foolproof.

In this case the telephone *did* have a 'mute' button, so the secretary had even less excuse.

'Hello.'

'I am sorry my voice is so "funny" – I had never thought I was so amusing.' Spanish Voice.

'She is young – and stupid.' Nick made sure the secretary could hear, and understand to whom he was referring, 'I'm sorry.'

'No matter. Opposite the cinema in Notting Hill Gate there is a café, on the North side. Go West from the tube exit for about a hundred metres . . .'

'Yes, I know it, but just hold your horses for a second . . .'

'It is the last piece of the jigsaw. It has taken much work, much persuasion, but now – justicia!' He said it in Spanish, triumphantly.

'What do I get if I go? More erroneous half truths, more names we can't use because the evidence is little more than hearsay?'

'The truth – la verdad.'

'That's what they all say. Truth depends on which way you look at it. Your truth, someone else's lies.'

'Not this. Tomorrow at eleven o'clock. Two people will approach you. Be alone. They know who you are, what you look like.'

'This is not the midnight movie –'

'Be there – *fool*!' Nick could feel the anger in the man's voice: 'You are amateurs, all of you. You, the girl, your Editor. It is part-time with you, you are like clerks.'

'Actually pal, I don't have to take this. My bloody *life* has been threatened, and my family's.'

'And still you do nothing? Don't you want *revenge*?'

'On who? Perhaps you'll tell me. Or will I find out tomorrow –' Nick couldn't resist it, 'mañana?'

There was a pause. 'Cynicism is weakness.'

'Actually I'm sick and tired of you, the story, Bianca – the whole lot. Anyway, I'm busy tomorrow, got a story to do.'

There was a canyon of silence from the other end, and Nick had the most enormous feeling of error, mistake and unprofessionalism. This was *business*, and he'd acted like a petulant child.

He said quickly: 'I'm sorry, that was uncalled for.'

'Be there.' The line went dead.

Breakfast was hope, dinner could mean disillusionment. Sunlight dappled the surface of the sturdy table Nick's Dad had made, across the Habitat mugs, and the white octagonal plates, as the three of them sat and ate breakfast.

The meal was quiet, but it was the quiet of ease rather than the sullen silence of other meals, other breakfasts, and Nick savoured it like a remembered note.

It was at moments like this, with the occasional glance and smile from Rebecca, the touch of his wife's hand, brushing against his accidentally as she reached for the

217

butter or the coffee jug, that made Nick realise why he so loved being married, why he loved his wife and child.

They were his rock, weren't they? They as individuals, as people to be cherished and cared for, and also as part of the institution that bound the three of them.

All the monstrous and preposterous edifices we erected for ourselves were as nought, he felt, compared to this seemingly humble, so obviously simple and honest construction.

He would have liked to somehow preserve such moments, freezing them in time, to return to them, as we return to museums, to remind ourselves of who we once were, and from whence we came.

He swallowed the last of his toast and drained his coffee.

'Well,' he stretched, 'I must go and see a man about a dog.' Nick's father used to say that to him when Nick was a kid, and Nick had hated it. It was obscure, deceitful, it meant . . . nothing, just separation.

He wondered why he himself said it occasionally, it was like carrying some unwanted memento around. To his surprise Rebecca said with exasperation.

'Why do you say that? When I was little I thought it meant you were going to buy me a puppy, but it just means you go off for ages and ages, and I never know when you're coming back.'

He pulled his daughter's head into his chest, aware that Jennifer was watching him intently. 'Then I'll never say it again, ever.' And he vowed to himself that he wouldn't. In some things lay continuity, in others merely the repetition of errors.

Nick had never realised that Rebecca hated that phrase as much as he himself had when he was a child. I was my father's son, she is her father's daughter. He felt strangely . . . the only words he could think of were . . . grown-up.

'You promise?'

'I promise-promise. But I bet if I said I was going to see a man about a – horse . . . then you wouldn't mind that, would you?'

'No Dad, never.'

'Hey, look at the time, I've got to work.'

Jennifer watched her husband like a secret detective looking for clues. He obviously did not know about her visit to Jessica's flat, and he could not know of her plans for the tape.

He doubted if he would have been so apparently smug and confident about the tape had it been an ordinary cassette tape that could have been played on the stereo deck.

They said all professions were a conspiracy against the laity, but the professions had their secrets they thought no-one was else was privy too, and therein lay their weakness. The sacred Nagra, the little reel-to-reel Nick thought kept it safe from prying ears.

Jennifer knew different now. He would see how much he had underestimated her.

He gave a kiss to each of them, and then walked down the street, towards the station, thinking: I'm happy, how easy it is to be happy.

When he left, Jennifer went to the bedroom and found the tape in the bedside drawer. She would deliver Jenny to school. Then she would return the car, take a train to Waterloo, and the Northern line Underground to Leicester Square. From there she would walk to Wardour Street, to her appointment.

There, whatever it cost, she would listen to the tape. She had to know. She put the tape into her handbag, closed the bedroom door, and came down the stairs, feeling like a spy, like a conspirator.

The cup of deceit grew on you, sip by sip, like an alcohol habit.

At the foot of the stairs Rebecca was waiting. Could she

see betrayal in her mother's face, for suddenly she said: 'Mummy, you do still love Daddy, don't you?'

Something like guilt crossed Jennifer's face: 'Of course I do darling,' she put an arm around Rebecca, 'what on earth made you ask me that?'

Rebecca shrugged with false schoolgirl nonchalance: 'Sometimes you argue – well, a lot lately.'

'Darling, all Mummies and Daddies argue, it doesn't mean anything.'

'I hate it when you do.'

'Then we'll do our best never to argue again. You love Daddy, don't you?'

'Yes,' she said. Her face was fierce, and her look seemed to accuse her mother. It was like a rebuke or a challenge. 'I love him lots and lots.'

Jennifer met her daughter's eyes and held her gaze: 'Then if we both love him, he's a very lucky man isn't he?'

'Yes.'

'And if you both still love Mummy . . .'

'We do Mummy, we do, I love you lots.' Rebecca flung her arms around her mother.

'Then everything's fine, my cherub.'

And in the handbag the tape rested, like a stolen crown of thorns.

Nick sipped his coffee and read The Independent, until he was joined by a man and a woman, both casually dressed, both – Nick estimated – in their early thirties.

'Nick Carter?' Nick folded his newspaper: 'Yes. Do you want coffee?'

'We ordered,' the man said, and within seconds, a waitress placed two cups of chocolate-black espresso in front of them.

'All ears,' Nick said.

'Are you taping this conversation?'

Nick gave an exasperated look: 'No.'

220

'How do we know you're not wired up?'

'Because I'm telling you.'

'It's not good enough, we could lose our jobs over this.'
So far the man had done all the speaking, and the woman
just watched him, almost clinically. Her look made him feel
uneasy.

Nick looked around him then slipped off his jacket:
'OK?'

The man, tousle-haired with a pock-marked complexion,
still breathed suspicion: 'What about *under* the shirt?'

Nick said, deadpan: 'Come round and have a feel.'

The man did, actually running his arms over Nick's body,
up to his armpits and around his back. Nick remembered the
other more skilful hands of the Special Branch bodyguard.
Then for a weapon – now for a concealed tape.

As the man ran his hands over him, Nick looked at
the other customers, but no-one was taking a blind bit
of notice.

Eventually the man sat down next to the woman, who
had never taken her eyes off Nick. He said: 'Sorry, but I
had to know.'

The woman spoke, and her accent was cultured and
confident: 'I am a doctor, and I work at St. Mary's Hospital,
Paddington.'

Nick said: 'Yes, near the station, I know it.'

'This gentleman is a contact tracer, do you know what
that is?'

'Not off hand.'

'If we believe someone has been in contact with an
individual suffering from a communicable disease, it is his
job to trace them and persuade them to seek treatment.
That way we can try to limit the spread of the disease.'

'Logical.'

'At St. Mary's,' the man said, 'we deal, amongst other
things, in sexually transmitted diseases, including the HIV
Virus.'

221

'AIDS.' Nick said.

A faint flicker of irritation passed over the doctor's face: 'Well, yes, we deal with patients who have fully blown AIDS, but we also trace people who are HIV positive. That means the virus is present in their blood. It does not mean that they will necessarily get AIDS.'

Nick shrugged: 'That's not what I hear.'

'Well, whatever you *hear*, Mr. Carter, I am a doctor, so why not rely on my version.'

'OK, sorry. So you find these people who may have been in contact with someone who is HIV positive, and you tell them, right?'

'Right.' the man said.

Nick bit his bottom lip: 'And I thought *I* had a difficult job. I wouldn't like to be you. But forgive me, I'm here because of a certain individual who keeps calling me, and clearly you know him.' Nick drank his now cold coffee. 'So, you know, what's the story?'

The doctor opened a small leather attaché case and took out some sheets of paper: 'These are originals, not copies, because with copies you might think they were clever forgeries.'

'Been done before,' Nick said, 'slip what you want someone to see under a real letterhead, and when the copy comes out it looks like one sheet of paper.'

'We have removed these documents without permission. We have taken this risk because we believe that there is a grave risk to public health, and also that there is a national scandal that should be exposed.'

Nick picked up the sheets, the blank sides facing him: 'Someone's health records?'

'In a matter of speaking.' the man said, 'We are breaking every ethical and moral rule we believe in to do this. And we wouldn't do it unless we felt that it was vital.'

The woman said: 'The names on that list – with addresses – were given to us six days ago. We believe each of the people on that list has had intercourse with a person carrying the HIV virus.'

And still Nick didn't get it.

He flipped the paper, and started to read the names. It was crazy, not possible, fantastic – beyond belief. It simply couldn't be true, could it? It was beyond their wildest dreams. Even the royal was on the list. It had to be a hoax, had to be, surely?

Nick said, 'You'll have to prove all this. If you can, that is.'

The woman tapped her attaché case with her finger: 'I have the referral from the American Hospital, Paris.' She paused: '63, Boulevard Victor Hugo, Neuilly.' She gave the address like an extra qualification, a balm to Nick's cynicism.

'Show me.'

She did.

Nick read the notes carefully. He said: 'Do you realise that some of the names on this list are people the Enquirer believes to have slept with Bianca Vasquez? Who is the . . . ?'

And then he knew, and he was aware of an enormous waterfall of noise in his ears, and everything in the cafe going small and indistinct.

How could he have been such a fool? The woman with AIDS, the patient at the American Hospital, WAS Bianca.

Chapter Fourteen

He heard the man's voice ringing in his ears like a distant tocsin. The patient was Bianca Vasquez. The patient was Bianca Vasquez. It rang like an approaching leper's bell.

The patient was Bianca.

And in an instant he was back in the room, back in Paris, the Place de la Concorde below him, as Bianca stepped out of her dress in one movement and stood naked before him.

Her beauty filled the room, and it was like standing before some work of art. Nick felt as if he were choking.

Her hand reached out, took the bundle of dollars and rasped it down the front of her body. It was as though there was no air left in the room, as though her presence had devoured it.

Nick felt he was losing his balance, that the whole world was tilting. Then, with amazement, he heard a voice, the voice of a man he knew was Nick Carter, coming from a long, long way away, and it was saying: 'Look, I'm sorry, I don't think I can do this.'

Bianca looked at him quizzically, a new expression on her face, as he got up and moved to the window, as he gazed down on the cars that scurried and fought around the Place.

On their honeymoon, he and Jennifer had dashed, helter skelter, hand in hand, crazy with love, through the gauntlet of cars, ignoring the horns, the shaken fists, risking life and limb.

And now, with what seemed like a lifetime in between,

he was just a few yards and a universe away from that spot.

He swallowed pride like phlegm, he tasted betrayal like blood.

He said, feebly: 'It's not the money, you see. You understand that? You can have the money.'

And he was not Nick Carter, not the real one from London, nor the fictional one from Hong Kong, he was a frightened creature, viscerally afraid, torn by something, terrified of some dark part of himself.

It was as though he had taken a mind altering drug, a drug that makes the recipient see things bend and change shape; where the inanimate comes alive.

And then, as though the drug had given him a moment's respite, he knew with a vicious and astonishing clarity exactly what he would do. Exactly what he had intended to do all along.

He looked out again at the Paris he had once loved, the Paris he was about to betray. He wanted to weep for betrayal, for the double, triple, multiple betrayal he knew he would now undertake.

He turned to the woman whose presence dominated the room. She said: 'You're just nervous.'

And he was not. Not now. When the traitor decides upon his treachery there is no room for nervousness, it is an irrelevance.

It was the moment for that treachery, for that betrayal. And there was not a second then that he doubted he would do it. The hesitation, the feeble voice from within, had been the last desperate plea for morality from a hopeless, pious rearguard long abandoned.

He knew there was no other world now; no past and no future. Just this amazing present circumscribed by the walls of the room.

She had abolished the past, forbidden the future. She

had insinuated the demon and exposed his world and his beliefs for what they really were, a sham.

His loyalties, his theories, his petty moralities, now lay trampled into the mud like defeated battlefield standards. She had touched him like a magician and turned him into nothing more than the component parts of himself.

Nick was now nothing less, nor more, than the sum of himself, the essence. She had carved out his soul by her presence.

She had lain it incarnate, before him, for the Beast had returned with a vengeance. He was rock hard, and he knew that he wanted Bianca more than anything, and it was not an empty phrase.

He understood at that precise moment why men died for women, killed them, killed for them. Why men abandoned families, and careers for them. Why some men went lovingly to the hangman for them.

It was for this; for the possible, actual, promised, remembered, past and future possession of such a woman. Nick knew that there had never been such a woman in his life; not the ultimate betrayal not Jenny, nor the affairs or one-night stands before his marriage.

This, *this* was why men would risk all for a woman, for the – it was so astonishingly simple – for the *moment*.

Never anything like this woman before, and never would be again. He had been allowed a glimpse at a pinnacle, for once only, and there was no God, no Devil, no reward, no punishment could possibly stop him.

He turned to her: 'You are the most beautiful, *exquisite* woman, ever, in the history of the world.'

She said: 'I am the most beautiful woman in the history of earth.'

She came towards him and he gazed at the luscious ripple of her muscles and skin, at the gentle undulation of her breasts, with their dark pointed nipples.

Her waist went in like the pinch of an hour-glass, and

he marvelled at the cropped and tiny triangle of the hair over her pubis.

'Men would die for you.'

She had reached him, and put her hands onto his shoulders, and they felt like balm against the heat of his now fevered skin.

Her breath was on his lips like the advance guard of hers, and he could see the whites of her eyes. There was a tiny rasping, sound, and a feeling like the touch of a delicate finger as her nipples brushed his shirt.

It was like a mild and pleasurable electric shock.

Bianca said: 'Would *you* die for me, Nick?'

He was like an insect suspended in solution, hanging in a void while time sped by outside, in the real world. 'Yes,' he said, meaning it, 'if you were my woman I would die for you.'

Bianca laughed, and it gave breeze to her breath, like a zephyr on his skin. 'But there is no hope of that, Nick, for you can never fully possess a woman like me. Ever. Until you die. That is so, isn't it Nick?'

She was torturing him, and he knew it, but what was torture against the promise she held? He said: 'No, you could never be my woman.'

'But for this one night, this –' her smile was wicked, '*fraction* . . . you can possess me.'

He was another man, or perhaps the man he really was and had hidden all these years: 'If they put me to death for possessing you, I would still do it.'

Her fingernails came down his cheek, became fingertips, the hard, the soft, the sweet the sour, the *balance*. 'You are strange. Unlike the others.'

'You . . .' he brought his hand up to her face, held the fingers a fraction away as though her skin might burn or freeze him, 'You are unique.'

And then there were no more words. She kissed him gently on the lips, and he closed his eyes, taking

228

the moisture of her mouth into his like pearls to savour.

She removed his clothes, and took him to the bed, seating him, propping him up against the fluffed pillows. He lay there naked, one leg raised at the knee, erect but not awkward, as she went to the open briefcase containing the dollars.

She removed several packages, split the wrappers with her thumbnail and as she climbed back onto the bed, without warning, sprayed the bills like an exploding pack of cards, so they cascaded onto Nick's body.

She climbed onto him, and rolled their bodies into the notes like autumn leaves, and the dollar bills began to stick on the new perspiration of their bodies.

Nick thought of Babes in the Wood. The money crackled under the weight of them, then her tongue darted into his mouth like a tiny serpent, flickering in and out. His hands were over her peach skin, stroking, rubbing, feeling the surface of her body as if it were some new and magical material.

He felt incredibly *alive*, and his cock felt as if it might burst with the blood that inflated him. She took a bill, put it in the palm of her hand, and closed both around his penis; Nick felt the strange embrace of currency shot through with the heat from Bianca's hand as she moved it slowly up and down the shaft of his cock.

He arched his back in the pleasure of it, as a skilled thumb found the sensitive nerve, the submerged tunnel of pleasure. Soon the note softened, wet with his thin fluid, and Bianca crumpled it, lifted his head so that he could see, put the crumpled paper ball in her mouth, chewed as if relishing the taste, then spat, chewed, spat and chewed until the ruined note was like some spoiled sexual confetti.

Nick brought the fingers of his right hand up the inside of her leg until he touched – rather, *sensed*, as

229

though his fingers had antennae – the first moist hair of her pubis.

He moved further, almost frightened, as if she might stop him, and then found that she was sodden. He thought of the small area of wetland near his home when he was a boy, the luscious green-ness of the clumps of grass half-submerged. He felt the raised Mount of Venus, the hair sodden and short, almost cropped like a crew-cut. Why was she wet? Why was she excited? Then he felt, with a half-gasp of surprise, the protrusion of a note from her vaginal entrance.

It was almost – obscene – and he felt a contraction in his stomach, at the dirtiness, the sensuality of it, and another bolt of energy shot through his agonised cock.

Her hand found his, a handful of notes thrust into his palm. She whispered, urgently: 'Put it inside me, all of it.' And incredibly, he did, like some financial rape, the power of money extended to the most intimate act. His eyes were closed, like a blind man, for he feared that if he opened them he would stop this sexual madness, and he did not want to stop. He was consumed by it, insane with it, he knew the joy of the truly mad.

He slid out the funneled note, and pushed in the crumpled notes, one after the other, feeling them soften with her moisture, cramming them like hidden treasure into a tiny crevice of a cave.

'Now eat me.'

He slid down to her thighs, and her scent invaded his throat. He was high, drunk, an addict, like an opera singer or a trapeze artiste, balanced high up on the wire.

Then he sipped the first taste of her; the slightly salty oyster flavour, and like a thirsty man he wanted more. His face was pressed into the moist moss of her, wet with her, and his mouth and tongue thrust deep into her pudenda for the forbidden feast.

He drank of her, hungrily, his face at the entrance

to her, the tip of his tongue, rigid like an extra cock, searching the hills, ridges and crevices of her sex.

At length she lifted his head, and rested it on the inside of her thigh, which he kissed, returning her juice to her skin. She made him kneel, legs at either side of her breasts, her arms outstretched as she took him in her mouth.

He watched her intently, watched her eyes, which never left his own as her mouth encircled his penis, and his hands caressed the small, arrogant mounds of her breasts and the twin castles of hardened nipple.

Her free hand had circled his buttocks, and he felt with what now was only mild surprise, her finger enter his anus. It went deep, and he felt a sense of occupation. Was that what women felt, someone, something, going to the core of them?

It withdrew, as if it had been just a reconnaissance. She was milking him into her mouth, pulling gently at his cock, so that he groaned in a delicious anguish. There was the rustle and crackle of paper, and then the touch of the note, and an odd sense of satisfaction as she slid it into his anus.

He withdrew slightly from her mouth, fascinated by the contrast of skin; her face, her hand, his penis as her pink tongue circled the tumescent end, and he glimpsed the white of her teeth as she bit him, gently and teasingly.

She rolled up onto him, riding him, hand flung back in exuberant attempt at balance, thrusting her pubis against the base of his cock, against the bone of his pelvis so that it burned and hurt. He buried his face into her neck, pulling her down so that her hair cascaded onto his, shielding them both like a forest of weeping willows.

Both hands gripped her amazing muscled buttocks. She danced like a marionette above him to his thrust, her smile of strange glee, frightening him, threatening him, urging him on to more endeavours.

It was all so *crazy*, and free, and then he ejaculated in a spastic spasm that arched his thighs upwards, made him cry out in a strangulated half scream, half moan, and she had to grip like a rodeo cowboy, with the inside of her calves to prevent toppling from him.

It went on and on, contractions like some bizarre pre-birth. Racking him, not with pain but absurd pleasure, propelling him outwards to some dangerous edge of himself.

And then it was over, and he knew that over meant over for ever, and he felt profound regret, not at what he had done, but that he would never, *ever*, in whatever the history of his life would be, have the opportunity to do this wonderful thing again with this woman.

What lay ahead was just the prison sentence of lies for the rest of his life. From now on it must be denial, to Jenny, to Jessica, to his employers, to the world, to everyone, and most of all to himself. For if he acknowledged this; this betrayal, this revelation of the real and potential him, then his life would fragment.

If he acknowledged this then he, literally, could not go on. He would have to lock it away in some tiny, secret cell of his mind, then lose the key, lose the chart that mapped the labyrinthine maze of corridors to the locked door. It was over, for ever.

Bianca was at the foot of the bed, kneeling, sitting slightly back, resting on her legs, which were wide apart, and she had a look of the greatest insolence and contempt on her face. In her left hand was another rolled cylinder of banknote, like the one she had pushed like a woman's substitute phallus, deep into his anus.

She spoke, and her tone was like some purple velvet gown of a poisoner: 'Look Nick. Look what I do. Look what I prefer. Look what makes me come.'

She held his eyes, and his never left hers. Snake and vermin, her cobra to his pathetic rat about to die.

She swayed slightly, nostrils flared like the dangerous, beautiful cobra hood, and then he saw the movement, his eyes flickered, he saw the hand and the rolled note move to the cropped pubis as she inserted the note into her vagina.

Her right hand probed the pubic hair, found the point of her pleasure and began to slowly circle, as the other hand slid the note in and out. He watched fascinated, beyond judgement, beyond feelings of shame, or humiliation or pity.

He did not know how long it went on, a minute, long minutes, a proportion of an hour? There was only her breathing, the hard coal eyes, blazing into his, her finger circling, body swaying back and forth like a dancer, the rhythmic in-out slide of the note.

Then he saw her tense, grimace, her teeth bared, her lips draw back like a snarling animal. Her left hand opened, the note fell, her right hand and finger circled quicker, more urgently, and her whole hand of splayed fingers was in her pubis, and she was crying out, gasp sobs, incomprehensible and in a foreign language.

And Nick was hard again, the fullness of his cock immediate, and triumphal. Her muscles stood out, like whipcord, as she tensed, went statue rigid, then fell forward, her head bowing, a waterfall of hair – almost like a gesture of submission to some power even greater than her power to entrance.

He knew she had insulted him, and his sex, and he did not care. Such concerns existed in the world outside this one, in the world of the true, the faithful, the normal and the civilised.

When her head came up, she was no longer defeated; that had lasted but a fraction. She was proud again and defiant. She saw his ready cock, and she smiled.

'Come to me.'

He did, and she positioned him so his cock was level

with her breasts, and he trembled with anticipation and nerves.

'Do it,' she said, 'do it to yourself, over me.' And he did, without hesitation or embarrassment, until he came with a repetition of spastic spasm, and saw his fluid cream her breasts.

She said: 'The pearl necklace.'

They showered, separately, and she dressed. Now he was flaccid and absurd, and the power of his money had gone, like an injection worn off.

She said to him: 'Would you still die for me Nick, now that the evil is out of you? Now I have performed the exorcism.'

He said to her, knowing she could never understand. 'You rid me of nothing – you brought something back.' He knew, of course, that she hated him, hated all the Nicks there must have been over the years, and once that would have made him care desperately but it no longer did.

'But I would still die for you,' Nick said, and he knew that absurdly it was true. What had happened had been a kind of truth for him, and he would not betray that truth, even to himself.

She surprised him, coming forward, giving him a long, lingering kiss, the kind of kiss a lover would give another, and then smiled with a venomous hatred.

'No, Nick. I think you would prefer *me* to die for *you*.' He feared she might strike him, there was a moment when he tensed as though a blow might come, but it was only words, innocent words.

She said: 'Let's see who dies first.' Then she spat something at Nick, something she had concealed inside her mouth next to her cheek. It hit him in the face, wetly and fell to the floor.

Bianca watched him pick up the hundred dollar bill, un-crumple it, smooth it out and look at it thoughtfully.

234

It was as when the young soldier had hurled the notes at her; too late payment for goods taken though not offered; a monetary excuse for rape. When he had spat the words: 'Puta.'

Bianca spat the money at all of them, *all* of them. She left the room, and Nick took this new aphrodisiac, went to the bathroom, tore the soiled note into small pieces and flushed them down the lavatory.

Nick had looked at his watch and seen that barely 45 minutes had passed. Then he had picked up the telephone and dialled Jessica's room.

'Jess, me.'

'Nick?' Her voice was like a knotted chord.

'Hook, line and sinker. Perfect.'

There was a whoop of amplified joy down the line: 'You got her. You lovely, lovely little bastard.'

'Went like a dream. I'll be down in two minutes. Jess?'

'Still here, get your arse down and join us, and bring the tape.'

'A word. Paddy in earshot?'

'No, he's in his room ransacking the mini-bar.'

'He doesn't touch the tape.'

'That's why he's here for God's sake.'

'The plan has changed. Just you and me. I make my excuse, you switch off the tape, end of story. That's all you need.'

There was silence.

'You still there Jess?'

'I'm here. Something happen up there?'

'Nothing! Do you understand me, Nothing!'

'Hey, I believe you, and I'm in the same hotel for Christ's sake, not Alaska.'

'I had to say certain things to get rid of her . . .'

'Fine.'

235

'You agree, or I'll put a match to the tape right now?'

'Shit, Nick, stop panicking, you have my word.'

'If you betray me on this I'll never forgive you.'

'Hey, ease up with the heaviness, you've just broken a great story. Get down here.'

'You've got your story.'

'We are heroes, my son, and Bianca is dead.'

And how prophetic that unwitting remark had proved. He put the telephone down.

He had known then that from that moment on it was all ultra-dangerous. It must never get out, ever, for if it did it would ruin his marriage and almost certainly his career too.

And it would cut something from under him, some foundation, some core belief.

So after Jessica had transcribed the tape he would take it, steal it if necessary, to make sure it was in his possession. And no-one would ever see it again.

Then, the seal upon his document of betrayal, he had gone back to the window and looked once more at the Place de la Concorde.

There they had guillotined the victims of the Terror and now the metal maelstrom whirled around it like a frenzied modern dance. The world had not changed, just him, irrevocably.

It had to be lies from that moment on and for the rest of his life. For he could never admit – least of all to himself – what had gone on in that room. To do so would be to demolish what he was, what he had constructed, and what he professed to believe.

And he had lied, just as he had promised himself. Lied fluently, lied professionally, lied above all to himself. Successfully too, for he had blotted it out of his mind, almost from his subconscious.

Nothing had happened in the room with Bianca. In a

supernatural way, he almost believed that that was true. As though what had happened, had happened in some other world, some other part of him.

But as he scuttled in the darkness of falsehood the searchlight of truth had been turned upon him, and he was caught, naked in its glare.

He had not been able to escape the truth because the truth simply . . . was. You could not deny the truth out of existence anymore than you could deny heat or cold.

A sentence turned in his head like the awful finality of a jury's verdict. I made love to Bianca. I had sex with Bianca. Bianca and I. I did it. I did it. And now she was . . .

The bell sounded. The patient was Bianca Vasquez.

The same voice, sonorous and ringing, cut into his reverie.

Chapter Fifteen

The doctor said: 'Are you OK?'

Nick looked up from the list, from the other world in which he now belonged, deep into the eyes of the messenger.

And he thought: She must know. Must. She must see it in his eyes, couldn't she see the difference now?

She said: 'You look faint. Are you squeamish about this kind of thing?'

'I'm fine. It's warm in here. I missed breakfast, had a bit of a skinful, last night.'

Bianca spitting the note at him, after saying: 'I think you would prefer me to die for you. Let's see who dies first.'

She had known, all along. We thought she was our victim, when we were hers. *I* was hers. Did she know she was about to be betrayed? Was it all planned?

Not through Annabelle, because if Annabelle had known, then she would never have let Nick make love to her. Thank God he had not made love to Jenny since Paris. Had he kissed her, had he passed on bodily fluids? Had he cut himself? He felt this deep, lacerating anger at himself, and a touch of horror – could he have infected Rebecca? He knew the myths of AIDS, and the so-called facts, but it was something the authorities had lied about ever since it first appeared.

It was the monster; the new Black Death, and who *really* knew how you got it? Only – Nick thought with growing terror – that when you got it, you died.

And now I shall die, banished like a leper, wasted and thin, racked by fevers, my face a shaven headed

239

convict face. I shall die and my wife and child will be shamed.

It was an awful medieval religious retribution. He did not believe in God, but he found himself saying inwardly: Once, God, I strayed just the once.

And the bitter cynic in him mocked his pitiful plea for its hypocrisy. And it said; That's what *everyone* says Nick, why me? It was only the once; I've lived a good life, I don't deserve this; it's unfair, someone else, oh God, not me, someone else, not me, *please*.

'Mr. Carter?'

'Yes, I'm fine, really.' The male had asked him the question, and now said: 'Every name on that list has been given to us as a sexual contact of the late Bianca Vasquez. She sent a posthumous letter to the American Hospital at Neuilly where she was first diagnosed as being HIV positive six months ago.'

'Why did she do that?'

The doctor said: 'We don't know – conscience, a sense of honesty? We'll never know because apparently she never said. Perhaps she simply wanted to prevent an epidemic.'

Nick was working like an automaton, but working. He said: 'Did she name *her* contact, the person she thought she might have got the disease from?'

'Yes,' the male contact tracer took the list, and brought a thumb down the names, stopping at one. 'Him. She had reason to believe that he was bi-sexual and promiscuous.'

Nick looked at the name. It was the Minister. Nick remembered the young man in the room when he had barged in. The man must have been homosexual. Christ this was enormous. Through it all, through the deepening sense of his own personal tragedy, Nick saw the social and political enormity of it all. A Minister of the Crown, a member of the royal family itself. And it was *his* story.

'How many people know about this?'

The doctor looked around her, like people do in spy films, suddenly and obviously frightened. 'Just a few. Frankly nobody wants to know. But everyone on this list will eventually have to be contacted.'

The tracer leaned in, speaking softly, also afraid:

'The hospital chief executive sent a personal hand-written letter to the Minister's office asking the Minister to come and see him, or to grant him an interview.'

'What happened?'

'The Minister came in a private car, stayed an hour, and left.'

'Was he tested?'

'Yes.'

'Positive?'

The doctor said: 'I could be struck off for this. Those geriatrics at the General Medical Council would ruin me.' She bit her lip: 'I can't believe we're even doing this.'

She looked to what was clearly her lover for advice. The contact tracer said: 'Tell him Shirley,' using her name, courageously for the first time, unafraid now: 'He's positive, Mr. Carter, he tested positive.'

Nick thought, Jesus, Jesus, Jesus, we've got the bastard, got him, got him. He lied, he lied. And then like the stab of the knife. And you, Nick, you too.

'Will you contact the others?'

'Yes,' the man said, 'we have a moral, ethical, and actually a statutory responsibility, too.'

'But,' Nick said, flatly, 'it will all be covered up, won't it? They'll put the locks on you at St. Mary's; need-to-know and official denials if as much as a whisper gets out.'

'Yes,' the doctor said, just as flatly, 'We've already been warned. Two men came this morning, policemen, but different, you know, in civilian clothes, but not like ordinary detectives.'

'Special Branch,' Nick said.

'They took away some paperwork, presumably concerned with the Minister's blood test. And they took the list of contacts Bianca supplied to the American Hospital.'

Nick felt the heat rising: 'You said *this* was the original. If it's a copy it means nothing.'

'*They* have the copy. We had more blank sheets of paper from the American Hospital. We typed out the original list again. It is now indistinguishable from the original. We were aware that the authorities would try to confiscate the list.'

Nick looked at them with new respect and new suspicion. 'You're political activists, aren't you?'

The doctor said: 'We believe in justice, in public morality and we believe in our country. Not what it *is*, but what it could be.'

'And you just *happened* to have a blank sheet of letter-headed paper from the American Hospital.'

'Paris is not far,' the man said.

'No, it's not. Neither is Tripoli in a private jet. And, of course, you could have obtained blank sheets and *forged* the whole thing, just for my benefit, then enacted this concerned charade.'

He looked at them both. Were they hoaxers, liars, activists trying to use him to fulfil some incredible political smear campaign? Did they lie, or did the Minister?

He said: 'I promise you that if this is a hoax, I will personally make it my business to hound you two for the rest of my life – and I'll have bugger all else to do.'

'It's the truth, you have our word.'

Their word. Nick laughed bitterly inside. If they were lying, then he risked his career. But if they were telling the truth then his life was in forfeit.

For a few minutes he had forgotten the awesome threat of what was to come.

He remembered being a schoolboy and playing a game

242

his Dad had challenged him to. His father had said to him: 'That postcard you sent to Jimmy, your friend, try to keep it in your mind all the time, never for a moment forget it.'

And Nick had said, that was easy, that he would simply keep it in his mind all the time. And within fifteen minutes he suddenly remembered: Jimmy's postcard! Which meant, of course, that he had previously *not* been thinking about it.

However good or bad something was, for periods of time the memory sadly – or mercifully – blacked it out.

But how could you forget that you were dying? He said to the doctor, out on the busy pavement: 'Will all these people be HIV positive, the people who had sex with Bianca?'

She shrugged: 'Not necessarily. it depends on how safe the sex was, how protected they were, by condoms for example, how much bodily fluids such as saliva or semen were exchanged.'

Nick nodded, numbly: 'And those that are will get AIDS and die, right?'

'No, again not necessarily. Those who *are* HIV positive stand a very high chance of developing full-blown AIDS, but it isn't absolutely certain.'

Nick gave a bitter laugh, inviting doom: 'But when you get AIDS you die.'

'Up to now most people do die, eventually, following sometimes a quite long and sometimes relatively normal life. But there are new developments, new drug experimentation, the more time passes the more hope there is.'

'Sure, sure.' Nick tucked the paper inside his jacket. He thought he smelled Spring in the air, a kind of warm fragrance, and thought, how inappropriate, how *cruel*.

'Don't let us down,' the man said, 'we're depending on you.'

'And who is "we"? Who is Spanish voice?'

They mimed incomprehension, and Nick said:

'He fixed the meeting. Have you met him, or just spoken to him on the telephone like me? Do you *know* who he is?'

Nick felt like a child again, wanting desperately to know a secret the rest of the gang are keeping from him.

'We know someone. Someone who knows the person of whom you speak?'

'And *this* someone, who is he?'

'Not a bad man.'

'Why the hell can't I know? My life has been on the line here, could be again.'

The doctor said: 'As God is my witness there is nothing sinister here, nothing of which you would disapprove. The contrary.'

'And the threats? To me, my family? Who is behind those?'

'Not us.'

'But you know who, don't you?'

'We've said enough.'

'One last thing,' Nick said, 'I must be losing my touch. You either show me your identification or this document is worthless.' They did, fulsomely. Passes with photographs sealed under plastic. Letters addressed to them in both personal and private capacities. Nick looked at them for a long time, noting addresses – if they *were* lovers they had separate flats.

'You brought all this especially.'

'Yes. We were surprised you hadn't asked earlier.'

'Believe it or not I had something on my mind.'

'Well,' the doctor said, 'you know where we live, where we work, that we're who we say we are. So if we *are* hoaxers you can ruin us, can't you?'

'You're speaking the truth,' Nick said, 'I can smell it on you both like bloody carbolic soap.'

'And you,' the man said, 'seem disappointed. Would you prefer it to be lies?'

'No,' Nick said, 'but I'm afraid it wouldn't be possible to explain.'

The couple walked away, not looking back, and Nick turned towards the Tube station, hesitated and then strode for the nearest pub.

He went in, ordered a double brandy, downed it, went to the toilet and threw up. When he'd recovered he took out the document and studied it as a man will study his death warrant, with incomprehension but fascination.

Bianca had named more than fifty contacts, but only one name that should have been on the list was missing.

His own. Why?

Had she wanted to spare him the humiliation if the list ever became public knowledge? And why would she do that? He was the one who had ruined her life, he was the one who had driven her to suicide.

Was it the opposite? Had she assumed the list would never become public knowledge, but that the recipients would simply be contacted and tested. Did she assume that Nick would never find out?

Had she wanted him to carry the deadly germ, to his wife perhaps, to other lovers?

Had his omission from the list been her blow from beyond the grave?

That lunchtime an airmail letter was dropped through the letterbox and into the hallway of the Richmond house. It was addressed to Nick and marked 'Personal'.

It was postmarked Molokai, Hawaii, and had been mailed by Mr. Yakamoto after Bianca's death, just as she had requested.

Nick could not know it, but it contained answers to his questions. He could not know it because when Jennifer returned from Soho she found the letter.

She did not open it. But she made a decision.

Chapter Sixteen

He ordered two more large brandies and drank them quickly until the alcohol began to trim the unravelled edge of his panic.

When he asked for another the barman said: 'You're starting early, won the pools or something?'

He retreated to his corner, hand wrapped around the glass. I will get AIDS now? Did it feel like this in the condemned cell, looking at the door through which you would go with obscene speed one early morning; through to the hood and the rope.

Was this what it was like to look at your own approaching death? Was there hope, any at all? Had he been protected when he was inside her, had she put a condom on him, he certainly had not had any with him.

He tried to think back, desperately putting the pieces together like a torn picture. It had all been so clear, so indelibly stamped in his memory, and now he felt like a man who had been on a bender, and there was just the awful oblivion of amnesia.

If he had been inside her without protection, then he was definitely at risk. He felt the most awful terror creeping over him like a chill. And if he had worn a condom, what about the other things they had done? Wasn't it all about blood, fluids – a flicker of hope, there had been no blood, no cuts, surely – but semen and saliva, they were fluids. And there had been semen and saliva, her juices.

He put his head in his hands and said to the darkness of his palms, Oh God, why me, why me, why ME? He would have to go to a private clinic, he had seen advertisements for one near Regents Park. He would go there and take the test.

But he already knew the answer, he would be HIV positive. It was something from a nightmare. That happened to other people, gays, drug addicts, the promiscuous business travellers, not to him. It wasn't fair!

He would never see his wife and child again, his parents, or his friends, he could never face them. He would go away, somewhere far, and wait for AIDS. He would turn into a living cadaver and then he would die.

It was like some divine retribution – and for what? For one act of lust. It wasn't fair. He tried to think. He had to do the story, even if he died, he would do the story. He would drag them down too like Samson in the temple.

But first he had to find somewhere, temporarily, some room in which he could hide away until it was done. He would try the cheap hotels around Paddington station, no-one would think to look for him there.

He downed the brandy, went to the pub's pay-phone and dialled his home.

After two rings the answering machine picked up and he said a silent prayer of thanks that his wife was not at home. He left a message saying that he was going out of town on a rush job, and did not know when he would return.

It was commonplace, and he did not think Jennifer would question it, or even ring the office, not for a couple of days at least, and then the die would almost certainly be cast.

He replaced the receiver and loosened his tie, feeling the sudden oppression of the pub's heat, the smell of stale beer and staler bodies – why did so much of public London smell like a zoo?

He stepped out into the comparative freshness of the air, into the exhaust fumes and the hot smell of cars and buses. Turning right he headed for Hyde Park, and as he did so a man who had entered shortly after him poked his head out of the pub doorway, saw the direction in which Nick was walking, and followed.

Jennifer walked through the sleaze and false glitter of Soho, past the peep shows and the games halls, threading through the caravanserai of red faced, overweight visitors, who shuffled aimlessly, blinded by the lying promise of sex the area seemed to offer.

She turned into Wardour Street, past the film offices, the labs and the private viewing theatres. Nick often came up here, she recalled, to review first run movies, and she'd accompanied him once. It had been a Rambo film, a half naked Sylvester Stallone being crucified by cruel Communists in some idiotic parody of Christ.

She'd hated the movie and loved the way they'd seen it. There'd been drinks first, and sandwiches and canapés. Then they'd moved in to a small movie theatre with large, comfortable seats, even armchairs that swivelled.

The wine followed them, and the sandwiches, and it had been like watching a movie in your own home, with friends, and refreshment. Only instead of a TV there was a large movie screen.

She'd drunk rather too much white wine, and she and Nick had held hands in the semi-darkness. Now it was like returning to the scene of a crime.

She found the address she had been given, ascended some stairs, and announced herself at a small counter. The man remembered her telephone call, and was as good as his word. Soon she was in a small store-room with a pair of earphones on her head and the tape unfolding before her.

She heard her husband's voice, and it shocked her, as though it was some voice from the past.

Jennifer was breathing quickly, her stomach knotted into a tight ball. There was conversation, rustling noises –

some of the conversation hard to pick up. Then it became clearer, and she listened intently to her husband – lying – pretending to be another person.

She felt deeply guilty now, like a voyeur seeing someone do something mean, or perverted. She tried to picture the room, her husband and Bianca, the Bianca who was – what was the phrase they used at inquests, that Nick had told her, "now lying dead". Nick and Bianca together. Money, a transaction, lies and deceit.

Jennifer felt tears in her eyes. Perhaps it would be better not to know, not to peer like a blind woman into this hidden, sound only world.

But the tape wound on, and she felt powerless to arrest its march. The unidentified sounds were the worst, the rustles, breathing – was it breathing? Or was it air-conditioning, or some noise from the tape? It was like being underwater, or being partially deaf. She heard Nick lying, apparently insouciant. His voice saying: 'Look, I'm jolly embarrassed . . .' and it seemed to her a parody, a bad parody. How had Bianca fallen for this? The insincerity reeked like foul breath. Couldn't Bianca sense it, smell it?

Rustling, rasping noises – tantalising and infuriating – what were they? – and then the voice of this beautiful, now dead, woman, this destroyed creature. 'You're quite sweet. Have you slept with many women?'

Jennifer held her breath. Nick saying: 'Enough.' Enough? Was this Nick, or the Man from Hong Kong? Had Nick slept with 'enough' women, or had his alter-ego?

And was she touching him as he spoke; was Nick touching her? The imagination was like a rack, torturing Jennifer. Had this woman turned him on, had she brought back his desire, where she, Jennifer, had failed?

The tears streamed down her face now. Tears for treachery, for the promise or threat of his, for the Pandora's box opened and impossible, now, to close.

Bianca said: 'I doubt it. Enough is a great deal.' Her voice was haunting, it made Jennifer think of – silk? – and there would be no more words for Bianca, ever, ever again. And Jennifer knew that whatever Bianca had done, was about to do now, on the tape, *nothing* could be worse than what had been done to Bianca.

Jennifer felt hate now, and it was not for Bianca. What made a woman become what Bianca had become? Money or power? And men controlled all those things.

Jennifer swore, viciously, under her breath 'Fuck you, Nick, fuck you, you bastard.'

Her husband's voice said: 'I would like to sleep with you – if that's possible.' It stabbed her like a knife, and she said again, 'Fuck you, Nick, *fuck* you.' He either meant it or he did not. He would sleep with her and Jennifer would hear it all, or he would leave as he said he had.

But by what right did he do this; to take the promise of sex into the bedroom with this stranger? By what right did he take what had been between Jennifer and him and fabricate it – if fabrication it proved – with this woman, Bianca.

And how could he, this *man* – yes, Jennifer thought with a sense of partisanship which shocked her – how dare this *man*, lie and cheat a woman who offered her body in return for money?

It seemed so basically wrong, and unfair. Double jeopardy. 'You bastard, Nick,' she said aloud.

Bianca asked for money, taking the bait, oblivious to the Judas who feigned helpless male-ness in front of her beauty. Jennifer felt a bile of hate for her husband, for journalists and newspapers, for anyone who could perpetrate this deceit.

The transaction unfolded, assaulting Jennifer's ears, and Bianca said: 'I think you are a man of honour.'

And Nick saying, in the voice that . . . God, the

251

voice Jennifer knew like her own; the voice *they* owned, together, as a couple, that she and Rebecca owned, the family voice of requests and complaints or banalities and small talk; the voice of dark, small hour exchanges, of love and lust, *that* beautiful, unbearable, hateful voice saying: 'Yes, I am a man of honour.'

The tears dragged down Jennifer's face like thorns. How could you, Nick? How could you do this as your livelihood?

There were more words, Nick being – what was his favourite word? – professional. Nick slowly pulling the wings off the entrapped and unsuspecting butterfly.

How I hate you Jennifer thought. For what you have become and for what I know that you are about to do. Bianca said: 'Haven't you dreamed of sleeping with Bianca Vasquez? Every man has.'

Was Bianca naked? Was Nick naked? Was he feasting his eyes on that famous, then infamous – now decaying – body? Was he erectile as he had not been with she, Jennifer, these many months?

She heard Bianca tell Nick to sit down. 'You're cold.' She must surely be touching him now, Jennifer thought in anguish. She heard the sound of what could only be the rustle of clothing, and an audible murmur. It came from Nick, and Jennifer knew it was of approval and admiration.

She burned inside. Were they having sex now, or just kissing? Was Bianca's tongue inside Nick's mouth? Had Nick even thought of her – his wife – at this moment of betrayal?

She waited with horrified fascination, waited for the explicit sounds of sex, and then to her disbelief she heard Nick speak.

It was almost as though it was the voice of someone else, an actor playing Nick. And he was saying the impossible words, the words of reprieve, of hope, of future, the words Jennifer had not dared to dream he might say.

The voice of Nick was clear, unambiguous, and it was saying: 'Look, I'm sorry, but I don't think I can do this.'

In front of Nick was the Serpentine, behind him the grassy half bowl of slope where the packed crowd had sat for the Stones' concert in 1969.

Nick and Jennifer had come down by train for it, and the images of the day hovered around him now like ghosts around a ruined Greek amphitheatre.

The poignant, expectant hippies, the belligerent, strutting Hells Angels. And the sneering, almost loutish Jagger in his absurd dress, inexplicably peeved at the cramped and sweating crowd, shouting to them: 'Are you gonna be quiet?' So he could read his poem for the fallen Brian Jones.

Then the butterflies, hundreds of them, some already half-dead from their confinement, scattering for their short-lived freedom, disappearing white into the scorched sky, eventually to die like the optimism of that hopeful generation.

A couple kissed, high up on the rim of the bowl. Had they even been alive when the Stones played? Could they feel the memories too, or was it illusion?

A man at the edge of the incline threw a stick for his dog, a small hairy creature, shapeless at this distance, and it scampered eagerly up the slope to retrieve it.

Nick watched it run, full of energy, half way up the slope, grabbing the stick between its jaws, then tumbling joyfully down to its master. But Nick's eye had caught something else too, the glimpse of a man standing, half obscured by a tree, at the top of the slope.

And he would not have registered it except for the fact that the man suddenly moved, turning – hiding? –

253

behind the tree. Then Nick saw him stride boldly away, off away from the direction of the Serpentine bridge, walking purposefully, but badly, like a awkward spear carrier in a poor Shakespeare production.

Something quickened in Nick, relegating the self pity. It was a sense of fear and an instinct for survival. The man had been watching him, Nick felt sure. Or was it simply coincidence, the return of paranoia like the surfacing of a dormant illness.

Nick sat down again on the bench, and tried to look left without making a too obvious move of his head. Down to the left, over 150 yards away, near the boat sheds, a man lounged. He was wearing a dark anorak, and smoking a cigarette. Nick tried to remember if the man had first been there when he sat down.

On impulse he turned his head, slowly, deliberately, staring down at the man. If he was innocent then Nick was too far away for the look to mean anything. But if he was not . . . ? The man threw down his cigarette, stubbed it out, and walked off without looking back.

Nick got up, slightly scared now, but with an odd sensation of elation, as though danger was proof of life. It did not take a great leap of imagination to believe that somehow *they* (once again, Nick thought with annoyance, who are *they*?) had had the doctor and the contact tracer followed, suspecting that they might do what, in fact, they *had* done.

Yet if 'they' were the police, and if the police had reason to arrest Nick, the doctor, and the contact tracer, then why had they not done so, either in the cafe, or when the three of them emerged?

But if 'they' were someone else, some police that dare not speak its name, who acted without clear cut judicial authority, then better that they wait to deal with one man, isolated in an uncrowded week day park.

Or if 'they' was some terror group or criminal conspiracy, would they not hesitate to kill him? The unease was fear now, and it acted as a cold shower might, it woke him, chilled him, made him want to struggle for warmth and survival.

Nick checked his pocket, patted it with one hand, reassuring himself that the documents incriminating so many, were still there.

And the fear was different now. Before, Nick had been frightened for his life, for the status quo of his quiet, suburban life outside work.

Frightened that somehow 'they' would hurt him or Jennifer or Rebecca. Now he felt sure that the only person they wanted was he, Nick. And with what can you threaten an already dead man?

He strode off towards the Serpentine Bridge, the opposite way from that he knew both his watchers had initially gone. Would there be more of them?

He would head towards Kensington High Street, past the Royal Gardens Hotel, and pick up a tube at the High St. Ken. Underground. He walked briskly, not hurriedly, a man out for an early Spring walk, a man with nothing to hide and nothing to fear.

Up the incline, swinging left onto the bridge, a few cars passing him. No-one in sight, except family groups, courting couples, pensioners slowly rationing out their loneliness.

He heard a car behind him as he crossed the bridge proper, saw it pass him – it was a Rover saloon, he noted – watched it suspiciously as it passed. Two men, staring straight ahead, bored businessmen, indifferent to their surroundings.

Nick paced on, saw the Rover slow, saw the passenger look out as if checking the menu on the strange structure that comprised a restaurant on the south side of the bridge.

Nick paused, checked the traffic and crossed the road to the other side of the bridge, leaning on the stone rail, pretending to look down at the Western side of the Serpentine as it curved into Kensington Gardens.

He could see from the corner of his eye that the Rover was still stationary. Nick turned and began to walk on. The passenger got out of the Rover, looking at a map.

Nick picked up his pace. The man looked across at Nick, a puzzled look on his face. Nick tried to make a judgment. The man was in his mid-Thirties, a little overweight. He was wearing a roll-neck sweater, casual slacks.

He shouted to Nick: 'Sorry mate, I'm lost, can you help?'

Nick ignored him, pressing on, feeling the document in his breast pocket like an extra heart. The man called again, something Nick didn't hear, or didn't care to hear.

The Rover began to move, pulling out from the kerb Nick could see it from the corner of his eye, and it was . . . coming into the right hand lane.

Nick began to run, knowing it was futile because clearly the Rover would overtake him, but also knowing he could do no other. The Rover sped past Nick on the wrong side of the road, screeching to a halt.

Nick darted left, across the bridge road, cutting behind the car. He saw doors opening, the man in the sweater nearest, starting to chase him, the other man still clambering out of the car.

Nick didn't feel he could out run him. He saw a metal advertising placard for Lyons Maid Ice Cream, lifted it, feeling the enormous weight, and swung it like a clumsy club.

The man tried to slow, skidded on the stone, and the contraption caught him on the lower leg in a glancing blow, and he stumbled and fell headlong.

The makeshift club's own weight and momentum took it from Nick's hands like an athletic hammer, and he ran. He was going straight, heading for the entrance near Queen's Gate and the former Iranian Embassy.

He could hear the footfalls of the second pursuer and wondered if the man would take a risk, turn back, and try to get his car to chase Nick.

Then Nick saw *another* man running across the exit road, clearly trying to block his escape. Nick lunged left, off the concreted road, onto the grass and the separated trees.

The clip-clop of his pursuer's feet on the concrete had become a dull thud-thud, but he could now hear the man's laboured breathing, and knew he was gaining.

The man trying to cut off his exit was still way off to the right, and with a lot of ground to make up. Should Nick shout for help? He doubted if there was air enough in his lungs, for every time he breathed in it was like stoking a red hot fire.

He had not run more than two hundred yards and already he was puffing and panting, his lungs scorched and raw.

This couldn't go on. He stopped, and turned, saw the man come to a stop. Nick said: 'What do you want? Tell me.'

The man chasing him stopped too, clearly also grateful for the respite: 'I'm a police officer.'

'Liar!'

'You have a stolen document.'

'Why aren't you in uniform?'

'C.I.D.'

'Show me your warrant card.'

The man lunged. But he was out of breath, and to Nick's own astonishment the kick he aimed caught the man on the leg, and his own momentum took him past Nick to fall headlong.

Nick ran.

The cut off man was gaining now, closing the gap

between himself and Nick. Nick tried to increase his pace, trying the bigger stamping stride he had once perfected playing rugby at school.

But his body didn't obey, the years mocking the memory, and he could only labour, feeling that his speed was dropping, realising with mounting fear that the man would cut him off.

It was a close run thing, but the cut off man made it with yards to spare, reaching the spot Nick must cross, turning, arms outspread, a look of something like triumph on his face.

And Nick felt a burst of vicious, cutting anger, almost of killing fury. He had once had to fight a boy at school, *had* to because the boy had tormented him for months, and Nick's friends had forced him into it. And Nick had been scared shitless until the fight started, and then after the first blows, the first hurting kick from his opponent, he had had only one aim in mind, and that was to *kill*, disable, *hurt*, this *thing* that represented all that had made his life a misery for so many months.

And it was thus now. Nick suddenly hated this man who symbolised all the agony of his changed life. He put every ounce of strength into his stride. The man realised that Nick would not slow for capture and stepped forward, arms outstretched, ready for the take. Nick feinted left, put all his weight on his left foot, saw the man go left, then thrust right in what should have been the perfect rugby sidestep.

It almost worked. But Nick was three decades older, the movement was rusty, unpractised, and it lacked the speed and pace of youth.

As Nick went right, the man recovered, getting an arm out blocking Nick in what was almost a stiff-arm tackle, threatening to halt his upper body while the lower half went on running. That would have left Nick flat on his back.

But his opponent was older too, and Nick heard a scream and a crack as his torso juddered the arm. But still it held. And the man's other arm was now clawing at Nick, trying to pull him into some cruel embrace.

It was too late for the hand off, that quick thrust of the rigid arm, pushing the opponent away. But not too late for a host of other things, long ago learned then tucked away in the veneer of middle-class non-violence.

Like outside the school gates thirty odd years ago, his tormentor kicking Nick in the testicles, and then that blind, red rage and Nick's hands going for the boy's eyes, mouth, throat, *anything*.

Nick jabbed out at the man's face, felt skin tear, went again, hand like a claw, felt some obscene contact with bulbous – not flesh – worse, ocular tissue, heard the man scream again.

Made the claw a fist, punched, straight, hard, repeatedly into the face, the mouth, the eyes, the windpipe, then felt the grip break and the man fall, crying.

And Nick was running again. He saw two horse-riders ahead of him, walking their charges around the sandy horse-track. He panted up to them, and gazed up beseechingly: 'Please help me. I'm being chased. They want to kill me. Please. Let me ride on the back of your horse, just to the edge of the park.'

As he said it he realised how absurd it must sound. The two women on horse-back looked down at him in the way that only those on horse-back can, as though they and the horses were one, centaurs looking down on the lesser two-legged breed.

'We'll get the police, if that's what you want,' the clearly older of the two women said.

'No!' Not the police, please.' What if it *was* the police? But he saw the immediate hardening of their looks, and the *suspicion*.

The elder said: 'I'm sorry, really. Come on Melissa.'

And before he could protest they kicked their horses into a canter, spattering him with sand.

And then the Rover appeared on the perimeter road, the man in the sweater at the wheel, the man whose leg Nick had hurt and he turned the car off the road into the dividing patch of grass between the road and the sand horse-track.

He jumped out, limping badly, and Nick saw a look on his face and realised with elation that it was *fear*. But the man had courage for he still closed with Nick, and it was a vicious free for all of kicking, punching, Nick determined to go on until there was nothing left, no breath no energy, and he felt the man subside under the rain of blows, the head go down, the hands go up, protecting now, sheltering, not striking.

At the end of everything Nick possessed he felt the man topple, and as he stumbled, begin to sway, Nick caught him with a stupid, swinging not-to-be-recommended punch, felt it hit the man's head, felt the awful, but beautiful – as some pain, rightfully incurred can be – hurt in his hand as he connected.

And as the man hit the ground, he kicked him with all his power in the torso. Then Nick carried on running.

He emerged in Knightsbridge, near the Sheraton, saw a cab with its For Hire sign lit up, and hailed it. As it slowed and he went for the door handle, his hand was beaten to it by a well-manicured one belonging to a woman who had two Harrods carrier bags in the other, and a Pekinese on the end of a long lead.

'Please,' Nick said desperately, 'I hailed this.'

'I beg your pardon, but you didn't.' The woman grabbed her nine tenths of the law, taking possession of the cab by the simple expedient of opening the door and clambering in, pulling the protesting Pekinese after her. Nick stood, too exhausted, too out of breath to stop her.

'I need this bloody cab,' he said through the open door.

'Yes, don't we all.'

Nick said to the cabby, in some desperate appeal for British fair play: 'Come on, mate, you saw me first. *Please*!'

He raised his eyebrows: 'Sorry squire, looks like you lost. Can't argue with her ladyship I shouldn't think.'

Nick said desperately: 'Fifty quid! I'll give you fifty quid to take me.'

The cabby shook his head, and jerked his thumb to the woman passenger who sat doggedly, staring out of the window as though the matter was beyond dispute: 'Give me a break, mate, she's already in. She'll scream blue bloody murder. Sorry, guv.'

Nick hated her. *Hated* her.

He watched the cab move off, scanned the traffic for more, but saw only purposeful ones, hire signs off, going about their business. He looked back towards Hyde Park, knowing there'd be more pursuers. He had to get somewhere safe and continue his journey to the office.

He thought of his original plan, before he'd been headed off, which was to get to High Street Kensington Underground. It was simpler now, the Knightsbridge Underground was only 150 yards away. They'd never find him there.

Jennifer arrived home and replaced the tape in its original position with the new found skill of those who have just graduated from the academy of deceit.

She went to the bedroom and lifted the silver framed photograph of the younger Nick and Jennifer, a picture taken shortly after Rebecca's birth.

Two strangers stared back at her. The man to whom she had been married for what seemed like all of her life, the man she thought she knew; and the woman she thought she had once been.

What, she wondered, was left for these two people

261

now, these two people who had escaped from the silver frame, grown older, and worse – incomparably worse – grown apart?

Nick dodged the traffic and crossed the road, heading for the Underground station. He flung a handful of coins into the ticket machine, punched a panel and grabbed his yellow ticket.

He descended the escalator taking two steps at a time, selected the far end of the platform, and backed up, panting and dishevelled, against the stone wall.

The train indicator said the next train was for Heathrow Airport, but it was one of the older type of indicators, and did not say – as the new ones did – how soon the train would arrive.

But it was a frequent line, it was around lunch-time, and Nick felt he would not have long to wait. The platform was already busy, and was filling with Knightsbridge shoppers, mostly women, clutching several carrier bags apiece.

He kept his back to the wall, examining the new arrivals – especially any lone males – with deep suspicion, moving even further away towards the tunnel mouth, if they came near him.

Nevertheless his confidence was growing. He felt sure he'd lost them at the edge of the park when he'd had the flailing fist fight with the last, lone, assailant. To summon up reinforcements they'd have to radio, or telephone.

Haggling for the cab had delayed him, but Knightsbridge was a big place, full of stores and cafés, and exit roads, so that a fleeing man could elude capture.

And if by some chance they discovered him here, it was not like a sparsely populated park, they would not dare harm him here. And he was sure now it was *not* the police – not any legitimate branch of it, anyway – so they couldn't simply perform an arrest.

A smartly dressed man in his mid-forties, carrying

a light-tan leather briefcase, stood a few yards away from Nick, apparently engrossed in a poster extolling the delights of Yugoslavia.

Then Nick saw the man look up at him and look away. Nick felt the fear start again. He doubled back, along the platform, weaving in and out of the waiting passengers, having to push and shove occasionally when they refused to part for him, conscious of the disdainful looks, aware that he smelled of brandy and sweat, and that he had flecks of blood on his clothing, which themselves were torn and stained.

At last he looked back, searching for briefcase man, and seeing no sign of any attempt to follow, stayed in place, in among the women, his camouflage and his protectors.

He felt the first ruffle of hot wind pushed out of the tunnel by the advancing train like some subterranean monster's foul breath.

The crowd moved slightly, as one, tensing, preparing itself for the possible push and shove when the train stopped. Nick shuffled to keep his place, and felt his foot tread on another behind him. Instinctively he turned to apologise.

Five feet away, off to the left, he saw the man with the briefcase looking fixedly ahead. The train thundered out of the tunnel and into the station with a clattering roar.

Again, his foot pressing onto another in the crush and movement, and he said, half turning: 'I'm sorry . . .' But the woman on whose foot he had trodden wasn't listening.

The noise was deafening, she probably couldn't hear him, but there was a look on her face as she met Nick's eyes – surprise? Guilt? Fear? All of them?

And unbelievably Nick felt her hands on his body, palms inwards for an embrace – shove? He was half turning, saying: 'What the hell –' and then he knew, and he fell left, going for the floor and the flower field of feet.

He was conscious of her face as it would be for ever imprinted on his mind. Brown eyes, red lipstick like a wide slash over the mouth, powder, too much of it, brown and flaky and deep in the large pored skin.

And the awful weight of her as he slipped from her push, and the terrible momentum, and the awful scream of fear, as it carried her into the void of temporary space in front of the screeching, braking train.

Nick fell hard and felt the breath whoosh out of his body, but heard the terrible scream, *screams* now as the passengers witnessed the deadly sight. There was a blinding flash and zap of electricity then a cacophony of shouts and screams as the train ran over her electrocuted body in an ear-splitting screech of brakes.

He got up, ribs hurting, pushing through the gibbering, crying, nauseated mass, recoiling on themselves, mouths and eyes like some Edward Munch painting.

The smart man who Nick thought had followed him, was now being sick with studied concentration over his tan briefcase.

Nick ran up the escalator, vaulted the ticket barriers, ignoring the cries of protest from the Underground officials, then he was out into Knightsbridge, running for all he was worth, past Harrods, running blindly, terrified, oblivious to the stares of the shoppers.

They would do anything now, stop at nothing to get the list. It didn't matter *who*, now, it only mattered that he got the list to the newspaper so that it would be published.

A black cab slowed near him, and he looked through sweat filled eyes, misted with fear, to see if it was For Hire, but instead he heard a voice, calling: 'Nick! *Nick*!' and he searched for the caller in trepidation.

The taxi door opened a fraction as the vehicle slowed, and he realised with an absurd sob of relief that it was a TV producer he knew.

He stopped running, hands next to his sides, almost a

physical and emotional wreck. She said: 'My God Nick, you look awful. Fancy jogging in Knightsbridge. And at your age too. Can I give you a lift somewhere?'

Between gasps for breath, he said: 'Yeh – you can – I wanna go to the Enquirer office.'

She pulled a face: 'Actually Nick, I was heading the other way.' Nick pushed past her, a fierce determination in his face; 'Not today you're not Elizabeth. Not today.'

She took a long, hard look at the exhausted, bloodied man. As he climbed onto the seat next to her, something seemed more elemental about him than she could ever remember.

'Whatever you say, my dear man. We seem to be going your way after all.'

'Jessica, it's Jennifer.'

'Yes?' There would be no repetition of their meeting, Jessica was determined about that.

'Have you seen Nick?,' Jessica groaned: 'I thought I'd made it very clear where I stand on all that.'

But Jennifer's tone seemed soft, conciliatory: 'It's nothing like that. When I got in there was a message saying he was going out of town. He seemed strange, upset. I need to speak to him urgently.'

'He had a meet with some people in West London.'

'Did he come back?'

'Don't know.' Then Jessica lied: 'There was some vague talk of him being sent to Glasgow. Maybe they diverted him to Heathrow to catch the Shuttle.' It was a common fiction to pretend you were going out of town. Jessica had used it herself in the dog days of her marriage.

Maybe Nick did have another woman, or maybe he just wanted a night away from Dunroamin.

'Oh,' there seemed deep disappointment in his wife's voice.

'If he comes in I'll give him the message.'

'Thanks.' She paused: 'Jessica, if he was there, you'd tell me, wouldn't you, you wouldn't cover for him if he was trying to avoid me?'

'Jennifer, I'm busy. Take your marital problems to Clare Rayner.'

There was a gasp. 'Christ, but you're a bitch. I'm beginning to realise now why people hate reporters so much.'

'Ask me how I sleep at night.' Jessica heard the receiver crash down.

Nick said: 'Bianca had AIDS. She believes she caught it from the Minister.'

'Jesus,' Jessica was curled like a spring.

'She's named fifty other people, BIG names. I have all the original documents. It's out of this world. It'll finish the government, it'll . . . it's hard to take it all in.'

'Royal? Tell me he's on the list Nick, you little darling.'

'He's on.'

'There is a God, there is a God!'

She had answered his summons and met him downstairs, in a side corridor off near the medical room. His appearance shocked her, but thoughts of that vanished when he showed her the list.

'And it's all true Jess, every word of it. I *know* it is. They even tried to kill me to get it back.' Nick described the chase and the nightmare on the Tube platform.

He was wild eyed, dishevelled, a little drunk, almost paranoid in his belief that they'd tried to kill him. But Jessica knew, with absolute conviction, that he was telling the truth.

'You believe me Jess, don't you?'

'Yes,' she said, 'I believe you. Every bloody word, my son.'

He handed her the documents like he was handing over

his first born: 'Guard it Jess, with your life. I'm going to get cleaned up, then I'm coming up and we're going to see Miles. Both of us.'

'No problem.'

'This he'll *have* to use. And if he pussyfoots around on this, I'm going to Paris Match, or Stern, or the Washington Post or something. They're not suppressing this.'

'Nick?' Jessica turned the envelope in her hands, her tongue licking at dry lips: 'Suppose *this* is a forgery?'

'It's not.'

'You don't know that. Two strangers in a cafe, the word of Spanish Voice. Suppose it's a deliberate plant? Do you realise the potential for libel damages here?'

'It's true Jess. It all fits. We've got to believe it. I've nearly lost my fucking life over this, no-one would go to those lengths to get hold of a forgery.' He shook his head: 'If I go down for this one, I'll go down big. I can't turn back. But I don't have to take you with me. You in or out?'

'Never seen you quite so determined.'

'Actually Jess, I've bugger all to lose if the truth were known. In or out?'

'In.'

The editor's secretary said: 'He's got two people with him I'm afraid.' Nick said: 'We'll wait.' He and Jessica plonked down on the leather sofa in the ante-room.

Within a minute they heard Miles' voice on the inter-com: 'Get Nick Carter would you?'

The woman smiled: 'Coincidence. You're in luck.' Then, into the speaker: 'Mr. Carter is here Mr. Rimmer and Jessica –'

But the two of them were in the office unannounced, and Miles was smiling his most unpleasant, insincere smile: 'Nick, how good to see you, Jessica! – They're like Siamese twins you know – please sit down.'

He'd addressed the Siamese twins remark to two men who sat on one of the matching white leather sofas, and who now struggled ungainly to their feet.

'Ah. These two gentleman are – well I'm sure they can introduce themselves.'

The taller and older of the two said: 'Detective Chief Superintendent Clew-Markham of the Special Branch. My colleague, Detecive Chief Inspector Lethbridge.'

Nick turned to the Editor: 'Miles may I speak with you privately for a moment?' The envelope in his hand seemed to wave like a provocative flag.

Miles said:

'Actually, Nick, with regret I have to say that these gentlemen, are here on business – business with you.'

Jessica watched the two men carefully, saw them subtly part, change position so that one was off to one side of Nick. She thought. This is an arrest. They *know*!

The older policeman said: 'Mr. Carter. Mr. Nicholas Carter?'

Nick said: 'I think that bit is indisputable.'

'I have a warrant for your arrest under the Official Secrets Act.'

'Bollocks,' Nick said.

Jessica saw a look on Nick's face, a snarl of fear and anger like an animal cornered, at bay.

'We have reason to believe you are in possession of stolen documents covered by the Act.'

'I won't let you, you bastards.'

The policeman produced a folded piece of paper. 'This is the warrant. Do you wish to see it?'

Nick turned to Miles: 'Bianca had AIDS Miles, and she's screwed the Minister, and pop stars and Christ knows who else. Are you going to let them do this?'

The younger policeman said in a hard voice: 'He has no choice Mr. Carter; and neither do you. Will you come with us peacefully?'

'It's all here,' Nick patted the envelope, 'Official Secrets my arse. This is a government cover-up. They tried to kill me to get it.'

He saw the Editor's patronising smile, the spread of the hands like Pilate washing his hands: 'The law must take its course.'

'Mr. Carter you are under arrest. I must warn you that anything you say may be taken down and used in evidence at your trial. Do you wish to say anything?'

'Yes. You're both a disgrace to your country.'

The younger policeman put out a hand: 'May I take that now?' Nick looked at Miles with the deepest of hatred: 'You realise what they're doing. If they take this we're finished.'

It happened in an instant. Jessica grabbed the envelope and darted for the door, leaping the glass coffee table like a hurdler. The older detective was nearer and tried to grab her but Nick lunged at him, crash tackling the man back onto the sofa.

The younger detective was surprisingly athletic for his bulk, he took the coffee table in one stride and slammed Jessica against the door with a creak of timber and crunch of bone.

She collapsed on the carpet, and the envelope fluttered free. The younger detective brushed himself down, breathing heavily and picked up the envelope.

With his other hand he hauled Jessica to her feet and said with apparent sincerity: 'I hope I didn't hurt you, but I couldn't let you run off with this, it's material evidence.'

Nick and the other policeman had disentangled themselves and the four protagonists stood awkwardly, as though embarrassed by what had happened.

Then the first detective said to Nick: 'I could put handcuffs on you after that. That was assault on a police officer.'

'And how,' Jessica demanded, regaining her breath, 'do you describe what that gorilla did?'

Nick said with a despairing tone: 'Miles, if you believe in *anything*, anything at all, you've got to stop this.' But Miles said nothing. He was thinking of Buckingham Palace, of the investiture, of that three letter accolade before his name. He had, he concluded, come a long way.

After his release Nick walked for a long time in the steady drizzle that had settled on West London. He doubted if they would try to harm him now, not now they had what they wanted.

He was safe, but he was finished. One threat of death had been lifted, and the other remained. In a few short months everything he had ever been had been destroyed. It had all seemed so permanent, and it had been nothing.

And, of course, when the results were confirmed, he would have to tell Annabelle. It was unimaginable. How did you tell someone you were HIV positive.

That you had possibly given them AIDS? Nick shivered with the horror of it.

There was no more proof of the story now, and if he mentioned the incident at the tube station to anyone else, they would merely think him paranoid. When he tried to raise the matter with the police they had shown him a copy of the Evening Standard.

The woman's death under the train was listed as an apparent suicide. She was in her thirties, lived alone, and her occupation was listed as civil servant.

Was he wrong? Had it been a suicide attempt in which he had become involved? Had he moved unwittingly into her path at the moment she planned to leap?

Or had it been an accident in which he'd played a part as the crowd moved forward and he fell to the ground, terrified of being pushed? Had that propelled the woman

onto the track? Had he, Nick, been partly responsible for
her death?

He leaned against a lamp-post, the thoughts torturing
him. The police had decided not to charge him, just a
caution this time. Of course, he was not to be allowed
his day in court.

Nick coughed and spat into a gutter black with water.
Bastards, all of them, Miles, the police, the government,
Spanish Voice, everyone. He hated *everyone*.

There was nothing left for him now. Tomorrow he
planned to go to the private clinic and get confirmation
of that which he was already sure. And afterwards?
Disappear in shame until the first symptoms appeared,
the night sweats, the sarcomas, the fatigue and weight
loss. Then a cocktail of alcohol and barbiturates and a
slow drunken slide into oblivion.

He caught his bedraggled image in the mirror of a
lighted shop window: 'Christ,' he said aloud, 'I look
like a bloody tramp.' He walked on, welcoming the
protective cloak of the rain and the night. Eventually,
at the end of her street he hesitated, engulfed by the all
embracing misery. Then he gave in, and turned, trudging
and squelching in his sodden shoes until he found the
right house.

He pressed the button over the nameplate, and
eventually heard the voice, high with suspicion: 'Yes?'

'It's me – Nick.'

The automatic-entry buzzer went, and he pushed
at the door, seeing her immediately framed in light
at the entrance to her flat at the end of the hallway.

When he reached her he said with a pathetic attempt
at flippancy: 'Penny for the Guy?'

'You look bloody awful.'

'Feel it,' he smiled, ruefully, 'released without charge.'

'And can't go home. By the way your wife called you,

271

she has something important to discuss. She and I had words. Sorry.'

'You never did get on. Can I come in?'

She stepped back into the hallway: 'Get in before you catch your death.' 'Thanks.'

As soon as she'd shut the front door, she turned him in the hall and pushed him like a reluctant school-kid, into the bathroom. He said: 'What's all this?'

'Clothes off, hot shower, I'll chuck you a dressing down in. Hot toddy when you get out. You look like a candidate for pneumonia.'

'What can I say, Jess?'

'Thanks. And don't complain that you look like a big tart with my dressing gown on. Sofa bed OK?'

'Great. I fucked up, didn't I? I really fucked up.'

'Show ain't over 'til the fat lady sings.'

'You wouldn't believe me if I told you the last time I heard that, and under what circumstances.'

'You must tell me one day.' Jessica closed the bathroom door and Nick began to peel off his sodden clothes.

He sipped the hot whisky and lemon while she watched him with a kind of maternal concern. He said: 'Thanks for what you tried to do this afternoon.'

'The envelope, you mean? Well, you looked too knackered to try. A gallant failure, a noble charge of the Light Brigade, another honourable British attempt to snatch victory from the jaws of defeat.'

She threw her head back and laughed uproariously.

'Glad *you* can see the funny side of this.'

'Oh but I can, Nick, I most assuredly can. Despite the fact that I'm black and blue all over where Mr. Plod slammed me against the door.'

She took a drink of her wine and began to laugh again, shaking her head, contorting her face when the wine went

272

down the wrong way. The laugh becoming a cough, then a laugh again.

Nick was becoming annoyed. 'Want to share the joke with me? It's finished now, you realise that do you? We had those fuckers nailed to the wall and I screwed it. And I'll never forgive myself for that – ever.'

He leaned back on the sofa, face desperate. Jessica poured herself some more wine: 'Oh I think you will Nick.'

'Yeh? You don't know me.'

'I think you will because you forget the greatest boon to espionage since secret ink.'

'Are you off your head?'

'Xerox! The copier Nick. When you were wiping the blood off yourself in the Gents I made five copies of those hospital records.' Nick sat bolt upright, spilling his hot whisky, feeling it burn his bare leg, ignoring it.

'You made *copies*! Fabulous, great.' Then his elation died. 'But it's no use. Copies will too easily look like a forgery, we needed the original and the police got that.'

'Says who?' Jessica's face was triumphant.

'Jess, we took it together to Miles' office.'

'Did we?'

'It *wasn't* the original?'

'No. But they thought I was so desperate to run off with it that it *must* be.'

'So they didn't check it, Christ Jess you're a genius.'

'I am. By the time they *had* checked, the original was long gone. Didn't they ask you about it?'

Nick shook his head wearily: 'They kept going on about the original and I kept telling them they'd got it. I just thought they were really checking if I was telling the truth.'

'You *were* mate, as *you* saw it.'

Nick upended his whisky and lemon, feeling the heat and the spirit flow into his veins. She'd saved it. He owed

273

her everything. He said, with undisguised admiration: 'How, Jess? And why?'

Returning to the seventh floor with the envelope she had seen the two men go into Miles' office, and concluded from the cut of their clothes and their manner that they were policemen. Why would they come direct to the Editor at *that* particular time? It could only be connected with Nick.

He would be summoned to see the Editor and the document confiscated. But if they suspected they had not obtained the original they might launch a full scale search of the office.

So she had made copies and secreted them and the original, in a place she felt they would never look. She'd put it in a cellophane bag and taped it to the inside of the water closet in the Ladies loo.

'You saw the Godfather?' Nick said with awe.

'Oh, they all do it. One day I plan to check all the loos in London, you'll find guns, jewels, drugs', they were both laughing.

'When did they come back?'

'After about half an hour, but they didn't even search, I think they knew then they were up merde rue sans paddle.'

'Brilliant.'

'And where is it now?' Nick asked, with a shade of anxiety.

'In the personal possession of the London correspondent of the Washington Post. Its existence has also been verified in front of a solicitor.'

She mentioned a name and Nick whistled: 'That's going for the top.'

'We've got them now. The Post also know that copies are going to Stern and Paris Match. Once those three publish, the British papers and the BBC and ITN will *have* to refer to it.'

'We smoked them out. You clever little sod. The Post will use it?'

'You saw the names on that list – American senators included, a British cabinet minister, pop stars – are you kidding? Our man from the Post is flying back to the 'States tomorrow with the original. *That's* how important they think it is.'

'They can't suppress it?'

'Impossible.'

He reached across and took her hand: 'What can I say Jessica? You're a bloody marvel.'

She returned his squeeze and the two of them felt the blood cross, doubling their energy: 'The shit, my dear Nicholas, is about ready to hit the fan.'

'And *we* will be fired.'

'*You* might be Nick, but I got my retaliation in first as the soccer managers say. I called Miles at home and resigned.'

'What did you say?' Nick leaned forward eagerly, wanting to hear the minutae of it. Jessica grabbed the wine bottle and drank straight from the neck. She said: 'What the hell, eh? I said to him that I couldn't work for any editor of any newspaper that connived in the suppression of a story like this.'

'And . . . ?'

'That he was a weasely-mouthed git with a yellow streak, bucking for a knighthood so badly he sat by and let his best reporter get arrested.'

Nick said: 'Second best, I'm looking at the best.'

'Whatever. Together we're the bestest.'

'You bet.'

'I also told him that he has one of the worst cases of halitosis I'd ever come across and given a choice between kissing him and a camel, well hello Morocco.'

Nick was holding his ribs: 'You lying little bugger you never said *any* of that.'

'Oh yeh?' Jessica produced her pocket tape recorder flipped the re-wind button, then the button marked 'Play', and Nick heard her voice. Nick said: 'Not the *Editor*?'

She said: 'If I can secretly tape the chairman I can tape that bow-tied horse-breath.' And she had, and it was exactly as she'd said it was. Down to the very last insult.

'You comfortable?'

'Thanks. Yeh.' He looked up from the floor-level sofabed. 'We're both out of work now. I'll call Miles first thing in the morning.'

'Good man, stout fellow. Now we make *real* money. The book! The film! There's a whole market of foreign magazines dying for first person stuff from us.'

She slipped the light switch and said from the illumination of the doorway: 'Sleep well.'

'Thanks.'

'Nick?'

'Yeh?'

'If you want my opinion, I think you'll be OK.' He didn't reply and she closed the door. As he lay there he wondered what she meant. His career? His marriage? She can't know about Bianca and the virus. She can't know I slept with Bianca.

But in his heart he knew that she did.

Chapter Seventeen

The smell of Spring had vanished like the false promise of a fickle lover, and now a cold breeze cut like loneliness across the unshaven stubble of Nick's face.

Nannies pushed prams containing the babies of others, and children ran, swaddled against the cold, pursued by anxious parents. Couples huddled into immobile statues of love, as Nick sat letting those of the other world parade before his eyes.

His heartbeat was normal, his hands rock steady, in fact he was amazed at his calm. He had thought perhaps that such a moment would make him weep or cry out or display for the first time the outpourings of some hidden well of emotion.

Instead, there was nothing – just a blankness, a void, an absence of feeling, like a terrible sense of peace. He had paid his bill, and walked out into the razor sharp wind, marching steadily, past the tube station, past the cricket ground, down past the shiny mosque with its tall minaret, and ended here in this park.

And now he sat, immobile, his hands in his pocket.

The test had proved negative. Nick did not have the virus. So now he must face this strange thing, the thing he thought he had abandoned, this thing called living. He must face Jennifer, he must face life without the security of the Enquirer, but most of all he must face life for the first time knowing something of what he was.

There was the awful responsibility of going on. He felt the cold through his trousers, felt the cold inside his nose, felt the clearing of his sinuses, and the thin fluid running unchecked onto his upper-lip. Un-selfconsciously he wiped his face with the back of his hand, snorting back the liquid.

When he'd actually received the result, at the precise moment before the doctor had told him it was negative, he felt like a man teetering on a fence, a man who can fall this way, or that. That, oblivion, this, hope, a future.

When the words finally came, for a split second, as when one touches either an icy cold object or an extremely hot one, it was almost impossible to know which; to know what the words meant.

Then they registered, 'I'm happy to tell you . . .' hitting home with the force of a fist, and he gave an audible gasp-groan of relief.

'But remember, our knowledge of this is in its infancy. It has been over six months since your contact, and that is time enough for the antibodies to have registered positive to HIV.'

Nick looked up, somehow registering the word 'but'.

'I'm clear, you said so.'

'Yes, you're clear. But there is a tiny, minute chance, that it has not registered yet.'

'Christ!' Nick felt himself go weak at the knees: 'I could still get it.'

'It is possible. An outside chance. But not probable.'

'My God, there's no reprieve.'

'I'd recommend a test every three months for the next three years.'

'Good God.'

The doctor's hand touched Nick's arm, clasped it, and Nick saw the hand mottled with age spots; like a father's. How strange to be held by a male hand, and how comforting.

The doctor said: 'Mr. Carter you are not HIV positive, and you almost certainly never will be as a result of this contact. I'm trying to be cautious, realistic.'

278

'Yes, realism. We must have realism.' Nick said it in a daze.

'Am I free . . . I have a wife.'

'Yes, you're free to have sex.'

'There is no possible way that I could . . . ?'

'You have tested negative to the AIDS antibodies, Mr. Carter.' The reassuring hand, squeezed: 'Go in peace. Sometimes that is not the message I have to deliver here.'

'No, of course not,' Nick turned, 'thank you.'

He didn't have AIDS. He was not HIV positive. The future was now, today, tomorrow, to be lived for itself, each hour. Looking out across the water he mouthed a prayer to a God in which he hardly believed.

A toy yacht with a dazzlingly white sail cut across the slight chop of the pond, and Nick watched it, bobbing against the tiny waves like some speeded up old movie reel.

The sky was still incredibly blue and it felt like re-birth. As he left the park and crossed the road he saw an Evening Standard bill outside a shop. It read: 'Bianca AIDS sensation. Palace Crisis. Minister Resigns.'

Nick walked past without buying a newspaper.

At Baker Street station he called Jennifer from a payphone and told her he was coming home.

They sat at the scrubbed-pine table as they had that morning barely a week ago, before Nick's world was shattered and re-built.

He remembered that moment, that breakfast with his wife and child, and how life had seemed good, and how much he felt he loved his wife and his daughter.

Now thankfully Rebecca was at school. Silence sat between him and Jennifer like a chaperone, and whatever trust had existed that morning lay shattered on the table like a carelessly damaged heirloom.

She poured the tea in silence, and then said: 'Actually, I was becoming convinced you'd left me for another woman. I called Jessica, the day you went. Believe it or not when you didn't come home, I became convinced you'd left me *for* Jessica.'

'We're not lovers, Jen, you have my word.'

'Yes?' She looked him directly in the eyes, 'then is there someone else?'

He met her gaze: 'No. There's no-one else. But there is something you have to know.'

'Like where you *have* been, for example?'

'No, not that. I've been in a hotel in Paddington.'

'You don't have to lie, you know.'

'I'm not.' He rummaged in his pocket and tossed a crumpled bill to her. He remembered every detail of its genteel poverty and loneliness, from the chipped washstand to the much-washed pink nylon sheets and the list of petty regulations hanging from the door hook.

'You're a journalist, getting receipts is your stock-in trade.'

'I don't want to waste words Jen. Have you seen the papers?'

Her hand encircled the mug, pulling it in defensively and Nick watched his wife's hands as though seeing them for the first time. She said: 'We could hardly miss them, could we? Me or Rebecca. And there's always the TV.'

Nick rasped a hand over his stubble, feeling the rough touch of the bristles, remembering how he had felt his father's face and been reassured by its stubble. I'm grown up now, he thought. I'm a man, my son.

'Well – I've resigned.'

'My God! Why? Good God, Nick, how will we live?'

'Like others. They live. We'll live. I'll work like other people do, and we'll survive.' He paused: 'If you want to.'

'*Want* to?'

'Go on, you and I. Something fundamental has happened to me, to you and I. If you don't want to go on, I'll move out, you can keep the house, I'll make sure you're well cared for, as long as I can see Rebecca at weekends –'

'Nick!'

Her hand went out tentatively, then bolder, and covered his like a leaf. And he looked down at them, hers and his, the mug of tea, like three objects in a still-life painting.

She said: 'Poor Nicky.' He could feel a terrible swell of misery in his throat like a cancer, paralysing his jaw. But he soldiered on, stumbling through his misery like a dogged grenadier.

'So, well basically, Jessica wants us to team up, go freelance, you know, write books and the like. But I'm finished with it all. I want out. Anything. Anywhere.'

'Why Nick, *why*?'

'Well . . .' he ran one finger of a free hand around the rim of the mug, making it squeak, 'because of Bianca, because of you and me – well, *me* actually, that is, not *you*. Because of me, what I've become . . .'

The knot of misery grew like a tree, and its branches clutched at his throat, paralysing his vocal chords.

'Nick. Nick, look at me.'

He did, and he had never seen such a nakedness between them, never seen them stripped to such raw elements: 'I listened to the tape of you and Bianca – all of it.'

'Yes?'

'I had to know about you and her.'

He closed his other hand across hers, making a little pile of hands: 'Well, now you know Jennifer. So you see my offer makes a lot of sense. All I will say – not in my defence, that would be absurd – but in mitigation – Christ, I sound like a lawyer – is that I would give everything if I could turn the clock back and not be in that room with her.'

'Yes,' the pile of hands became four. 'When I first heard it I *hated* you Nick, God how I bloody hated you. The deceit of it, how could you do that?'

He shrugged: 'Because I'm a man.'

'But I've had a lot of time to think since then. Lying in that bed alone, I've tried to think, to see it from your point of view.'

Nick smiled with genuine amusement: 'From *my* point of view, Jen, are you mad? You heard the whole tape and you tried to see it from *my* point of view.'

'I heard every word,' her hands formed theirs into a little tower now, intertwining her fingers with his; 'I don't know if you touched her, kissed her, felt her breasts before you made your excuse and I *don't* want to know, *Nick!*'

Her look silenced any protest he could have made.

'All I know is what I heard last,' her nails were biting into the skin of his fingers now, 'I heard my beautiful, lovely husband saying; "Look, I'm sorry, but I don't think I can do this."'

And Nick realised she was crying, and it was not from hatred or bitterness or betrayal or despair, it was from love and gratitude at what she thought had happened.

The old Nick would have seized on that, sensing the narrow advantage, pursuing it for the short-term gain, oblivious to the future loss. But he was another person now, and he had not suffered what he had suffered to go back to the old ways.

He detached a hand, reached up and lifted his wife's tear-stained face: 'Jen, listen to me, you have to know the truth about what happened.'

'No!' She detached a hand and pointed an accusing finger: 'No fantasies, Nick, no male bravado, no trying to prove you're a super stud to try and wriggle out of

282

this marriage. I *heard* the bloody tape, I *heard* it. From start to finish.'

'What about after my excuse, did you listen to that bit?'

She wiped her eyes: 'There's nothing after that, it's blank.'

Nick said: 'That's not possible.'

She looked at him with a kind of blazing anger or pride: 'Isn't it? Well, don't tell me you got up and switched it off with her standing in the room. Because I know you Nick, you *bastard* . . .' her venom rocked him, 'even if you could get away with that, you *wouldn't*. And do you know why?'

'No,' Nick said quietly, 'I don't.'

'Because you're too professional. Even if you did want to screw her, even if you were capable – my God, did she turn you on Nick, did she? – you wouldn't, not if it meant risking the story.'

Nick felt like a raft on a stream, taken down by the rush of the water, turning and spinning with its power and swirl.

'You know me better than anyone Jen.'

'Yes, I bloody do.'

They leaned back from the table, temporarily parting, Jennifer slightly out of breath, the two of them like gladiators after the first clash, the first drawing of blood.

At length, she said: 'I shouldn't have done it, it was a terrible deceitful thing to do. To have doubted you like that. But I had to know.'

'You had that right. I've been deceitful too, in all kinds of ways you wouldn't believe possible.'

'Is there anything left for us?'

He looked out of the kitchen door, down the garden to the stone lion statue that sat like a lone sentinel next to the privet hedge. God, how long had that been there? Objects anchored you with the chains of time and memory.

283

He said: 'It's up to you.'

'No, Nick, it's up to us. You and me, me and you, Mr. and Mrs, the couple, the singular. In or out, Nick. I'll cast my vote first, one of us has to, and I vote "Yes."'

Her eyes were ablaze with a kind of madness, and he realised he had never seen this side of his wife, this determination, this righteous anger.

'I vote Yes, too. That makes two Yesses.'

'Will it ever be the same?'

'No, it will *never* be the same, I'm sure of that, but it will be different, and different can be OK.' He realised he was choking on his tears.

'I'll settle for OK, right now.' She stood up and reached for him, spilling her tea which stained the wood like a birthmark, and she was holding him, and he was saying: 'Jen, *Jen*, I'm so sorry.'

But she was choking off the words with kisses, and the petal soft flutters had been replaced by something more vigorous and basic as her tongue sought his, and he could feel the raw and bony outline of her pelvis thrust against him, and he realised he was growing like some horny teenager out of control.

'I love you Nick, love you, love you.'

And he could smell her, the soap and the freshness, the tiny scents of the garden and the cold air on her skin. And that familiar, amazing body against his. There was a rush of passion to his brain like the blood that inflamed his cock, and he was saying: 'I love you too Jen, God, I love you, really.'

Then it was fumbles and embracing, and a walk crawl, and a two-legged step out of clothes to the stairs, hands glad to be home, running around like crazed pets; items of clothing discarded in a paper chase of passion, onto the stairs, step by step to the bedroom.

He was stripped to the waist, she too, her bra pulled off, still fastened and he saw her breasts like old friends, more diamond-shaped than he ever remembered them, the nipples sitting up waiting for the suck of his lips.

Jennifer threw her head back and moaned like an animal, and her hand felt the length of his hardened penis through the cloth of his trousers, and he felt her shudder of pleasure.

He fumbled under her dress for her pants which were wet like tissue paper, and tore them in his hurry to get them off her.

'Oh Christ, Nick, right up me please. Your hand, all of it,' and he did, cupping his fingers, scooping into her, hearing the delicious suck of it, and her gritted-teeth moan and cry at the violent, welcomed, invited assault.

She fumbled at his zip, pulling at the waistband of his trousers and the elastic top of his underpants until his cock swung clear, then she pulled him backwards onto the bed, and he stumbled onto her, caught absurdly in the tangle of his sliding trousers.

He was on his knees over her, pushing her skirt up around her waist, finding her, himself, then guiding himself in, her hand helping – inside her without preamble, exulting in her squeals and cries, then drowned them as his tongue met hers their jaws and teeth clashing like jarring swordsmen.

Her legs were up, back like a gymnast, then hooked on his shoulders, drawing him further in with an amazing strength, and he drove into her, on and on, in a crazed rythmn, driven by some animal passion for her.

Glued by sweat and sex and lust, he pounded into her, hearing the strange swamp noises of sex; her cries, high, low, like pain, like impossible pleasure, and then she was shuddering, rocking, aagghing, and it was aagh-God, no, no, no, yes . . . yes . . . yes . . . that's it . . . yes . . . that's . . . oh-God-*yes* . . . fucking yes, fucking . . . oh fucking Christ, *yes*!'

And he was going too, eyes closed, feeling the space shot

of his own orgasm, racing for the stars, tearing his soul out, hurling it away, emptying the very core of his body.

When at last he found and met her eyes they were almost crossed, glazed like someone on the brink of death or the distant border of some mental ecstasy. He remembered what the French had called some orgasms: Le petit mort – the little death.

Then she focused, found his eyes, gritted her teeth and said with a hard passion that almost scared him: 'I don't care who you've done it with or who you do it with. Just keep fucking *me* Nick, that's all.'

Jessica said: 'Personally I think you're being a fool.'

He shrugged: 'Perhaps. But I know when I've had enough. I think reporters have a shelf-life, and mine's over. Anyway, I think I'll quite like public relations.'

'Poacher turned gamekeeper. This I gotta see.'

'My first job is to take a load of freeloading motoring correspondents to Milan for the weekend. Fiat have got a new saloon out.'

'Oh wow, watch out, Nick. After you've wined and dined them and paid their hotel bills and lent them a new car to swan around in they may get real mad and criticise the design of the ashtrays.'

Nick raised his glass: 'That's not my concern. I think the whole business is as corrupt as – hell, Jess, it *is* time to get out, I can't think of a comparison.'

'Newspaper corruption makes Caligula's dinner table look like –

'*A vicarage tea party*.' They said it in unison, laughing.

'Seriously though Jess, I won't miss the deceit, the lying and the sheer, God I don't know, the sheer *amorality* of it all.'

She addressed a non-existent bystander: 'And this is the man going into *public relations*. But hey Nick, the book is still on, right? The Bianca Vasquez Affair. We've got a lot of interest, here *and* in the States.'

'Yes, I'm in for the book. I forgot the first rule of newspapers, *never* resign, wait until they fire you. That way you get the money.'

'Oh stuff their money.' Jessica paused, sipped her wine slowly, then eyed him thoughtfully and said: 'Everything tickety-boo down at Dunroamin?'

'Couldn't be better. We're off to Bali in a month or so, just me and Jen. Becky'll be on a riding holiday, so me and the trouble and strife are going on a second honeymoon.'

She toasted him: 'To Darby and Joan.'

He lifted his glass: 'How about you? Anybody in the offing?'

Jessica shrugged: 'A probable, two possibles. Working on it.'

When they'd finished lunch, split the bill, looked for an excuse to linger and found none, at last Nick said: 'I might as well get this over with. Actually, you saved my marriage. Thanks for what you did with the tape. Jen somehow got hold of a Nagra and played it.'

Jessica whistled: 'Cheeky sod! Anyway, what part have I played in this?'

'Don't be coy Jess. You know what went on in that room as well as I do.'

'Do I?' She gave him an amused little look. 'I just transcribed the tape up to your elegant excuse and then you descended on me like the Hound of the Baskervilles, remember?'

'Come on Jess.'

'That was it, I swear.'

'You're pulling my plonker.'

'Look idiot-head. I got up to the excuse bit and a bit past, and then I switched off. I have no reason to lie about this. Anyway after you made your excuse there was a clicking noise and a long, long silence. God's honour I didn't touch the fucking thing. May He strike me dead this minute if I lie.'

He didn't. Nick bit his lip, and said at length.

'But you know that wasn't the end of it?'

'Sure I know.'

'How? How if you didn't hear the tape?'

She gave him the kind of look one would give to a particularly dense child: 'Because you're a *man*, Nick, for God's sake. She was a stunner. How could you possibly see that woman naked and *not* do something. You'd have to be a zombie.'

'And you expected that all along, did you, some sexual activity?'

'Sexual activity? What is this Nick, a Californian seminar or something? I expected you to screw her, get a blow job, something, anything.'

He stared sullenly at the table.

'Well I paid the price.'

'Come on you're negative, you must be. You're so goddamned happy with wifey you're glowing.'

'You knew I was scared shitless about that, didn't you? That night, at your flat.'

'Yeh,' she put her hand on his between the coffee cups, 'I don't want to make light of it. I can't imagine the fear you must have gone through. But all's well that ends well, eh?'

'I suppose so.'

'It'll be our secret. Send me forty grand in a brown envelope or I'm going to scrawl your secret all over London.'

He looked up and she was laughing, and he found, to his astonishment that he was too.

Suddenly serious, she said: 'Look, I've really *got* to go, but remember that I *didn't* tamper with that tape. If you ask me, it was switched off straight after you made your excuse.'

Nick said: 'I swear to God, Jess, I didn't. And I couldn't if I'd wanted to. She was standing right in the room. It would have blown the whole thing.'

'Well, if *I* didn't touch it, and *you* didn't switch it off, that only leaves one person.'

'Bianca?'

'Could she have got near it?'

He tried to remember the darkened room, the traffic going round the Place de la Concorde, but it all seemed to have faded now like an old, sepia snapshot.

'I don't see how. I mean, she was near to me – I think – and I went to the window, said I couldn't go through with it. I don't see how she could.'

'And if she did Nick, then she knew there *was* a tape in the first place. And even if she just discovered it by accident, she would have known then that it was a set-up. All she had to do was destroy the tape.'

'Let's get a cab together.' They left the restaurant, hailed a cab and took it to Waterloo. As it edged past the tapas bars and the restaurants, Nick said: 'If she knew – then either she turned up knowing, or went through with it. Almost as though she wanted to be discovered.'

'Hold on, sunshine, let's not jump to fancy conclusions. Tapes and tape-recorders are notoriously unreliable. I think you just had a lucky technical break.'

'Yeh, that'll be it.' He looked out at the traffic choked normality of the London streets, loving it: 'I'll miss hearing from old Manuel.'

'Spanish Voice? Yeh, I wonder who he is?'

Nick shook his head: 'He'll probably turn out to be some out-of-work actor hired to give it a flavour of intrigue.'

'Yeh, likely, but the question is, by *whom*? And who was doing all the nasty stuff?'

Whoever it was, Nick thought, it was too late for them now. The government was toppling, a general election likely, the Palace with its knickers in a twist, the American

Press raging with it, a few pop and sports stars with their careers on definite hold, a new debate about public and private morality, about AIDS, about . . . and who cared? Nick didn't. He realised that he truly didn't.

The cab crawled up the cobbled incline to the station's back entrance: 'Let's have lunch when I get back from Bali. This time strictly on Globe Public Relations.'

'Why not. Orso is nice and expensive.'

'Keep in touch Jess. Come down and have dinner with us.'

'Jilly Cooper says that's London-speak for "good-bye"?'

'Actually, Jess, maybe I never told you this but in my own silly way I love you.'

'Oh fuck off, Nick, please. What do you think this is, an episode of Thirtysomething?' Then she kissed him hard, and not without passion: 'Go on smart-arse, you'll miss your train.'

Chapter Eighteen

Through the open French windows, from where they sat the two men could look out across the lawns and the tiered gardens. Across the balustraded steps and the neatly trimmed high hedges, past the arrogant statues and the still fountains, way out across the rolling Downs where the mist still hung like icing on a dark cake.

One of the men was at least twenty years older than the other, but he was slim, grey-haired, and was aquiline of feature. His skin was also pallored like a man who has spent a lifetime in rooms where the sun rarely reaches.

The other looked older than his fifty-two years, his face racked by the lines of pain that had somehow creased, and crumpled him.

As he sipped his tea a close observer would have seen a deep, grey scar across the back of his hand. It needed no such close observation to see the second – a jagged tear, almost crucifix like, on the patch of his right cheek. It was here that the first bullet had penetrated, smashing his upper jaw, shattering his teeth, before it was deflected downwards, missing his tongue, to exit through the flesh of the bottom of his mouth. The scar there was concealed by the flesh of the double chins.

There were two other such scars on his body, now hidden from view. One on his belly, the other on his back, marking the entrance and exit wounds of the passage of another bullet.

He was bald and stocky, going to overweight now, but his eyes still burned with some fierceness the ageing, given up body belied.

The man put down his cup, stood up, and walked

awkwardly to the open French windows. Even after more than ten years he could not get used to the artificial leg, and at nights he dreamed his was still whole, and often awoke, feeling the ghost of his long-lost limb.

He turned to the grey-haired man: 'It's very beautiful here, she would have loved it here when she was a girl.'

'Yes,' Sir Percival said kindly, 'it is rather beautiful.' He paused and put down his own cup: 'You must miss her very much.'

The man turned: 'I miss the girl, Percival. I miss my child. I didn't know the woman.'

'At least we have seen justice done.'

The man sighed a deep, terrible sigh:

'Ah, yes. Justicia!'

'When will you return to the United Nations?'

'Tomorrow.'

'I shall accompany you to the airport. You will allow me?'

'Of course.'

He turned awkwardly, dragging the artificial limb, and looked out across the Downs. Sir Percival said: 'All those years ago, when we were young men, we believed in the same things. Remember?'

'Yes,' the man said, still facing out across the countryside, 'I remember.'

'In what did we believe, Javier, and have we achieved it?'

The scarred face turned: 'Justicia y verdad.'

'Justice and truth.'

'When we spoke those nights, over chess, I never believed I would ever have to put my principles into practice in such a personal matter.'

'Twenty-five years is a long time.'

'I many times wish I had died in that ditch rather than lived to this future.' The head bowed. Sir Percival got up, walked to his friend and put a comforting arm around the man's shoulders.

'Could I have done more to find her, then?'

'You were barely alive when the Sandinistas found you. Then your leg had to be amputated. For months you hovered between life and death, what COULD you have done?'

Sir Percival said at last: 'You will remember that I became aware of your plight through MI6, they had good contacts with the Sandinistas. We acted as conduits for the Americans after they severed ties. I learned Angelita's body was not found. I did everything possible. I tried embassies, the Red Cross, refugee camps. There was no trace.'

'I was grateful Percival.'

'When you contacted me I immediately agreed to help. Bianca was becoming known to us. She was making dangerous friends, although we did not know at that time that she was . . .' he hesitated, tailed off, unwilling to say the words to his friend.

'You could have done no more than you did, Javier. Would you have preferred that she had died in that ditch with your wife and sons?' Sir Percival asked it as kindly as he could.

The man looked up like a sad dog to its master: 'Why didn't I die? Perhaps it would have been better.'

'Because . . .' Sir Percival moved to the tea table, 'because you were meant to live.'

He motioned Javier back to the chair and the civilised unreality of the tea, the china cups and saucers, the silver teapot, the lightly baked scones, the thick yellow cream and blood red jam.

'I'll be mother,' he poured more pale Earl Grey, and the two men drank in silence for a while.

'Why did you agree to help me put a stop to my daughter's activities, to the men who used her?'

'Because you believed in the things I believed; justice, truth.'

'You were retired, you could have washed your hands of it.'

'I was made to retire, Javier, diplomatic ill-health. I did not jump I was pushed. A cushioned landing of course, car, index-linked pension . . .'

'Why? Your reputation was unrivalled.'

'I love my country. I saw it rotting from within. I began to see it at close hand – Ulster, mostly. Northern Ireland has poisoned our Army and police like Algeria did to the French.'

'Corruption?'

'Financial, political, sexual. Sometimes blackmail, even murder, here at least once, more than once in Ulster. I tried to clean it up, I believed I was succeeding. Then someone decided I must go.'

'Why didn't you speak out, for God's sake? Your contacts told you about the royal and Bianca, you told me that yourself. You could have created a sensation.'

Sir Percival replaced his tea-cup with a delicate 'ping' as china met china: 'England, Javier, remember this is England,' he wagged an admonishing finger.

'The Official Secrets Act, to which I was signatory, forbade me on pain of imprisonment from speaking out.'

'Then memoirs, a newspaper article, something.'

'I would have been stopped, an injunction sought, the book banned, the newspaper threatened. It is the way of things here.'

'So I gave you your opportunity.'

'Yes. Expose Bianca, using a newspaper. That would open the gates, and the resulting flood would sweep away some of the human sludge that clogs our system. But I could not know, Javier, that it would have such a devastating effect on your daughter. If I had known that, I would have desisted from it all. Nothing is worth a human life.'

Javier held himself erect, fighting the tears: 'It was the illness. It was already too late for Angelita.'

'Regrets?'

'A million.' Silence and tears and sadness hung in the room like mist. Sir Percival spoke, lightly: 'You never told me how you learned that Angelita was Bianca, or that she was prostituting herself.'

Javier got up once more and went back to the French windows. He said, speaking as if to himself: 'I met her Percival.'

'Met her?'

'A diplomatic reception in New York. Managua had sent me to try to build bridges with the Reagan administration. I had a meeting at the UN. I had seen Bianca's face in magazines, of course, but I never, in my wildest dreams . . .' he halted.

'You spoke with her?'

'Suddenly she was in front of me, and I was introduced. It was like peering into the face of a ghost, a dead person come back to life. I knew instantly.'

'Did she –'

'It was like a lightning bolt, I felt I was choking. I knew, I knew, Percival, the eyes, the eyes.'

'She said nothing?'

'No. But I saw it in her face, just for a fraction. Recognition! Then it was gone, and it was though a shutter had come down.'

'Did you try to get her alone, to speak to her?'

'Before I left I went up beside her. She was looking at a picture on the wall. It was Picasso's Guernica. At that moment it was a picture of my soul. Destroyed, jagged. She knew I was there but she did not turn. She could not look me in the eyes, I know it. I whipered her name, "Angelita." She did not turn. I left.'

'Did she try to contact you – afterwards, secretly, privately?'

'No.' Javier said it harshly, 'there was nothing. She was no longer Angelita, no longer my little angel. She was Bianca, and by then I knew what Bianca was.'

'How?'

'In the cruellest way possible Percival.' There was deep sadness etched into the scarred face.

'The Reagan administration hated us, we were clients of the evil empire, but we were still desperately short of arms, and the Contras were beginning to make their presence felt. There was a man . . .' Javier said a name, and Sir Percival nodded.

Everyone knew him.

'A rich man, a celebrity, an arms dealer a man known for his exotic and bizarre taste in sex. He could get us arms, for a price. The deal was done; rifles, machine guns, three helicopters, two patrol boats, ammunition, even medical supplies.'

'You had no choice but to deal with him.'

'No choice, and the deal was a good one. He offered me a bonus of half a million American dollars. To be paid into a private Swiss account, of course.'

'It is his way.'

'I told him it was impossible for me to accept the money.' Javier shrugged, and then tears began to stream down his face: 'So he offered me something else instead, something he felt I would treasure. He offered me a night of sex with Bianca.'

Sir Percival shrunk back in horror: 'Javier, I can't imagine . . .'

'Yes, Percival, without realising it he had offered me the body of my own daughter.'

The woman arrived from London in time to join the two men for dinner. Her hair was shorter than it had been, and was cut more severely. She wore a plain black, tailored suit, a simple watch, little jewellery.

While the men drank claret, she sipped at Malvern spring water, and ate sparingly. She said little, mostly listening to the conversation of the two men, occasionally interjecting with a comment or observation of her own.

For most of the time she seemed lost in thought. She looked like a business-woman, perhaps a civil servant. Above all she looked sad.

After a male servant had poured the two men cognac, lit two cigars and left a silver pot of coffee, Sir Percival said, addressing the other two:

'There will be a General Election. I was telephoned tonight by a member of the Cabinet. The PM is set on it.'

'You favour the other side?' The Nicaraguan asked.

Sir Percival shrugged and blew out smoke in great blue billows. The smoke seemed to irritate the girl and she wafted a hand.

'I have no political stance – despite my friendship with you Javier,' he gave a mock bow of the head, 'If the incumbents are returned it will be without certain, shall I say, *individuals*, and on the solemn promise that they will clean up the stable of corruption and intrigue this nation's governmental process has become. The *other* side are dead set on it.'

'What about the Metropolitan Police, and the Intelligence Services?' The woman asked the question.

'Our man at the top will go, quietly, before the end of the year, whichever party is elected. Ill-health, a desire to spend more time with his family, whatever reason.'

'And the Met?' the woman said, doggedly.

'A new commissioner, probably some trials, an independent police complaints commission with tough powers of enquiry and subpoena.'

The woman nodded, as though satisfied.

'Many of us have long been aware,' Sir Percival continued, re-lighting his cigar, 'that certain sections of this government see the intelligence services and the police as an arm of their policies.'

'Can the rot be stopped?' Again the woman.

'Our latter-day Duke of Clarence has left the country to seek treatment. I would imagine it will be a long time before any member of the royal family, Minister, or Honourable Member dares to talk one morality and live another.'

'Why does it mean so much to you, Sir Percival?' the woman asked.

'Just because,' he waved a hand to encompass the dinner table, the antiques, the ancestral paintings, 'just because I live like this does not mean I believe in government that is rotten and corrupt, that abuses the unwritten constitution of laws on which the rule of our nation exists.'

'Noblesse oblige?' the Nicaraguan asked.

'I don't know what that means,' the woman said. 'It means nobility has its obligations, my dear. It means that those with wealth and power have a duty not to abuse it.'

'And they were?'

'So many of the nobility, old and new. Those with the nobility of money, of power, of rank and influence, the nobility of the elected representatives.'

He lifted his glass: 'I offer you a toast. To Jerusalem, in England's green and pleasant land.'

'Jerusalem!'

The woman looked into her glass as though the answer to something might be there in the nothingness of the clear liquid.

Sir Percival said: 'In this case the ends justified the means. There had to be a starting point, a lever to pry open the lid. And then . . . la verdad.'

'Truth,' the Nicaraguan said, to the woman. 'Truth is so precious, it must be surrounded by a bodyguard of lies.'

'And liars?' she asked, throwing back her head and

298

downing the bitter, black Nicaraguan coffee that had stood untouched before her.

'Yes, my dear,' Sir Percival placed his hand on hers, 'sometimes by a bodyguard of liars. You came to care for him didn't you?'

'A little. Just a little. And now I fear for him. I fear it isn't over.'

'Shall you go to New York?'

'Yes, and then to Managua. With Chamorro things will be easier with the Americans.' She pushed her chair back, as though suddenly tired of the conversation: 'Actually I'm quite weary. I'd like to go to my room now.'

'Of course.' Both men stood.

'Good night Javier, goodnight Sir Percival. Despite the impression I may have given, I have no regrets about my part in it.'

Both men said, as one: 'Good night, Annabelle.'

Rebecca got a new horse, despite everything. Now Nick and Jennifer watched her proudly as she rode around the field at the pony club.

The two of them were tanned and relaxed, and held hands as they sat together on the wooden fence: 'Isn't she just brilliant, Jen? Don't you think she handles it to the manner born?'

'He! Handles *him*, horses are never *it*, and yes she does.'

Nick looked out proudly at his daughter, and on a whim turned to his wife: 'Maybe we should have had a brother for her, or a sister.'

'You *mean* that?'

'Dunno, really. Is there still time?'

She pulled him in close: 'Not really. I mean, it's possible, but I could have a hard time, all that amniocentesis stuff. And to be honest I'm not sure I want to go through the nappies routine again. Do you?'

He shook his head: 'Not really. I'm happy with the three of us.'

'Me too.'

'Fancy a pub lunch when Hopalong Cassidy gets through?' 'Yeh, why not.'

She pulled a face: 'Nick, do you realise that after Bali, and with Red Rum out there, we have reached our mid-Forties with hardly a penny to our names.'

'Come on. We've got the house, my pension rights are intact –'

'Wowee. We've got a daughter with the tastes of Jackie Onassis, and your salary has dropped by around seventeen thousand pounds a year.'

'W-e-e-ll . . .'

'So will you please tell me why I've never felt so happy in my entire life.'

'Can I write on both sides of the paper at once?' And she pushed him off the fence onto the grass, where he lay on his back, laughing uproariously.

*   *   *

The doorbell rang. Nick shouted: 'I'll get it. It'll be Jessica, she's bringing some stuff round for the book.'

He fastened his towelling robe, went into the hall and opened the front door. It was not Jessica, it was a dark-skinned man with a black, bushy beard. Nick thought: My God, Jehovah's Witnesses.

The man smiled, showing a perfect set of even white teeth, and Nick thought. Here comes the message, I'll just bet he happens to be in the area talking to people about the Bible.

'Mr. Carter?'

'Yes?' Nick was surprised.

'Nick Carter of the Enquirer?'

'Was, but I've left now, I . . .'

The man's hand came up in a silver arc and punched Nick in the stomach, and Nick thought crazily: Why is his hand made of silver, and then he saw the gush of blood and felt the delayed, searing, awful pain.

And he realised, with horror, that he was being butchered. The knife came up again, Nick thrust out his arm instinctively, and screamed as the blade carved through into the bone.

Behind the man he suddenly saw a contorted face, and it was screaming. Jessica. Then the jagged blade came up, Nick tried to move but stumbled, and it pierced his breastbone, first cutting through robe, flesh and muscle.

He saw an arc of blood, saw it hang as if in slow motion, like a rippled curtain, he kicked out feebly, heard the screams and the cries, saw the man turn, lashing out with his other hand, saw Jessica flailing, spitting, demented . . .

He was gone, pushing her aside with such force she fell sideways into the garden, and then Nick was crumpling, the hall tilting at a crazy angle.

He reached out to grab something that might keep him in this world, but there seemed to be nothing fixed or permanent, and one hand was holding on to the butchered meat of his intestines in some apparently futile act of aesthetics.

Jennifer was screaming, Jess shouting, and he saw a face close to his, Jessica's, felt a curled fist press into his wound, tried to scream from the pain, but felt only a foam of red bubbles on his lips.

He squinted, tried to focus, saw this fierce face against his, and heard Jessica saying: 'Stay awake, don't sleep. Don't die Nick, don't die you bastard, don't fucking die. I forbid it.'

He smiled.

'Don't die, not now. Not now Nick.'

The Daimler purred along the M4 motorway towards Heathrow Airport, and Javier said: 'An utter tragedy.'

Sir Percival nodded: 'He's still alive according to the latest bulletin. Intensive care, ventilator. He might still make it.'

'Why would the Grey Wolves let their assassin loose against a reporter?

Sir Percival looked out at the grey, dreary England he loved: 'He frustrated their plans, the female too. She's under armed guard now, but I suspect the man is long gone.'

'They hated the reporter enough to want to kill him?'

'He exposed Bianca before she had time to fulfil their role for her. To get the assassin into the House of Commons to kill the Prime Minister or the Foreign Secretary.'

'My God.'

'Their stance on terrorism has been unyielding, and both are perceived as friends of Israel. The Enquirer frustrated that, so they did what the ancient Greeks did, they tried to kill the messenger of bad news.'

Javier said:, 'Pour encourager les autres?'

'Possibly. They could not know it was our doing, yours, mine, Annabelle's. That the reporters, the newspaper, were just tools.'

'She is deeply upset. She had grown fond of him. Do you think they were lovers?'

Sir Percival shook his head: 'I think not.'

The Daimler passed the penultimate exit before the airport turn-off. Javier said: 'It could never have been done without her.'

'No. She played her role to perfection. The tethered goat for journalistic ambition. First outraged, always slightly stupid, always willing to be manipulated, always willing to be bought, at a price.'

The Nicaraguan tried to read his friend's face and failed. There was no reason not to ask, not now: 'Percival, I have never asked before, and it is none of my business, but . . .'

Sir Percival said: 'Go on.'

'I know this country, its rules and its social system. A man like you, of your age and standing, a girl like Annabelle. Normally, surely, you would never meet, how . . . ?' His eyebrows were raised in query.

Sir Percival gave a wry smile: 'Aha, you suspect she is my mistress. That I condemn and persecute others for what I do myself?'

'A mischievous thought, no more.'

The car came off the motor-way, and into the airport entry road, gliding almost soundlessly into the fluorescent-lit tunnel beneath the northern runway.

'Please do tell.'

'Twenty-eight years ago, before I was head of the Intelligence services, I perpetrated that most cliched of clichés. I had a relationship with my secretary. Actually relationship is too grand a word. I had sex with her once. A moment of weakness for both of us, deeply regretted on both sides. She was a married woman, our backgrounds, I . . .'

'I understand Percival.'

'She became pregnant. She wished nothing from me, not even my name on the birth certificate. Her husband believed the child his. But true to her word she kept me informed of the child's progress.'

The Nicaraguan said: 'Bianca was my child – Annabelle is yours.'

'Yes. I was amused when she became a model, somewhat shocked when she began to bare her breasts for the popular newspapers. Then her mother wrote to me. She feared her daughter had become a prostitute and was abusing narcotics.'

Suddenly the sadness was in Sir Percival's eyes, as though he and his friend had swopped masks.

'That is why you understood my agony?'

The Daimler emerged from the tunnel and followed the directions for Terminal 3.

'Yes', Sir Percival said, 'it seemed like Divine Judgement on us both, those believers in truth and justice.'

'Does she know – that you are her father, I mean?'

'No! Most emphatically not. I contacted her through – well, I think you will understand that a former head of British Intelligence has many sources, many ways of achieving things.'

'She readily agreed to help?'

'Eventually. I think she was looking for a way out, a way to be . . . *decent* again. She became the bait, the decoy, and she did it brilliantly.'

'And you never told me that *she* was *your* daughter.'

'The need to know, Javier, first rule of intelligence work.'

The Daimler glided to a halt outside the unloading area of Terminal 3. 'And you'll never tell her?'

'She'll learn when I die. She'll get the money, Patwick Manor, everything.'

The Nicaraguan beamed: 'Then the newspapers will say that she was your secret mistress.' Sir Percival's eyes twinkled: 'Never, Javier, believe what you read in the newspapers.'

At the kerbside the two men embraced: 'Goodbye old friend, and thank you. Thank you for everything.'

'Goodbye Javier.'

'Shall we ever meet again?'

Sir Percival's firm gaze flickered for an instant, and he said: 'No. I do not think so.'

'How long, Percival?' the Nicaraguan said, kindly; 'I have never dared speak of it before. Months? Years?'

Sir Percival shook his head: 'Such a strange illness. Various prognostications. Who knows? A year perhaps, shorter if I am foolish and rush about like a young man.'

'Come to Managua, the climate will suit you. England is so *cold*.'

He gripped the Nicaraguan's hand: 'No Javier, I shall die at Patwick Manor. I rather think that would be fitting.'

A look of urgency crossed the other man's face: 'Then tell her, Percival. Tell her before you die. Don't let her learn afterwards that she was loved. Tell her that you are her father. Tell her that you love her. Do it *now*, before she leaves England.'

He looked down: 'I only wish I could say those words to *my* daughter.'

Sir Percival smiled: 'Goodbye, Javier.' They embraced again, then the chauffeur took the Nicaraguan's luggage, and walked to the terminal building.

The Nicaraguan walked with him, turned once and waved, then did not look back.

Several hours later, at the spot where the two older men had embraced for the last time, a black London taxi drew up, and its passenger stepped out.

He was swarthy but newly clean-shaven. He carried just a small leather weekend bag, and he paid the driver with two crisp, notes.

The passenger then went inside Terminal Three to the check-in desk for Syrian Arab Airlines and presented the return half of a Business Class ticket, Damascus-London-Damascus.

A close examination would have revealed two deep scratches, concealed with female make-up, running from his right eye, down his right cheek.

Jessica had made those scratches. The Grey Wolves of Jaffa were bringing their man home.

Jennifer stood at the end of the garden, head bowed in the dusk of the failing day, and in her hand she held the Nagra tape in its cardboard sleeve.

She knelt down, slid the tape from its sleeve and flipped the green metal spools onto the lawn, watching the tape

305

unroll onto the grass. She took a small oblong canister from her cardigan pocket, unscrewed the metal cap and sprinkled liquid over the jumbled tape.

Stepping back several paces, she removed a box of matches from her other pocket, selected one and struck it, throwing it onto the petrol-soaked tape.

There was a 'whoomph', a gush of flame, and the make-shift pyre took light, the tape unravelling in the flames, writhing and burning like an agonised brown snake.

From beneath her blouse, Jennifer slid the blue letter with its colourful stamp and distinctive blue and red candy airmail edging.

It was addressed to Nick, and marked 'Personal'. Jennifer had no idea how Bianca had obtained her husband's home address, or who had posted it for her, for the date-stamp showed it was mailed after Bianca's suicide.

But Jennifer was in no doubt who had written it, for the woman's name was written in elegant, flowing script across the back of the envelope. Bianca Vasquez.

The letter had arrived the day that Jennifer returned from Soho after hearing the tape – the same day that Nick had gone missing for almost a week.

She had hidden it, and not told Nick of its existence, terrified of what Bianca might have to say. Terrified that by opening it she might release some evil spirit into the house, some legacy of Bianca that would destroy what Jennifer and Nick had so painfully rebuilt.

Now the letter sat in her hand like the stubborn, unwanted souvenir of a despised voyage.

She looked at it one more time, then threw it into the flames.

It browned, curled, caught and burned in a few seconds, and soon its black, charred fragments began to rise on the heat, up into the darkened sky.

It was over now. She shivered, pulled the cardigan

306

closer to her, turned and walked back towards the house.

Looking up she saw Nick's white, wasted face peering from his sick bed next to the window. He was staring down at her, down at the dying flames.

Jennifer smiled.

'The opera ain't over 'til the fat lady sings.'

Dan Cook, baseball commentator, US TV April, 1978.

Often wrongly attributed to Dick Motta, coach of the Washington Bullets, who adopted the phrase.